Baby Momma 4

Baby Momma 4

Ni'chelle Genovese

www.urbanbooks.net

Urban Books, LLC
97 N18th Street
Wyandanch, NY 11798

ISBN 13: 978-1-60162-644-8
ISBN 10: 1-60162-644-4

First Trade Paperback Printing April 2016
Printed in the United States of America

10 9 8 7 6 5 4 3 2 1

Distributed by Kensington Publishing Corp.
Submit orders to:
Customer Service
400 Hahn Road
Westminster, MD 21157-4627
Phone: 1-800-733-3000
Fax: 1-800-659-2436

Baby Momma 4

by

Ni'chelle Genovese

Acknowledgments

To the creator of all things, including this wonderful talent that I've been blessed with—I give God all the glory.

I owe an extra special thank-you to the entire Urban Books family. Carl and Martha, both of you are amazing to work with, and I am forever grateful for all that you do. To Joylynn, I couldn't ask for a better literary agent. You're the only person who can curse me out without using a single curse word.

Thank you, Smiley, for such a dope-dope-dope cover. I still get chills whenever I look at it.

Follow me on Twitter, Instagram, Facebook, and Pinterest @NichelleG4.

"You never really understand a person until you consider things from his point of view . . . until you climb into his skin. And walk around in it."

—Harper Lee, *To Kill A Mockingbird*

Prologue

I

Four Years Ago
Washington, DC

I pulled frigid air in through my nose, letting it fill my lungs, freeze my insides. I'd spent the last week shut away inside a room no bigger than a broom closet. The smell of my own waste still filled my nose. I cringed at the gritty texture of my own filth and dirt crusted underneath my nails.

The wind whipped around me, sent my hair cutting into my cheeks. If I had any sense, I would've dressed a little more rugged, worn something other than leggings and my favorite sweater. It was just some old, ratty, cotton-ball-thick-thing that was the color of coffee with two creams. It wasn't name brand or anything special. But it was one of the last things my dad had given me before we fell out, so I loved it just as much as I hated it. I didn't appreciate the fact that I'd probably die wearing the damn thing. But, it's not like I knew that a week ago when I put it on.

My arms were wrapped around my body tighter than a straitjacket. I clenched and unclenched teeth to keep them from chattering from the cold and maybe from fear. I'm not sure which one. But I was feeling this sickening never-ending roller-coaster drop kind of feeling.

Adrenaline sent tremors of terror through my body, rocking my ankles, knocking my knees together. I forced one foot forward, and then the other, shuffling across gravel, tattered cigarette butts, and busted up pennies that might have been wishes. When I couldn't go any farther, I looked out over the tips of my shoes barely hanging over the gunmetal-black edge of the bridge. Silvery-black waves rippled across the water beneath me. It looked so close and so terrifyingly far that it took my breath away. The pounding from my heart rocked my whole body.

There was a heavy churning ache in my chest as I guided my feet forward. I opened my eyes long enough to blink. I inhaled, throwing all of my weight forward, curling into myself. Not in my worst nightmares had I ever imagined something like this. I was curling into myself. My nails cut into my skin through my sweater. I hunched forward, plunging through the air like I was trying to split my back open and spread wings before I reached the bottom.

Air rushed into my face, beating against my skin so hard and fast I couldn't get a breath in to scream. My stomach floated in my chest, tingling the same way it did when I rode the roller coasters at Busch Gardens. There were so many thoughts fighting, fading, and clouding my head that holding onto a single one was like grabbing at smoke. All except one—the last one—and it was more of a feeling than a thought. It felt worse than everything I'd been through that'd got me up on that bridge in the first place. It was even worse than the falling in itself.

The scream that finally tore its way up my throat should've hovered me over the water. It should've frozen time, or caught God's ear so he'd hear me and give me a do-over. Regret exploded in my brain, spreading into my soul as I hit the freezing waves like a concrete wall. The shocking cold water instantly numbed my skin, jarred my bones, shaking my insides. After everything I'd done, I was going to die with you in my belly and I'd forgotten . . . Well, no, I didn't forget. I just didn't get a chance to give you a name.

II

March

There was a soft beep coming from somewhere nearby. My heart sent throbbing pulses of pain to my temples that synced with the beeping in my ears. I tried to swallow, but the inside of my mouth felt like sandpaper. All of my body parts were waking up individually. Feeling came back to my limbs one by one in the form of pins and needles as my senses came back.

The smell of onions, Black & Mild smoke, and something familiar met my nose. Somewhere outside my room, a man was speaking in a rough, quiet whisper.

"Yo, I know you ain't *still* talkin' about that shit? How long ago was that job though?"

He paused to make several long honking sounds with his nose. I gagged as he snorted up and swallowed snot.

"A'ight, well, *if and when* she wake up, I'll let you know so you can have that revenge chat or get that revenge pussy. The bitch probably brain-damaged, but shit, if you wanna talk to or fuck a comatose ho, it's whateva. You the same nigga who was like fuck the spiders, fuck karma. And where that shit get yo' ass?" *That* was the familiar smell I smelled. It was Tariq. He doused himself in Egyptian Musk body oil, and I swear that smell could travel through the walls. It was enough to pry my eyelids open. As things slowly came into focus, a chilly breeze came through a window beside my bed. The unfiltered sunlight hurt my eyes, but it was the best kind of hurt I'd ever felt. It meant I was alive. Everything was bright green with flashes of electric-blue sky. The air felt and smelled like it was the beginning of spring, but that was impossible because from what I remembered, it was just hot and humid out. It was just July.

Flashes of silvery-black water came rushing up to my mind. Tears welled up in my eyes. All of the hurt and disloyalty washed over me. I survived. Oh God, I'd survived. But something was different. My body felt different. I dragged my hand toward my stomach, squeezing my eyes shut tight. That warm fullness that I'd felt in my belly for so many months was gone. My stomach wasn't even round anymore.

Tariq's footsteps echoed across the hardwood floor. They weren't moving toward me. A bottle hissed open, the cap bounced, making a soft metallic whir before falling flat with a tiny *plink*. Women moaned loud over the sound of sleazy music. He was watching porn.

I fought against the invisible weights holding my body down. Looking around didn't seem to take as much effort as moving, so I concentrated on that. It almost broke my heart to see that the room was damn near empty. There had to be something I could use to help me somewhere. A heart monitor and a clear plastic bag hung beside my bed on one side. I turned to examine the other side of the room, cringing when I realized the oniony smell was coming from my own body. *Well, at least, I know that nigga wasn't getting his kicks by sponging me down every day.*

Moldy dark brown and black water stains marked the ceiling. The dark wood floor looked bare and dusty except for a small worn-out rug by the opened bedroom door. I couldn't see much of the rest of the house from my angle.

A small scratched oak nightstand sat beside the bed with extra IV bags lined up along the top of it. Relief hit me in a wave when I saw the dingy-yellowed cordless phone. Moving took nearly all of the energy I had, but I managed to lean as close to the side of the bed as I possibly could.

The beeping from the heart monitor sped up as I tried to lift my arms. It felt damn near impossible, like one of those dreams where you're half-awake and half-asleep. The volume on the television lowered. I leaned back toward the center as shoes clipped across the floor in the direction of my room. Snapping my eyes shut, I tried to take slow, deep breaths while focusing on the birds chirping outside. I could sense his presence standing in the open doorway. The frame creaked under the weight of his back.

I could see Tariq's face in my head. He used to have a nasty habit of sticking his hand in his pocket whenever he saw me, and that action in itself disgusted me. Someone told me niggas do that so they could stroke themselves whenever they see something they like. He would always stare at me for a second too long with his hand in his pocket. At least he was smart enough not to try anything with me.

Beer sloshed in a bottle. He gulped long and deep before his footsteps disappeared back down the hall. I waited until the television turned back up. This time, I scooted millimeter by millimeter while rhyming the lyrics to "I'm on One" in my head. It was my favorite Drake song, and it was the same tempo as the beeps from the heart monitor. I was beyond pleased with myself when the beeping didn't change its tempo. I called the only person I could trust.

My voice came out in a scratchy croak.

"Shandy?" I said into the phone.

I wasn't expecting to not be able to talk. The thought hadn't crossed my mind.

"This me," she snapped back. "And who the hell is this?"

I almost smiled. That was my Shan, always feisty as hell.

"It's me girl, Novie," I whispered.

"Oh my God! If somebody's playin' on my shit, I swear I'm gonna find you and—"

"Yeah, I need you to find me. I just woke up. I don't know where I am. Tariq is here."

"Girl, I know where you're at. I came to see you. That fool was trying to holla so hard too. Lady J had you moved; she said it would be quieter if they put you somewhere other than the house."

I wanted to scream, laugh, and cry all at the same time. It was getting harder to keep my heart from racing. Fresh tears were just waiting to fall from my eyes.

"I need you to go to the Anytime Fitness and get my ho-bag. You still got the key I gave you, right?" I asked.

"It's around my neck as we speak," Shan replied.

"Nobody can know that you're going to get it or that I called you," I told her in as firm a voice as I could.

There wasn't enough money in my bag to get me far. I'd pinched off of it way too many times to help Shandy pay a bill or to buy something cute. But there were clothes, a phone with a clean sim card, and an extra ID in there. It was everything I'd need to get out of this shit and get myself together. Daddy didn't like Swiss; he never did. I wasn't ready to face my parents, not yet, anyway.

Shandy clicked her tongue. "Tariq has been trying to get at me all this time, anyway. Offerin' to take me and the little one to the Cheesecake and whatnot. He ain't gonna be a problem."

I nodded even though Shandy couldn't see me. Hearing about her baby made a wall of toothpicks well up in my throat. I hesitated just before hanging up. There was one more thing I needed to know

"Shan? My baby? Have you heard anything . . . about my baby?"

I held my breath waiting for her answer. If I was alive he needed to be alive too. This was our second chance, and I'd have to make up for what I did for the rest of our lives. Shandy hesitated. The tension made my pulse start racing.

"Okay, Novie." She said my name in that after-school-special-tone of voice. It was that let's-sit-down-and-talk-so-you-don't-fall-down-tone of voice. "Girl, you know there will be plenty of time to talk about all that once I get you safe and—"

My arm was starting to shake. The muscles in my shoulder were on fire. I slid the phone back onto its cradle before Shan could finish not answering my question. The television volume lowered again. I knew he was coming this time, and he'd see my chest heaving and my body shaking. He'd see the tears running down my cheeks, and he'd either kill me, or let me go, or somehow, I'd escape. I tensed every muscle that I could control as his heavy feet slammed across the floor. The monitor sped up, but I couldn't stop the sound of my heart breaking if I'd wanted to.

And then he stopped dead in his tracks, turned, and went back toward the living room, toward the sound of his cell ringing from wherever he'd left it.

"What up, Shandy? I won't expectin' to hear from you. Girl, I'm on watch until tomorrow. Shiiiiiit, for all that, I might can get away for a few hours. It ain't like this thing here is goin' anywhere anytime soon."

I relaxed deep into the thin mattress. Lord knows I loved my homegirl to death. I'd owe her my life for this.

NOVIE

1

Where It All Began

A Maine coon the size of a baby lion trekked across the lawn. It found the perfect spot, sprawled out under a tree that provided shade, and yawned. The cat's tail flicked back and forth as it stared lazily up at a baby squirrel lounging on a feeder no more than a foot above its head. *Exactly,* I thought. It was too damn hot for all that running, chasing, and climbing bullshit. Just like it was too damn hot for me to be sitting up in this nigga's car waiting for him to get these damn Erykah Badu tickets from this mystery *associate*.

I waved a club flyer back and forth trying to cool myself down. *Club Tryst. Humph, when did this nigga have the time to go there, and where was I? He probably went with his damn associates*. That ain't even sound right coming from him. Was *associate* the new word of the day on Madden or *Call of Duty?* Where did he pick that shit up from? Javion didn't have associates. He was raised by his grandma in East Philly, he had a bum-ass-squad of niggas, and they lived where bum-ass-niggas lived . . . with their mommas or their baby mommas.

I craned my neck to stare up at the strip-mall-sized mansion in front of me. A fleet of shiny black cars stared back at me. Swiss was up to or getting into some shit; I could feel it. He didn't know anybody with that kind of paper, and if they had it, they didn't get it legally.

I cranked the AC in his Camaro up as high as it would go, running my finger through the frosty condensation that formed in the corner of the windows. He had one of those weird man-obsessions with his car. Washed and hand dried it twice a day, just like his ass, topped off all the levels, covered it good night, fingered it good morning. Okay I'm exaggerating. But I wasn't about to be sitting with the shit on "midlow and not high because high runs out the Freon," as he'd say.

I crossed and uncrossed my legs. Drummed my nails along the dash. None of this was sitting right with me. He'd used the word *associate*. I'm not saying my baby ain't bright as day, but niggas don't lie well. It's not in their genetic makeup. This was all starting to remind me of a book Shandy couldn't pull her face out of, where the nigga was inside fucking his wife all while the side chick sat waiting in the car. *Baby Momma,* that was the name of that book. I don't think Swiss would do some shit like that. Nah, not with the way he thirst after this ass and these hips. But you could never tell with niggas these days.

I tried to ease my mind by rummaging through his shit. I couldn't think of any other reason why the nigga would leave me unattended to go in some random's—my bad—some *associate's* house and take forever just to get concert tickets. *Humph. Guess they had to make the paper, mix the ink, and print them out too.*

I rifled through Burger King and miscellaneous take-out receipts in the armrest. As much as he cleaned his car, you'd think he'd throw away some of these receipts. I'd flopped down the driver-side visor when I noticed an old blue something creeping past. The sun reflected off the glass, preventing me from seeing inside. Blinking away sunspots, I fumbled, trying to put the visor back. *It has to be a confused pizza delivery guy or something.* I was so focused on the car I didn't see the bushy spider until it plopped down out of the visor onto my lap. A gas bubble squeezed its way out of my back end, and a screech came out the other as I limbo'd over the center console, screaming bloody murder. I was halfway in the backseat before I realized it wasn't a spider. It was front-row, center stage, Erykah Badu tickets. And the show was starting in less than an hour.

Sweat appeared on my upper lip. Even though it was frosty cold in the car, I was blazing hot and furious. The front door was still closed, and there wasn't a sign of anyone moving around inside the house. A quick glance over my shoulder confirmed that damn blue car was still there too. It'd parked on the street with the front bumper sticking out into the driveway enough for me to see it. Every second made me feel like screaming or climbing out of my skin.

I snatched the keys out of the ignition and eased my French-pedi'd toes back into my gold heels. Swiss was the first dude I'd ever met who found a woman in heels sexier than seeing her naked. He bought more shoes for me than I bought for myself. He defended it by telling me how he loved to follow my long legs down to my pedicured toes peeking out of something sexy. Made him want to tear all up into this more than any lingerie ever would. Thinking about him thinking about me in my heels made me want to tear that fucking door down.

I eased myself out of the car, careful not to slam the door, then quickly adjusted my sundress straps out of habit. *Let me walk in on this fool doing some shit; he'd feel all of this sexy-ass heel digging in that ass. Got me out here sweating and he's probably in there slurping lemonade outta her belly button.*

Sweat made my hands cold and sticky. I hesitated on the welcome mat for a bare second.

The sun-beaten door handle was hot to the touch. It seared into my clammy, nervous skin. If this fool was in here doing something he shouldn't have been doing, there was no way in hell I was gonna ring the doorbell. That would give him enough time to straighten himself up. I was surprised when I pressed down on the handle and it moved easily. Icy-cold air blasted across my face and neck as I eased the door open. I stepped into the foyer. *I am definitely not in DC anymore.*

Tall, bright green bamboo plants lined the foyer. I stared up at them with my mouth momentarily hanging open in awe. Red, green, and gold parakeets chirped and flitted around the tops of bamboo stalks up near the glass-domed ceiling. It was real cute in a Peter-Pan'ish kind of way, but fuck that bamboo and them birds. Where was this fool? I moved across the spotless floor, careful to keep my heels from clicking against the surface. Three long dark hallways spread out in front of me. I headed toward the one in the middle.

My ears were set to super sonar. I wiped my sweaty palms off on the front of my dress when a soft moan caught my ear. I paused . . . listening so hard I gave myself a headache. A second moan louder than the first one set my feet in motion toward the first door on the hallway to my right. *I will kill this nigga and his ho. He got the wrong one if he thinks he can play me like I'm boo-boo the goddamn fool.*

"*Shhh.* It feels good, don't it? I know you wanna tell daddy you like that shit," Javion said with a chuckle. "And I want you to stay just like this."

Javion's hushed voice was followed by the sound of his own low, husky moan. Betrayal stabbed me in the chest. That was *my* moan. That sound was supposed to be meant for me. I stepped into what looked like a small entertainment room. My lips were already forming every word that I was about to pop off at his lying, cheating ass. I've never felt so stupid or so humiliated. So blindly dumb. My mouth opened, but no words came out. My peep-toes peeped the mental stop sign slamming to a halt before the rest of my body got the message. I damn near did a full-front bow.

Her knees were spread, hands planted shoulder-width apart. I blinked, blinked twice, and then I blinked again to be sure the girl I was looking at was the same girl who'd opened the door. She was kneeling on top of the pool table in the middle of the room. Her skin was shockingly white against the black fabric. It matched her long hair piled into a high, messy ponytail on top of her head.

"I thought I told you to wait in the car," Javion's voice was dark and angry.

The girl's eyes were like headlights as they locked with mine. She couldn't have been more than nineteen or twenty. I had to force myself to look past the black tape across her mouth. I felt her degradation, along with my own confusion as I followed the handle of a broom sticking out of her ass like a stiff horse's tail. Javion's hand held the other end of it straight and stiff. A pistol was in his other hand, aimed in the direction of her head.

That couldn't be Javion. My Javion was a teddy bear and an HVAC repairman who listened to Future and fucked me to Jeremih. This Javion looked malicious, like something straight out of a Quentin Tarantino movie. He was sitting in a bright blue and white paisley patterned armchair pulled up to the edge of the pool table. Covering his face was a bright crimson-red ski mask.

His usually cheerful eyes were resentful and hard as he glared in my direction. I was scared to move any closer to this stranger of a man who I felt like I suddenly didn't know. The girl on the table whimpered when his hand shifted.

"Shhh. I know, I know," Javion hushed her like he was soothing a frightened animal. "I need you to hold that for daddy, just a little bit longer."

His eyes were on me all while he talked to her, like this was completely normal.

A deep voice boomed through the house, "That was a good workout! You know the best way to work off that freshman fifteen is to hit the treadmill. Your mom never liked working out but . . ."

The voice traveled through the house, echoing off the walls.

"Ashley?" he called out again.

The girl responded with a muffled shriek.

He was getting closer, his voice was getting louder.

Either the giant was coming down the beanstalk, or my heart was slamming against my chest so hard that it felt like the house was shaking all around me. I automatically looked to Javion for help because I had no idea what else to do, but he wasn't even paying me any mind.

"Ash, you got company? I thought I heard the doorbe—"

The owner of that deep, booming voice stopped just in the hallway. He had to have been at least seven feet tall. His wide-muscled body took up the entire door frame as he stepped forward in a pair of sweats, with sweat raining down his bare chest.

When push comes to shove, I'll take the stranger I know over the stranger I don't know. I instinctively backed myself toward Javion until I was standing a good distance behind his chair. I needed to keep myself a good distance from Javion too. As far as I could tell, he was on the other end of crazy for me right now, his own self. I wasn't trying to be in arm's reach of either one of they asses. Javion sat still and quit, like he just wanted the nigga to visually eat up the moment, roll it around in his brain, and digest it. That's exactly what happened too. The man's deep golden tanned skin went sickly pale. His grizzly squared jaw moved back and forth under the blond beard covering it, and his eyes narrowed to slits on Javion.

Javion finally broke the silence. "We gave you an extension, Beau. You missed it. The boss says I need to relieve you of a few obligations. Said maybe that would help you free up the finances to repay your obligation to him."

Beau raised his big meaty hands in the air. His heart broke the second he saw the girl on the table in front of Javion. You could see it all over his face and in his eyes. He was furious, scared shitless, and completely helpless—with no option left but to beg.

"Look, man, you don't have to do this. Please," he begged. "She's my only child. My baby girl." His bright blue eyes were glassy with tears. "I'm so sorry, Ash, baby. Daddy is so fucking sorry," he spoke to the girl on the table his voice shaky and cracking.

Beau raked his hands through his short blond hair, ruffling it into a spiky mess. He was shaking when he talked to Javion. "I swear on my life I'll get you your money. All I've got to do is win my next match. I'm guaranteed to win. I'll have it. All of it, I swear. Take my car, take whatever you need—"

"Not good enough," Javion answered.

Javion stood. I cringed at the pitiful sound the girl made when he twisted his hand holding the broom. This was a part of the game I never saw or experienced. It made the inside of my mouth get that uncontrollably wet feeling you get just before you vomit.

"You have until midnight to pay up," Javion said in a cold, flat voice. "Or I'll be making a trip to baby girl's dorm to finish this. Um, Chandler Hall at William and Mary University, if I remember correctly."

With that, he let the broom drop before turning the gun on Beau. Javion grabbed me by my elbow, calmly marching me toward the front door. I kept looking back, expecting to see Beau running after us with a gun blazing or on the phone calling the police.

"He ain't gonna do shit, so stop checkin'," Javion said as he opened my car door.

My eyes were full of questions, but I was still a little too shook up to do more than sort through my rambling thoughts. *What just happened? What the fuck kind of pervert ties a girl up and shoves a broom up her ass? Is that the kind of shit he enjoys?*

I slid my shades on, trying not to look at the house through the rose tint of my sunglasses. Hopefully, they'd be enough to hide my face if Beau or his daughter were in a window with a camera phone snapping pictures of their attacker. My phone lit up. It was finally charged. I tried to stop my fingers from shaking so I could check my missed messages or log onto Facebook. I needed to do something—anything—to take my mind off what I'd just seen. Javion walked around the back of the car toward the driver's side.

Thudump!

Something slammed up against the back of the car so hard it rocked in place. I jumped in my seat dropping my phone.

"Oh shit!" Javion shouted.

The worst of the worst scenarios flashed through my head. All that tie-'em-up hostage craziness had my ass so discombobulated, I'd completely forgotten to tell him about the blue car. *God, if this nigga is shot or is stabbed, it'd be my fault.*

2

A Complex Electra Complex

I turned completely around in the seat, my nails dug into the leather of the headrest. I was expecting to see blood splatters or five dudes in black wife beaters with crowbars and tire irons. My eyebrows shot up at what looked like a long black weave bobbing up and down. She started screaming down at what I think was Javion on the ground.

"Nigga! I can't believe you! I cannot fucking believe you right now!" she yelled, stomping her foot over and over.

"Tinesha, *stop!* Stop, nigga, you're pregnant," Javion yelled back.

She gave a final stomp. She stopped putting her hands on her sides. Tinesha was huffing like she was practicing her damn Lamaze. Javion hopped up, minus his ski mask. Light brown dirt speckled the side of his face and head. He tried to dust off the front of his jeans.

"Nigga, if you don't calm the fuck down, you about to get everybody caught up out this bitch."

"Nigga, the only person 'bout to get caught up is you and *that bitch*. I told *you,* this baby is yours, and you handle it by hiding from me? You ain't no man—you ain't shit," she huffed, all while pointing in my direction with her chest heaving.

"Get the hell on with that. You out here trippin' over nothing. I'll deal with you later," Javion talked quickly over his shoulder as he marched toward the driver-side door.

"You'll have to back me over to get out of here, bitch! I ain't goin' nowhere until you handle this shit like you're supposed to!" Tinesha stood behind the car with her arms spread out.

"What the fucking fuck, Javion," I snapped as soon as he opened the car door.

Sweat ran down the side of his face. He completely ignored me and started the car, throwing it into reverse.

"Move, Tinesha, I ain't playin' with you," he yelled out the window at her.

I punched him in his arm for ignoring me. I didn't sign up for either one of these bullshit situations. Yeah, he might've helped out with a bill or two and got my hair done whenever I wanted, but it wasn't worth all of this.

Tinesha posted up behind the car. "Hit me then, bitch. You man enough to take a life, but you ain't man enough to raise one? Huh? *Really*, nigga?"

She pulled off a shoe, hurling it at the car. For a pregnant woman who looked about to bust, she sure as hell had a lot of fight in her.

Javion turned the wheel to the far right, punching the gas. The car made a small arc as we backed around her. A few inches to the left and that would've been all she wrote. She gave us the finger so hard I bet she sprained her wrist.

I stared at the side of Javion's head with my arms crossed tight over my chest.

"Novie, that kid probably ain't even mine. She was fuckin' with one of my homeboys who was always doin' his thing on the side. Shit, we got drunk, she made her move, and I hit it a couple of times but stopped because my boy said they were good. She was being greedy, and I don't do sloppy seconds," he explained. "Then she called me outta the blue a month ago, talking about she's seven months along. Nah, that ain't me. It can't be."

I didn't know who or what to believe. Another woman would explain all the late-night trips and phone calls, but what I'd just seen this nigga do back in that house explained that shit just as well.

"So what if it is your baby?" I asked.

The corners of his mouth turned downward as if just thinking about a baby with her turned his stomach. "If it's mine, and my boy don't kill me for the disrespect, I'll do my part. But it ain't mine. It can't be. I ain't ready for that shit, and definitely not with her."

I wrestled with the idea of him having a baby with another woman. We'd only been seeing each other for four months. It definitely wasn't enough time for me to get crazy attached to him, but it was enough time for me to feel comfortable being with him. I could rock with the idea of us being together for now, but if that baby was his, I'd have to let him go. I didn't want to deal with any men and their unstable baby mommas.

I scooped my phone up. Shandy had sent me a text.

Javion watched me out of the corner of his eye.

I never asked him his business concerning who called or texted him, but he was sure as hell nosy enough to constantly ask me about mine.

"Whatsup? You got somewhere else to be?" he asked.

"It depends on whether or not you telling me what just went on in that house."

"*Spppsht.* That? That shit was just work," he answered nonchalantly.

I sucked my teeth. "Don't hit me with that bullshit. That was more than *just work,* and you know it."

"All right, Novie. Your boy back there is some kind of UFC World Champ. His dumb ass blacked out, had some kind of posttraumatic fight meltdown and snapped his wife's neck because of steroids. Boss straightened it all out. Kept him out of jail, kept his record clean, let him keep that title belt too, and now that nigga's bitch ass acting funny about paying. It's just work, like I said."

The look I'd seen on Beau's and his daughter's face, I couldn't shake it. Nobody deserved to be humiliated like that.

I crossed my arms and turned so I could face him. "So, basically, you help rich people get away with murder? And you went after his *daughter,* who didn't have shit to do with what he did? If that ain't fucked up." The bracelets jingled on my wrist as the palm of my hand fell hard and fast across the back of Javion's head. If we weren't so far away from my house I'd have gotten out and walked. I slumped back into the soft leather of the seat and stared at the sun dipping in and out of the clouds overhead.

Yes, I was raised in the game, but it was different type of game. Back in the day, Ramsey Evans was one of the youngest dudes in the game; he was a computer hacker who ran dope in and out of North Carolina and South Carolina. His daughter had a thing for *The Hunger Games* and *Comic Con.* They went to every convention every year. She wanted a live deer-hunting contest at one of them. Ramsey went above and beyond and hired the actors from the movie; he even gave people real bows and arrows. Almost caused a stampede when the deer came crashing across the stage waving its antlers, but he paid for a show, so he got one. You had Ewoks, Storm Troopers, and Wonder Women all shooting their arrows, not sure if their target was an animatronic or a real deer.

When it collapsed and the head fell off, people gasped. Ramsey . . . lying there with tape over his mouth so he couldn't scream. His hands and his legs were tied together. Daddy took over after that. That's how he did things. He would handle business like a Nigerian warlord when he needed to. But he never *touched* people's kids. He had boundaries, rules; there was a code of ethics that he followed. Javion left a bad taste in my mouth with his child's play. I couldn't respect a man that did shit like that.

"Novie," Javion said my name like it was an excuse. He sucked on his bottom lip and alternated between watching the road and watching me. "*This* is what I do in order to make these stacks we burn through like kindlin'. It's why I expect you to wait in the car when I tell you to wait in the car. It's not just me; it's a family thing, so I'm with my people. We do a lot of infamous shit for famous and financially privileged motherfuckers like him. Sometimes they ask for more than they can afford, and when they do, we have to scare up their payment."

A family thing, okay. I guess that would explain why I hadn't met or seen so much as a picture of any of his kin. If we weren't trying to take it slow and really build whatever this thing was that we had, I'd have started pressing him about this secret-squirrel family business.

I decided to try my luck. "So, who is this boss that you work for?"

He focused on the road in front of him. "Can't answer that."

"You move weight too? Have you been doing this for a long time? Have you ever killed anyone?" I fired the questions at him one by one as they popped into my head.

"*Novie*," he yelled slamming his hand against the steering wheel. "Chill with the questions. I already told you a helluva lot more than I should have. So let it go. I ain't telling you anything else."

I put my head back against the headrest and closed my eyes, unsure of why I wasn't scared or completely turned off by what he really did for a living. As much as I hated what my dad did for a living, I don't know why I kept falling for niggas who followed in his footsteps.

GENESIS KANE

3

The World Is Ruled by Favors and Fools

I parked on the street and stepped out, taking in a deep breath of the city. Summer was just starting to spread her legs after a long, celibate winter. You could smell it in the air, almost taste it on the tip of your tongue. It was that energy that made niggas anxious to get out of the house and into some bullshit. That shit that kept my plate full of cases, clients, and pretty faces needing favors.

The Metropolitan PD was my last stop before calling it a night. I liked to check in from time to time to see who or what had been brought in. I kept at least three officers in my back pocket at every station in and out of the area. They scratched my back, and when it was necessary, I watched theirs.

Dim fluorescent lights lit up the grubby interior of the station. It wasn't nearly as busy as I would have expected for a Friday night.

"Oh ho ho, now, looks like Santa stopped by extra, extra early. Hide your convicts and hide your wives. Genesis Kane is prowling the building."

I'd recognize that Boston-proper accent anywhere. Officer Squatton strutted over, giving me a rough pat on the shoulder. All the legal aides back at the office called him "The Fucksquatch." I'm close to six feet two, and even I had to look up slightly to make eye contact. He was a big, less hairy version of a Sasquatch with a fondness for women who weren't fond back.

I shook his oversized sweaty hand.

"Squatton, I get a feeling that ugly leer on your face you call a smile means you might have something for me."

Squatton's eyes shifted up and down the corridor uneasily before he motioned for me to move in closer. "I need you to do me a solid."

His mouth barely moved. "See, I got this abuse of authority and misuse of a service weapon thing coming down on me, and I need you to do your thing. But this one is major."

Those were serious violations, so I crossed it off of my easy list. He'd already come through on a couple of big asks for me, so I rocked back on the balls of my feet and gave him the go-ahead.

"Me and my partner were answering a call, see? Prostitution, loitering . . . I don't know, I was gonna figure it out when I got there. Everybody scattered. Rook took the front, I swept the rear. Pretty little thing too, nice tight ass. Might or might not have been hiding beside a brownstone. I let her feel my gun." He ran his hand over the butt of his holstered weapon. "And was about to let her feel *my gun*." Squatton grabbed his junk with a leering sideways grin on his face. "But my rookie partner came crashing through the bushes like a fucking Himalayan pygmy boar. Who the fuck doesn't stand down, when you say 'stand down' on the mic? I ain't even bring her in. Told her get the fuck outta there. Well, she got picked up the next day. But that ain't even the shit-shit," Squatton hissed through his teeth.

Squatton was a dog gnawing on a thick piece of rawhide. He leaned so close, I could see the bloody chewed, chapped, and cracked skin peeling away on his dry lips.

"Outside a hotel downtown, some undercovers were posted up, watching this new kid. A local heavy hitter who's been dropping bodies all over DC. He goes by the name of Face. They see the girl come out of the hotel last night, assume she's either a prosty or a customer. The guys drag her in. She has coke on her. They turn the heat up when she starts hollering about 'the other night.' Sarge is sayin' they gotta look into it. Her name's Saniah Sutton. Tell me you can fix this shit. It's my hands. They the problem. I'll get therapy, go to rehab. I'll do whatever. Just let me retire with a clean badge."

And The Fucksquatch strikes again.

"Can she identify you?" I asked, seriously considering the severity of the situation.

"Eh, she didn't look back, just got up and ran. But all she has to do is say where she was. They know where me and the rook were."

"Show me what you've got and I'll see what I can do."

Squatton grinned from ear to ear. He turned on his heel and led me down the hall with an extra bounce in his step. Hell, I didn't say I would or could do anything. I always say what I mean, and I said I'd see what I could do. It depended on what I was working with.

I sank my shoulders back onto the murky-grey painted wall as I waited in the interrogation room, or the box, as it was called. The lights overhead flickered, making a steady, loud, mechanical hum. A tiny little thing with long, dark, wavy hair falling all over her head covering most of her face was shoved through the door in some in-take pants and shirt so big they looked like they'd fall off her. She was younger, prettier than I expected, with creamy almond-brown skin.

"Tsk, tsk, tsk!" I peeled myself off the wall, pressing toward her slowly. I pulled out a chair, offering her a place to sit. "What would a bad thing like Face be doing with a sweet little thing like you?"

She twisted and untwisted her fingers together, staring at the door like she was about to get ambushed and eaten alive.

"You don't know my brother," she whispered, her voice was shaky and uneven. Her watery eyes shifted over the artificial wooden lines in the cheap table, tracing the dirty cup rings and coffee stains.

I pulled my card out of my lapel pocket. "So let me help you help this brother of yours. What's his name, Face?" I said, easing it across the table. I slowly waved it with two fingers like a white flag, a peace offering. "Genesis Kane. I represent the officer you're filing a complaint against."

"I don't care about that shit. I just wanted to bargain with them so they'd let me go, but it's too late now. I'm not saying nothing about nobody. Leave my brother out of this. He's been so fucking paranoid lately, he don't even sit down to take a shit. As soon as he hears about me being here, he's gonna freak out." She nodded at the scar on my lip. "What's it like living with that on your face?" she asked.

Caught off guard, I didn't have a ready answer. Sometimes I forgot about the twisted sand-colored skin that ran up across the top of my lip. Most people acted like they didn't see it, or they saw it and acted like it wasn't there. I can't think of anyone who just came out and asked about it. I shrugged, "I never really—"

"You don't think about it, right? Because it's not some shit like this." She pulled back her thick veil of hair with confident fingers. The flesh around her left ear down to the bottom of her cheek was scarred, jagged. I almost winced at the pink and brown skin healed over and woven together like a third-degree quilt. "My own brother did this to me. And it's even worse if you're against him. He does it to your whole face, all the way down to the neck. He lets the skin fester and the flies set in and maggots come. That's why they call him 'Face.' Y'all might, well kill me."

I couldn't swallow. My collar felt tight around my neck. I was normally prepared for anything, and I mean anything, but this was so left field. The metal chair legs squealed across the floor. Squatton was right in my face as soon as the door opened.

"What she say? That was the fastest head-fucking you've ever done. What did you tell her? You head-fucked the shit out of her, didn't you?" He was whispering a thousand words a minute, hovering around me like a zealous admirer.

"Not this time. This might not be your night." I wagged my finger back and forth. "You might actually have something I can't un-fuck for once."

Squatton slammed his fist into the concrete wall. His head fell back. He stared up at the ceiling with his jaw clenched, his hand limp at his side. It was probably shattered or broken.

"This can go only one of two ways," I told him. "If she stays here, that complaint is going forward. If she walks right now. No questions asked. All is forgiven."

His Adam's apple bobbed in his throat. Squatton knew either way he was fucked. Even if she walked, the guys building the case would smell something funny. Squatton just so happened to be on duty when she miraculously disappeared. Footsteps echoed down some hallway in the distance reminding us we weren't the only ones in the building. Air whistled through his nostrils with each breath.

Squatton leaned his head back against the wall. "Hey, Kane, remember that favor you asked me for? Ahh?" He rolled his head back and forth across the wall like a rolling pin.

I cracked the bones in my suddenly stiff neck, left, then right.

"It was a rape case, right? You wanted some evidence to *disappear*," he said in a smart-ass tone.

"What's your point, Squatton?"

His head stopped rolling across the wall; he looked me in the eye. "Now, I need you to make something *disappear* for me. Out of my jail. I'm gonna give you that bitch and everything she came in here with. You sign that book up front. Anybody asks why she walked, I'm gonna say *her attorney* got her out."

A few minutes later, I laid several oversized ziplock bags containing Saniah's belongings on the table.

"Here's your shit. Get dressed and meet me out front. I'll take you wherever you need to go." I laid her things neatly on the table in front of her.

She stopped wringing her hands. Her tongue darted across her lips. She pulled her bottom lip in between her teeth, debating on whether or not this shit was really happening.

"That's it?" she asked.

I nodded. "That's it."

"What do you do, again?" she asked in genuine awe. "Are you an attorney or an angel?"

I chuckled, feeling somewhat redeemed by her appreciation. "I do a little bit of everything," I stated with a wink. "The real question is, what am I not? Now hurry up. I was trying to grab some Chinese before they switch over to that late-night garbage they use for the drunks and after-hours crowds."

Live music floated on the warm night air. It was jazzy, up-tempo, tuba-heavy, something to keep the tourists out spending their dollars. It made the city sound like New Orleans during Mardi Gras. Saniah didn't give the precinct a second thought as she rushed outside in a cream-colored sundress. It clung to her full hips, which I did not mind watching as she walked in front of me. It also showed off the roundness of belly when she turned to take in her surroundings. My eyes lingered for a moment longer than I intended, but she didn't notice. Squatton left out the fact that he'd perv'd up a pregnant girl. The baggy prison clothes had kept all parts of that from showing.

I opened the back door for her, making sure to seat her somewhere in sight. I don't like the awkwardness of strangers riding all up in my personal space. And I never liked someone sitting in my blind spot.

"Where do you want me to take you?" I adjusted the rearview so I could see her face.

She stopped fiddling with her phone long enough to turn these big damsel-in-distress eyes onto me.

"Do we have that whole confidentiality thing like they give them on *Law and Order* or naw?" she asked.

"Yeah, technically, I can't say a word."

"Yes, gawd!" She dug through her purse. "And all my shit is still here too. *Woop!*" She celebrated, and then she put something up to her nose . . . and snorted. Twice. Wiping it clean with the back of her hand.

This bitch was actually doing coke in my car, in front of me, and she was pregnant.

"Oh, I needed that. Um, Genesis, right?" she asked as she opened the car door. "Look, I'm sorry for getting you involved. Me and my brother are misunderstood; always have been. He would never put his hands on me. I exaggerated a little, and I'm sorry." She sighed dramatically. "It's all about territory. I hear Sammie Knox has way more territory than him or his bitch need." She started rubbing her belly with a slick grin on her face. "I came up with an easy way to get it. Y'all niggas'll do damn near anything for a son, though. For a little prince."

The corners of my mouth turned down into a bitter frown. "Nah, not all of us. Just another hand to slap away, if you ask me."

"That's why I ain't ask you," was her smart-ass reply. She started to close the door but turned back as if it was an afterthought. "Oh, and my face? Car accident. Like I said, my brother's misunderstood. But, thank you for your help. I'll do you a favor and make sure Javion don't fuck you up when he comes back to execute everyone in that police station." She sashayed away, hips swaying, hair bouncing, and an energetic dance to her step. She sidestepped puddles, twirled to the sound of the band, and faded into the night like a ghost.

A sinister shiver ran across the back of my neck. It traveled across my cheeks, tugging at the scar above my lip until it throbbed. Favors. I didn't want shit from them; then I'd owe them something back. I was so sick of hearing that word.

Suddenly, food was the farthest thing from my mind. My gut was filled with anxious, twisting snakes of dread, all knotting together, making my mood sour as fuck. The SUV rocked from the weight of my fist slamming into the steering wheel. I cursed to relieve some of my frustration, but it didn't help.

I could feel that shit. Sense it with everything in me. The same way I could pick up on a judge who'd lean in my favor, or a juror who'd fuck up my client. I felt it when I'd asked Squatton for that favor so many months ago, and he made the evidence disappear on that rape case, and I felt it now. Only it was stronger. Way worse than before. I'd fucked up, and it was telling me I was going to regret some part of this night. Some part of this shit was going to haunt me for the rest of my life.

4

Hello, Kitty

Almond-coconut-scented steam swirled around me, clouding the air, fogging up the mirrors and my view of the city from the sixteenth floor. With a sigh, I eased down into the half-moon-shaped tub that could've easily fit a small swim team. Soft coconut shavings brushed against my skin underneath the bubbles.

I drained the water from my washcloth, draped it over my face, and lay my head back, enjoying my few moments of peace and quiet. The bathroom door creaked open. The sound of the evening news drifted in from the TV downstairs. *"An armed assailant flees from police down H Street after robbing a CVS. A double homicide has police looking for this woman. We'll tell you more at ten."*

I tuned out the grisly news, listening to see if I could hear Elgin trying to sneak in. Elgin was Javion's spoiled rotten, ugly as hell, hairless cat.

"Look here, little freak cat," I grumbled from underneath the washcloth, "leave my goddamn panties alone. Elgin, I swear on my life if I have to get out this tub, I'm gonna snatch you up by your little hairless balls and put you outside with the real cats," I warned.

It still wasn't exactly clear as to *what* he was doing to my panties once he got ahold of them. I don't know if he was eating or shredding the damn things, but every now and again, Javion would find a pair and swear up and down I was leaving them on purpose. Like I was on some kind of female territorial marking spree or some shit. All I know is I'd lost half my brand-new Frederick's of Hollywood collection over here, and I wasn't trying to buy anymore until they had another sale.

Hell, I ain't even *like* cats, let alone men with cats. Javion got a pass because he had more checks on the "date him" side than the "don't date him" side of the scale. He was single, fine as hell, with zero kids, and he had a good job. Shit, on top of all that, he was a straight man in DC, so that got him a double check-plus. So, yeah, I could definitely overlook his creepy panty-freak cat and his hustle for all of those perks.

With that thought, my washcloth was slung off of my face. It landed in the corner with a wet *splat. Mmm, let me find out he ain't playing tonight. Wonder if he wants to pretend to be the dirty plumber again?* The last time we got down in the bathroom, we had to take showers afterward just to get clean. It took every towel in the place to soak all the water up off the floor.

I kept my eyes closed, waiting for him to make the next move. My skin tingled in anticipation of whatever fun Javion had planned for us tonight.

"Humph, looks like I found me a mermaid. Didn't know they made 'em in black."

My eyes snapped open. A woman with a thick New York accent had me scooting to the farthest corner of the tub as I glared up at a different kind of hairless cat.

"Who the fuck are you?" I snapped in her direction, scanning the bathroom for something to cover myself with. "Javion," I shouted at the top of my lungs. *Where the fuck is he?* There wasn't a towel anywhere close, and my cell was in the bedroom on the charger. Elgin tipped in and plopped down at the heels of this colossal cat lady who was either smirking or frowning down at me. It was hard to tell which one since she'd had the kind of plastic surgery that was usually only for superrich and famous people. The kind that gave them all meaty lips and oversized cheekbones with stiff, puffy eyebrows. It was the kind where you didn't know if they were *all the way crazy* or just really confused kind of crazy. It would've made a hell of a difference in helping me figure out whether I needed to get out of the tub and all the way beat her ass or just slap her around until she figured out where she was.

"Hey, babe, sorry I took so long. The front door was cracked. I think the maintenance guy must've stopped by or . . ." Javion answered on his way up the stairs.

Whatever apology or excuse he had brewing on his lips dropped along with the expression on his face. He stopped dead in his tracks just outside the bathroom door. His eyes locked on the woman standing over me.

"*What* are you doing here, McKenzie?" Javion asked in a cold, flat voice.

She had the nerve to toss her long golden hair over her shoulder before letting out a long sigh, like we were boring her.

"I been calling all night, but you ain't been answering. *Now* I see why. You was obviously busy. Boss man sent me to get your pull for the day. I let myself in."

Javion tipped his head back, giving her a suspicious look. "I've been taking in my own drop for two years. Why would he send you out here?" he asked suspiciously.

Before I could blink, I found myself staring down the barrel of a gun. It came out of her purse so fast, I didn't have time to react.

The water made a solid splashing sound from my jaw dropping down into it. I looked toward Javion with my eyes begging for help.

"You ain't seen the news. Beau, that wrestler, and his daughter were killed. Assassination style. Cops pulled your girl's prints from the door handle. Been looking for her all day. Boss man don't know her. He said you're done, and she's dead."

Javion wouldn't look my way. He just stood there rubbing his hand across the back of his neck. McKenzie was eagerly eating him up in eyefuls. I wanted to tell him to handle this bitch or man the fuck up, but I was too scared to speak.

"A'ight, McKenzie, let me give him a call. I did my job, and I scared the nigga like I was supposed to. He said he'd pay tonight, and we left. If this has to be done I want to handle it. I'll give you twenty grand if you give me five minutes."

McKenzie thought his offer over. She swept me with an ugly sideways glare before stomping away.

"*Miho*, when you gonna give me a chance? You need to stop fuckin' with these foo-foo-frilly stranger bitches," McKenzie said as they walked away.

Javion's answer was inaudible as they went downstairs. *I know he didn't just let that stranger bitch call me a stranger bitch.* If I was speaking to my dad, I'd have some real hitters out here so fast. Having my life threatened was nothing new, but this whole wanted-for-murder shit had me so hot, it's a wonder I didn't make the bathwater boil. Frustrated and over the whole situation, I got up, sloshing water all across the tile floor as I dripped my way into the bedroom.

Eavesdropping on their conversation didn't even interest me as I made my way down the hall. Javion had just offered to kill me himself. He didn't fight the bitch or curse her out. This nigga was just as bad as the rest. In my book, all men were cowards when it came to stepping up for a woman.

I let out a small gasp when I saw the damn cat propped up on my overnight bag. The way he could creep from room to room freaked me the fuck out. After unceremoniously shoving him aside, I pulled out some jeans and a T-shirt, tugging them over my still damp skin. My sandals were soundless on the hardwood floor as I crept down the stairs and out the door.

How could I be so stupid? First, that pregnant bitch pops up, and now this. I should've known he was too good to be true. This was the reason why I was so cautious about letting someone in. This dude wasn't even a top-nigga. My freedom was at risk, and my name was out there, all because of Javion. Daddy would have my ass if he knew what kind of shit I'd let happen. Not cool . . . This was not cool at all.

5

Mommy Issues

The next morning, I woke Shandy up, telling her we owed Momma and Daddy a visit. Fucking around with Javion, I was probably gonna need their help, whether I liked it or not.

Every charcoal grill on every back porch, deck, and in every backyard in DC must've all been going at the same time. You could smell the ribs, hot dogs, and hamburgers. As soon as I rolled my window down, the smoky heat pressed its way into the car, swallowing whatever air-conditioning it came in contact with.

Javion had been blowing me up ever since I left. He was doing everything in his power to get into my personal space so he could read all into my headspace. And I just wanted some me-time and by me-time, I mean time with me and anyone *except* him. A part of me accepted what he did like it was second nature. The perks that came with dating him were unbelievable. It didn't even bother me, knowing that I'd have to watch my back and his. It didn't bother me knowing if something went down while we were together, I'd be guilty by association. And that, in itself, my acceptance and understanding bothered me more than anything.

My parents' place was off-limits to everyone except Shandy. Since Momma had sent me some mysterious 9-1-1 texts and wasn't returning my calls, we were homeward bound.

"Damn, Novie, can you move any slower? Got a bitch titties sweatin' and shit. I need the power of a good turn up in me so bad right now!" Shandy sat in the backseat fanning her double FFs furiously. She was the prettiest girl I knew with bright, slanted, cat eyes and clear baby-smooth skin. Somebody was mixed somewhere in her family because her hair grew thick and wavy, no relaxer necessary. But if you wanted to see somebody get real ugly, try to throw shade about her weight. I dare you.

Shandy wasn't fat, but she was plumper than what most would classify as thick. She'd been rocking corsets and waist cinchers to sit her titties up and push her booty out before it was even the thing. Don't get me wrong; she was more than comfortable in her skin, but she had no problem snapping if you tried to play her to the left because of it. Another half hour and all of my bestie's NARS foundation would be melting down her chin and into one of the many expensive shirtdresses she splurged on.

I shrugged. "My bad, girl. I'm just pissed we're here and not hittin' up one of these cookouts."

"It's all good." She stared longingly out the window. "I've got to put in some serious work, though. Find me a sponsor, sling some coochie for cash, or start movin' some serious dope. I was supposed to have two of these houses by now."

I cut my eyes at her over my shoulder. She knew better than to play around like that. Not when my dad was the infamous Sammie Knox. When the streets heard Knox was coming, it was like saying Bloody Mary in the mirror three times.

"Oh, don't look at me like that, Novie. You know I'm just all in my feelings, looking at these pretty houses when I just lost my grant. How the hell am I supposed to pay for my last year of school now? Me and my baby girl need this in our life."

She fussed over Aris Monique Patterson in the car seat next to her. I tried to tell her I don't know how many times, that people wouldn't see Aris and say *heiress*. She'd need an extra *r* or an *e* up in there, but you can't tell Shandy anything once her mind is made up.

"Lawd," Shandy let out a dramatic sigh. "I'm so glad I'm not breast-feeding anymore. I need me a drink and a blunt so bad. I hope Lady J ain't acting funny. You know how stingy she get with her liquor."

I met her wide, worried eyes in the rearview. Momma, or Lady J, as she liked to be called, because *Misses* sounded old, would be all right. "Stop worrying, Shandy. Everything'll be fine."

The tires crunched over the sandy cobblestone driveway through the small forest of pine trees and small oaks toward the four-story glass-front palace that belonged to my parents. Mixed feelings welled up inside me, clawing at the back of my throat. I needed them but hated spending more time than necessary with them. Somebody always wound up needing a favor, and their favors never worked out in my favor. I'd started to say just that as we stood outside the double French doors. I was clawing through my purse, digging around for my spare key. Shandy was busy fretting over Aris in her stroller.

I found it wedged in between the prongs of a fork at the bottom of my purse and made a mental note to clean it out or switch to a smaller bag.

"Ma?" I called out, stepping over a lonely pump with a broken heel. The wall was splattered with cotton candy pink Louboutin polish. Glass shards from the bottle were scattered across the floor. The outside of the house was always plain and simple, but inside, the house looked like a war zone.

"Novie? Hey, boo." She came rushing around the corner with her arms out, all flushed and out of breath. She was stylishly put together as usual, in a light blue dress that stopped just above her knees.

"What are you doing here?" She pulled me into an awkward hug then grabbed Shandy and did the same.

"What am I doing here? Really? What's up with the 9-1-1 texts, and what in the world happened up in here?" I dropped my purse on the side table by the front door. "Daddy?" I called out. My eyes were searchlights as I scanned the foyer and the main hallway.

"Your dad ain't home, Novie." She folded her hands across her arms saying how-dare-he-not-be-here, and how-dare-you-question-me, and I-dare-you-to-say-one-more-thing all in that one look.

"Um, Lady J, I think I need to change Aris. Do you mind . . . um, if I use the restroom?" Shandy could sense a family matter like an animal senses danger. She scooped Aris up out of her stroller, resting her head on her shoulder underneath her chin.

"Make yourself at home. Use the one across from the guest room down the hall to the left." She gave Shandy a serious look. "Just keep the noise down, *please.*"

I wondered what that was about as she waved Shandy off down one hall before swooping in to block me from going anywhere.

"Okay, Ma, what's really going on? Daddy hasn't answered one of my calls, and he always answers. Did you do something to him? Y'all have a fight?" I spun around her in the direction of the living room.

She was in hot pursuit trailing after me toward the living room. "Novie, bring your ass here. I need to explain something to you."

I stormed the living room like a one-woman SWAT team. She'd changed all the furniture again. It wasn't the make-you-cringe, we-rich-bitch, pink and gold Versace collection anymore. Thank the Lord. That either went out of style, or somebody she knew had something too close to it. Now it was dark cappuccino-brown, Italian leather ottomans, tall, glossy, floor lamps, brown carpeting. A high-backed leather sofa sat with matching armchairs beside it. But something stunk; it smelled rancid, like old Chinese food and sour washrags. I covered my nose with my hand. Heavy curtains were drawn, throwing the living room into semidarkness. I jerked to a stop in front of the couch, feeling like I'd swallowed a rock the size of my foot. "What the fuck?" I whispered involuntarily when my eyes locked on the pregnant girl shivering on a couch in a tattered, stained sundress. She was skinny as hell, but still very pregnant.

She was hog-tied, with her mouth taped shut, staring back at me for help.

I took a step back when I saw the vomit on the floor in front of the sofa. "What the fuck is this?" I asked. I couldn't even look my mother in the eyes as I pointed down at her. "What the hell is goin' on up in here?" I demanded in a shaky whisper. This couldn't be business related. It was against the rules to bring any of that into the house.

"I told you we needed to talk." There was an edge to her voice that wasn't there before. Fury was exploding in her eyes. "You wanna know what this is?" She chuckled, then giggled, and then she doubled over laughing until she had tears in her eyes. When she finally regained her composure, the venom was back. "Sammie supposedly left on business. *Late* Friday night the doorbell rings. And it's that ho, right there. I don't know what she was on, but the bitch was higher than caviar. Telling me how she and

Sammie been together. Showing me a goddamn slide show on her phone. Telling me she's pregnant. She thought she was gonna come up to *my* house. Disrespect me to *my* face. Gonna tell me about *my* husband and the life she about to live with him. *That's* what this is."

"Oh, shit. Daddy did what . . . she came here and . . . oh, damn."

There were always rumors about Daddy's women. I was always suspicious, but I never really knew for sure.

"These new-age bitches," she spat. "They don't understand the levels to this shit." She sneered down at the girl on the couch. "If you trading pussy for the nigga's time and trinkets, you don't come to *my* front door. I'm his *wife*. *He,* and only he, addresses me. You just another one of Sammie's hoes."

The girl wildly shook her head back and forth. She was saying something, but I couldn't make anything out with the tape over her mouth. And then her body went rigid; her back arched like an electric current surged through the chair. The veins in her neck protruded like plastic straws under her skin. She started squirming and groaning like she was possessed. She squeezed her eyes shut and alternated between clenching her jaw and straining against her ropes. Momma didn't seem the least bit concerned. She checked the hands on her petite rose-gold watch.

"I thought he'd have come home by now. Her contractions are about ten minutes apart," she stated in the most matter-of-fact tone.

Her contractions? I wanted to scream until my throat burned, but I screamed them in my head instead. This was it; she'd finally completely lost it. I knew it would happen one day, and we were there. She wasn't even bothered by the cheating or upset that Daddy might have another baby; she was just upset that the woman had the nerve to approach her.

"Lady J! Lady J, it's Sammie!" Tariq, Daddy's second in command, yelled from the direction of the foyer.

The tone of his voice made the blood drain from our faces. My knees were wobbly as I forced them to steer me in the direction of Tariq's gruff voice as we rushed to see what had him worked up. Tariq read like a brick wall. Outside of working, if it didn't involve weights, weapons, or warfare, the nigga wasn't interested. He never so much as sneezed loud, let alone yelled. Daddy kept him tethered to his side like a two-year-old on a harness. Our eyes met across the foyer as he rushed inside.

NOVIE

6

Fake Falls Away, and the Real Gets Realer

Tariq, in all of his Egyptian musk-scented presence, filled the doorway. I had to keep myself in the moment. That smell always took me back. Made my scar ache. His chest was heaving; he bent down, put his hands on his knees, and took a steadying breath. "We were handling business when somebody opened up on us at a light. Didn't see who did it. Sammie needs you to patch him up. We can't risk a doctor's office right now, okay?"

Momma nodded and kept on nodding. She was still nodding after Tariq left to get Daddy. That's when I realized that most women don't start out completely crazy. No, they're usually driven there. The change takes place in the space of an inhale, like zero to a hundred and eighty-three with no seat belt in a two-seater called love. In my momma's case, the driver was my daddy. And as crazy as she was about him, she'd go just as crazy over him, and he'd do the same thing for her in his own weird way.

She jumped when I reached for her.

"Ma? What do you need me to do?" I asked on the verge of tears, but I swallowed them back.

"You know I'm here too, Lady J," Shandy announced. She scurried away to secure Aris out of the way in her stroller.

Momma's lip quivered before she tightened it. She stopped shaking and steadied herself. Her eyes darted to the door and back. "Go move that bitch to the garage before he knows she's here. I'll have Tariq put him in the back bedroom. We'll just have to deal with her later."

I nodded, pulling Shandy with me. I needed to explain what she was about to see before we got in the living room, and she screamed the roof down on us. Hell, I needed to prepare myself to see that shit again before we got in there.

My stomach pitched. I turned and threw up orange against the far wall and dry heaved until there was nothing left. *Oh my God. What has she done? What did I let happen?*

Shandy turned away, closing her eyes at the sight of the dead with her head turned and her eyes staring through us. They would probably haunt me for the rest of my life. Shandy yanked on my arm so hard she almost pulled it out of the socket.

"Novie!" She got up on her tiptoes staring, fascinated with her body.

I prayed by some miraculous force she was alive, and I'd only imagined she was dead or just looked dead. When Shandy brushed past me, I knew it wasn't the case. I could see it lying there quietly, but I didn't want to believe it. I'd always thought babies were supposed to scream and cry when they were born. Shandy scooped up the slick baby with a look of awe on her face as Momma sailed into the living room with blood on her cheek and the front of her dress.

"How do I save a fool in one room and lose a fool in the other. *Fuck*." Momma cursed under her breath as she tapped her finger against the tip of her nose. "Your daddy is fine. But please . . . Please, tell me she ain't dead."

All I could do was shake my head.

She looked in Shandy's direction. Her finger stopped midtap. It hovered in the air, asking the question on both of our minds. How real was Shandy's loyalty to our family?

Momma crossed the room. "Shandy?" She sounded like they were about to discuss the weather. "You know we've got a lot going on right now. You know we have to get rid of *everything*, right?" Momma reached for the baby in Shandy's arms. The extra emphasis she'd put on the word *everything* was the spark that ignited the tension-fueled air.

Shandy's eyes went wild, her face turned savage. "You ain't takin' Aris away from me! Not again!" She hissed at us, showing all of her teeth, holding the baby protectively in her arms.

"Shandy, that's not Aris," Momma cooed at her. "Aris is upstairs right where you left her. That baby that *you're* holding is a *real* little boy." She talked real slow, as if she was explaining everything to a five-year-old.

And then she turned to me with this soothe-your-savage-friend look on her face, and I threw my hands up, thinking, *I didn't unleash the beast; you did.* Hell, I didn't know what to do, especially since the Aris that we'd left sitting in the stroller in the other room wasn't even a real baby. Yes, Aris looked like a real newborn; she even wore clothes, diapers, and baby powder. But the only person she was real to and had ever been real to was Shandy. People would come up to see her and walk away with the creepy OMG-she-got-a-fake-baby face. Most of our friends understood, and the ones who didn't get it would turn a blind eye or disappear.

Shandy's mom was addicted to OxyContin and alcohol. Swiss ran away before he finished high school. When we were fourteen, her mama pimped her out to one of her boyfriends for pill money. When Shandy got pregnant, her mom said she was useless, and she kicked her out of her house. We took her in; even had her looking forward to having the baby. We were all a little devastated when Shandy lost the baby at seven months. Then Momma got a doll that cost more than a diamond. It was weird in the beginning, but it worked, so we kept going along with it because we thought one day Shandy would snap out of it. The funny thing is, we'd been going along with it for the last seven years. Her momma was in a home for mentally unstable women now. All the drinking and drugs fucked her mind up.

"Okay, Shan," Momma's voice was whisper soft. "You can keep the baby. I'll help you with it, give you everything you need."

Ma, I mouthed silently while looking at her like she'd just grown an extra head and her extra head just said all kinds of bullshit in a foreign language. Shandy didn't need a baby and definitely not one that might be my half brother, who's Mom we might as well be accomplices to murder for. He was living evidence.

But it seemed to be exactly what Shandy needed to hear. She started to calm down.

"Shandy, you'll need to stay out of sight for a little while. And then you just tell everyone he's yours, and we're good. You aren't going to talk about where he came from or how you got him. He's your baby."

We both watched her. The baby whined a little, but he didn't cry.

Shandy furrowed her forehead. She rocked the baby, her whole body swayed back and forth, from side to side as she contemplated what had been said.

"Why do you keep saying *he*?" She propped the baby up.

He was shiny and slick, covered in another woman's blood and fluids. Shandy displayed his tiny twig and berries with his umbilical cord dangling down the side of her arm still attached to his mother. "*Aris* is a *girl*. Y'all start drinkin' without me?" She scrunched her face up at us like we were the crazy ones in the room.

I pinched the bridge of my nose between my fingers. There was too much going on right now. I could feel a good strong headache coming on. *What the fuck kind of Norman Bates shit were we about to spawn into the world?*

"Novie, go get Tariq. Tell him come clean this mess." She waved her hand in the direction of the couch while pulling me out of hearing distance. "Baby, it's not as bad as you think. People are already used to seeing her with that doll, and she's already a little heavy."

"I'm so done with this family. I really can't cope with you right now, Ma."

"Grow up, little girl," she spat in a sharp whisper. "You have one more year at Howard, and you still ain't picked a major yet. So what? You want to get a job, work until you die? Well, that tuition, those books, your car . . . all of it's paid for in red. We never bullshit you about this life, so you step up or get stepped over."

I traced the patterns into the carpet between my shoes. Her words hurt my pride just as much as they cut into hurt my heart. Shandy had started singing to the baby from behind us. It was something melodic but eerie. I tried to tune her out.

Momma grabbed my chin; she yanked my face up until I met her eyes. They were sad, but they were hard.

"We're gonna need you to do us a small favor."

I knew it was coming. The way the word rolled off her lips. She made favors sound like they were owed and not courtesies.

"What is it?" I had so much attitude in my voice.

Whatever this favor was had to be important. Momma overlooked my disrespect to grab something off the fireplace mantel. Five gold letters stood out on the white card she held up between her fingers.

"That girl had this on her. This attorney . . . Genesis Kane. I looked into him. He's been deputized as a voluntary prosecutor for the district courts when they're backed up. I don't care what or how you do it. You get to him. Find out why she was talking to him, what he might know. I need to make sure your daddy didn't fuck around, *fuckin' around*."

GENESIS

7

King of Hearts

The thick mahogany shades covering the floor-to-ceiling windows slid up without a sound, letting in the glow from the city at night. From up here, you didn't see the buildings or the traffic. You didn't hear the busy heartbeat of the city. I specifically chose this penthouse for the master bedroom's view of the Potomac River. It was the most majestic shit I'd ever seen, a reminder to keep me on my king game. I put all the shit from the other night behind me with a long weekend of uppers, downers, and all-arounders. Scotch, Xanax, hash oil, shit I don't even know. I zoned out on it, my vision blurred, and blood rushed to my head. My other head.

She was butt-ass naked with perfectly perky titties, a gift from her husband. They didn't quite match the age spots on her hands or the wrinkled sagging skin on her midsection, a gift from her son. She wasn't my type in any way, shape, or form. I liked my women with thick hips, dick-sucking lips, and those thighs that a dude could get lost in like quicksand. But I hyped myself up.

I growled, dug my fingers into her hip, making red marks in her flesh. She woke up from a sound sleep as I rolled her onto her stomach. I spread her legs from one end of the bed to the other. Her pussy was still glossy, creamy, full from my earlier deposits. I don't know about most niggas, but I don't like dipping in my own leftovers. Not only did it turn me off, but it made her shit feel like sliding into a bowl of warm Jell-O. I wanted to knock her upside the head, but I grilled her like I'm-about-tear-this-shit-up. My dick wouldn't go down if I wanted it to. I'd taken too many Viagras for that. So I eased inside her, filled her up, fucked her until she begged me to stop, and I ain't stop until she couldn't beg me anymore.

"*Mmm* . . . Damn, I wish I could just roll over and go right back to sleep. But thank you, Kane," she purred with a satisfied smile when we were done. "*Where* were you when I was still single? I swear, spending one night with you beats an entire session at my rejuvenation day spa. I feel like I'm glowing." She stretched, and then scooted in closer to lay her head on my chest. Her hair and skin still held the scent of the Marlboro Skylines she chain-smoked. It never went away, no matter how much expensive lotion and perfume she used, or how often she washed. I hated that scent. If a smell could tell a story, hers would sound like guilty marathon sex in a shady motel on cum-stained sheets. That's why I never delayed the timer on the blinds. If I didn't have anything to focus on, fucking her would be torture.

The combination of stale smoke, sweat, and J'adore Dior filled my nostrils. As my phone buzzed its way across the nightstand, I ignored it; didn't even glance in its direction. I gave her shoulders a warm squeeze. I hid my disgust for her the same way I usually hid my distaste for trashy white women, flashy, loud-mouthed niggas, and laws, in general. I tucked it away behind a façade of fake friendliness. Paula was oblivious as usual. She placed a warm kiss underneath my chin.

"Somebody else trying to squeeze in already?" She pressed her lips together into a duck-faced pout. "I'm not leaving until you're completely drained, so if you've got more, give it up."

With the tip of her perfectly painted period-bloodred nail, she *booped* the tip of my nose. I moved my head away just slightly. I hated that shit too. I barely touched my own face with my bare hands. And here she was touching my nose and stroking my cheek with her bright whore-red nail polish, flashing at me like a germy warning sign. Only hookers and whores wore red lips or red nails. But Paula Schaefer was listed in *Forbes* magazine as one of the richest women in the world. As VP of Schaefer and Brockman, she could make anyone into anything she wanted them to be. And since I didn't need to be the world's richest man . . . and all I wanted was a small part of that fortune in a fraction of that time, I smiled bright, kissed her on her forehead, and said whatever she needed to hear.

"I think you wore me out. How about you let me have some time off to recuperate?" I got up and headed for my master bath with Paula hot on my heels.

"Ugh! I'll tell you this much, one kid and your bladder shrinks to the size of a fucking walnut. I've got to pee so bad." She sped past me into the bathroom, unleashing a hiss of a stream into the toilet.

I braced my bare shoulders against the wall. "You know there are four other bathrooms in here that you can use besides mine?" I reminded her for what had to be the hundredth time.

"I know. I know. You don't have to be so possessive. Sharing is caring, Kane. Jeez, I couldn't hold it. But I've been thinking and . . . How would you feel about coming in and taking care of the paperwork . . . one day this week?"

The toilet flushed, and Paula was right there, back in front in front of me, hand extended, waiting to shake on making me a partner in the firm. No wash, no hand sanitizer, nothing. I reached for it, wondering how many million-dollar deals went down over some sorry sex and a pissy handshake. The sooner we made this partner thing official, the better off I'd be. It'd take me a minute to figure out how to break things off, but the idea of sending her husband an anonymous tip wasn't looking that bad.

She got dressed while rambling about whether she should have red, white, or some new amber wine at a dinner party for her husband. I'd just be a member of the bachelor's club for the rest of my life. You marry a woman, and then she plans all of your parties and vacations with the nigga she's fucking. I'll pass.

"Kane," Paula called from the doorway, "I've got the paper for you and doughnuts."

"Doughnuts?" I rarely ate doughnuts, and Paula didn't eat anything white. Something to do with good carbs and bad carbs, or I would've told her to keep and eat the doughnuts. Instead of making a big deal out of it, I said thanks and endured another smoky good-bye kiss.

My phone buzzed its way across the table as I was making my way back inside. I was in such a rush to answer it, I missed the last step. Bile rose up the back of my throat. The muscles in my stomach shuddered. The Dunkin' doughnut box was lying on its side on the floor right next to my foot where I'd dropped it. And if you followed the glossy globs of congealed blood that trailed out of it for about a foot, you'd find the fat, bloody-red pig's heart that'd rolled out of it when it fell.

It took me an extra hour to pull myself together enough to clean that mess up. This wasn't the first one, but it was the biggest. It'd started small with what might've been a mouse or a canary heart, and every so often, I'd get another one. I just never knew when or where. Why didn't I call the police? *Because I'm not a fucking snitch.* I was an attorney with a long and buried past that I didn't need or want anybody digging around in. It was most likely a crazy fuck-buddy-turned-friend who wasn't happy with the new status. All it'd take was some new dick, and she'd forget about me and terrorize that nigga with her gory heart story. Or she'd show herself. Either way, I had real shit to take care of.

On top of that, the texts were from Fucksquatch. It was urgent, and he wanted me to meet him at the station in an hour. We always kept our meetings to the ten p.m. time frame. After shift change, they were on a skeleton crew until morning. I checked my watch wondering what the hell else he could have gotten into in a few days. Knowing him, it'd probably be in my best interest to get out there sooner than later. But if this shit had anything to do with Saniah's complaint, he was on his own; my work was done.

I parked in my favorite illegal spot next to the hydrant in front of the precinct. Squatton needed to make this quick so I could get into the office and sign those papers while they were still on Paula's mind. The moment the door closed behind me, I knew something wasn't right. But it was too late to turn back.

"And here's the man of the hour. Genesis Kane. Am I right?"

A pile of bloody massacred cops lay behind the dude who'd stepped forward. The ones that weren't dead yet were lined up along the wall. Four men who I would've mistaken for computer technicians stood behind him with grim faces. Their Polo shirts and khakis were covered in too much blood; their posture was too aggressive for some IT work. I had an idea who he was, but I wasn't 100 percent.

There wasn't any point bullshitting. "Okay, I'm here. What do you want?"

He tossed Squatton's phone in his direction. It clattered to the floor in front of his shackled feet. Squatton had a look in his eyes like he was about to shit a freight train. He doubled over, making a sound that was somewhere between a laugh and a desperate wail.

"Where the fuck *is my sister*!" He slammed his fists into his forehead, dragged his hands down his face like he was trying to pull off his skin. His movements were jerky, mechanical, as he stormed toward the front desk and grabbed the bloody hunting knife off the counter.

The pack of officers shifted behind him mumbled, cried . . . prayed.

"On my life, you better start spilling secrets before I start spilling blood," he demanded. He moved in on a stocky female cop. "How many of those liars, I mean lawyers, out there know your secret, Kane?" he asked.

What secret did this bottom-feeder think he had on me? This nigga was on that Pablo Escobar. That scared the truth out of you or would draw blood until you told a good lie. That was my first thought. Thinking on my feet was how I made my living. The legal game was worse than being a fake fortune-teller. People lie to stay alive, and you don't have any choice but to learn the truth about them from their actions, their mannerisms. And this nigga didn't come across as a territory-hungry power-thirsty alpha nigga. I played to that, didn't ask any questions, or give him any decisions to make. And prayed that I was right.

"Saniah, right? I helped her get out of here. So give me a little time to check on her. I just need a few days." I sounded a helluva lot calmer than I felt. Sweat was starting to soak through the pits of my shirt.

He stalked the floor in front of the desk.

"She called me." He pointed the knife at his head. "She told me about you. My sister, Face."

The tip of the blade pointed at me.

I wasn't paying attention to a word he'd said or was about to say. "Your sister Saniah . . . is Face? Not you?" I asked. That was one for the record books. That scrawny little pregnant chick was taking over the drug game, scaring these cops and street niggas out of their turf all because they thought she was her brother. The pieces were still clunky, but they were all starting to fit together: her scar, the name; the only piece missing was her.

It was as if he hadn't even heard me. "For whatever reason, my sister likes you. But Face always liked keeping weird shit in jars, like ladybugs and butterflies. I should fuckin' kill you. But today ain't your day. So go. But you owe me, Ladybug. Remember who you owe."

NOVIE

8

Always Keep a Spare Tire

Two vodka cranberries later and I was still tossing and turning. Every time I closed my eyes, I thought about Beau and his daughter, or the pregnant girl and the baby boy who Shandy was hell-bent on raising like a baby girl. I felt sick to my stomach. Out of all the sick and fucked-up shit that my parents had done over the years, that was the worst. The one person who I'd normally talk to, Shandy, was caught right up in the middle of it.

The bright green numbers on the clock beside my bed changed to three a.m. I gave up on sleep and got dressed, and then I just started driving. That always helped me sort shit out. Every set of headlights that came up in the rearview had my chest thumping and my hands sweating. I should've asked my mom to help, but the timing was off. I cracked the windows, settling on a satellite radio station that played mostly old-school R&B. I just knew those blue lights would come flashing after me. I grabbed the pack of Newport Lights in my armrest. No one knew I smoked. Not even Shandy, my bestie/roommate.

The match flared, filling my nose with the smell of smoke and burning sulfur. As weird as it sounds, I loved the smell of burning matches, and I hated the smell from cigarette smoke. The end of the cigarette glowed bright red as I took a long, slow drag. I could feel some of the nervous tension leaving my body as I exhaled carefully, blowing a stinky cloud of smoke out the window. I'd become a pro at smoking and keeping the stink out of my hair and clothes.

I called my other bestie Denise. We were so much alike that we got on each other's nerves. She was cool as hell, but she'd talk about you like a dog the second you turned your back. Aside from Shandy, Denise was the only other person who could maybe talk some sense in to me at a time when my life was making no sense at all.

"What's wrong, Novie?" Denise yawned extra loud and long into the phone. "I'm answering in case this is an emergency. But I'm hanging up if you need me to get out of my bed and leave this house." She went off as soon as she picked up the phone.

I let out an exasperated sigh into the phone. "Dang, girl, I ain't even said anything. Why every time I call something's gotta be wrong? I was just . . . um." Well, damn, maybe I did only call her when something was wrong because I was drawing a blank, trying to think of another reason. "I was just being nosy; can't sleep. What did you get into tonight?"

"You ain't fooling nobody, but anyway, girl, I tried to get something up in me, but I'm about to fire this nigga Stephen from my little lineup."

I took another pull from my cigarette, digging through my mental Rolodex of Denise's fuck-buddies and ran-dom-run-bys. There were too many nameless faces for me to narrow it down. I drew a blank. "Fire who?" I asked, blowing wispy white smoke into the air.

"Stephen. The little white guy I been talkin' to from my job. I told you about him, the new supervisor with the dick-bulge. I've been trying to find out if he packin' or just *packin'*, like stuffing that jank with socks or something, but that nigga stay bringin' me chicken for lunch. I mean, yo, what the hell he think? All black people just like chicken?"

I did my best to keep from laughing. "Heffa, since when did you stop liking chicken?"

"Huh? I ain't say I don't like it. I love that shit. But that nigga just be bringin' it to me all unsolicited and whatnot. KFC, Chick-fil-A, Church's—that's all I get. I'm over it."

I giggled into the phone. I don't know what was funnier, hearing how mad she was about the chicken or hearing her call this white dude nigga the whole time. That was my girl, though.

"Oh, and I used all that coconut oil you let me borrow," she continued. "I found this little recipe on Pinterest for a hair conditioner. That stuff works, and Heather said it smells good too. Can you give massages with that shit? I'm gonna get her to rub me down."

"Hold up, who the hell is Heather? Girl, I'm gonna make some picture flash cards of all your *friends*. I can't keep up with who you're into, or who's getting into you. Is that the new girl you're talking to? You, Chicken Little, Hannah Montana, and whoever else ain't about to be using up all of my stuff for whatever it is y'all do," I warned her.

Ever since Denise went through the big chop a couple of months back, she'd been obsessed about growing her hair. She'd been trying to talk me into it, but I wasn't ready to let go of my perms and flat irons. Not yet, anyway. She could've at least asked before using up all my stuff, but that would've been too much, like right?

"Why you gotta play like that, Novie? Her name is Heather. But what the hell are you doing heading to Javion's?"

"No, I'm going somewhere else."

"Wait, I knew something was up with your little phone call. What's the matter? You been spendin' every weekend up in your little love nest. And now you goin' somewhere else? Do I need to get my little cousins to fuck him up, with his young-looking ass? Oh, let me guess. He lied about his little age? I told you that nigga was a twenty-five-lie. What is he, seventeen, nineteen?"

I bust out laughing. He really was a very, very young-looking twenty-five. I gave Denise a quick recap of my day, leaving out the part about Shandy and the baby.

"Well, damn, how are you going to get all that shit cleared up? You can't turn yourself in. There's no guarantee that they'll believe you," Denise pointed out the obvious.

I took a deep breath, paused, and exhaled my answer into the phone.

"I'm going to Krypton."

"Oh, *hell* to the naw. I know you ain't talkin' about *Kryptonite,* Novie."

I cringed even though she couldn't see me. The tone of Denise's voice said one hand was on her hip while she gave every word with a self-righteous head wiggle.

"Kryptonite in the flesh," I answered weakly.

"I'm coming to get you because your ass is obviously on somethin'. That nigga is off-fucking-limits. Sammie is gonna kick your ass, and he's gonna skin that nigga alive when he finds out what you're up to."

My teeth tugged at my lower lip. Just thinking about Swiss put a smile on my face.

"That's why my dad ain't gonna find out," I answered in a smart-ass tone.

There was also a chance that Swiss could help me with my problem since I didn't get a chance to ask my dad for help.

"Novie, miss me with all that. You are way too forgiving after what you went through . . . and that nigga . . . You've always been *too forgiving*." She took some of the harshness out of her voice. "I know you still have your little feelings for Swiss, but does Shandy know you're still messing with her brother? Family or not, Swiss ain't never been shit and never will be. Girl, we were barely out of high school. How many men go around fuckin' they baby sister's only best friend in the *whole world*, just to fuck her over? Only my no-good, bullshit brother would do that. You had to let go of a man, but she let go of family behind that shit. Wrong is wrong. You shouldn't pick something up after God's smacked it out of your hand."

Yeah yeah yeah, I know. I was always deeply grateful but guilt-tripped, knowing Shandy was loyal enough to cut her own brother off. She was obviously stronger than I, I thought. I couldn't cut him off completely, and every time I did, I somehow found my way back or he found me.

I cleared my throat. "You know I was just having a moment. Talking to you about all that actually helped. The moment has passed." I lied to get her mind off the subject.

The line beeped in my ear. "Speaking of the devil. Javion's callin' me. Probably to apologize and clear all this up. I'll let him buy us a few new Michael Kors purses or something before I fully accept his apology."

"Yassss. That's my bitch! I need a new clutch too. Make him get one in pink boa or some exotic shit. Hit me back if it sounds like he can't fix this." Denise all but oozed into the phone.

Instead of answering Javion's call, I turned my phone completely off. It only took me six sticks of spearmint gum and thirty minutes to make the drive from DC to

Woodbridge. My jaw was sore from chewing so much gum, but I didn't want to get to my destination smelling like Smokey the Bear. I promised myself a smoke on the way back home, and that eased some of my anxiety.

If there was one thing my momma always told me, it was to make sure I kept a spare tire. My palms got hot and sweaty on the steering wheel at the sight of Swiss's muddy work truck sitting in the driveway. I gave my hair a quick check in the mirror. The steam from my bath knocked all my curls out, leaving me with no other option than to tuck the sides behind my ears.

The front door swung open as I walked up to the house. He stood in the door in a pair of oil-stained coveralls barely hanging around his waist. Despite my conversation with Denise, I couldn't stop the smile from spreading across my face. Swiss was my spare tire. We'd been off and on for the last three years, but we could never claim each other, so we'd fall together, and then we'd fall apart. Swiss always called it an *understanding*. I called it stubborn denial.

"I missed you, Novie-star!" Swiss sang out my name in his deep, raspy voice returning my smile. "Am I off punishment?"

His thick bottom lip was drawn in between his teeth as I climbed the last step toward him. I stepped into the heat of his body, inhaling the smell of him. It was masculine, metal, motor oil, almond butter, and sweat. His locks were loose, hanging down the middle of his back, brushing against my hands wrapped around his shoulders.

There was a low rumble in his chest when he pulled back and cupped an ass cheek in each hand. He slowly dragged me toward him the way a bulldozer pulls earth. He parted my lips with his and fucked my mouth with his tongue. Shockwaves danced across the tops of my teeth. He stole my breath and breathed it right back. It was some kind of tantric CPR. Swiss was the only man in the world who could tell me exactly what he'd do to my pussy without ever saying a word. When I was panting, soaking wet, and wobbly, cool air replaced the heat of his lips.

"You can't be leavin' a nigga like that," he said in a quiet voice, pressing his forehead against mine.

"I know," I whispered. "I missed you too."

His warm gingerbread-colored eyes stared hard into mine. He seemed more bothered or hurt than usual. I was stubborn, always put up a fight, and he was trying to figure out why I was throwing in the towel so easily this time. My eyes felt hot thinking about everything. I'd been working extra hard at avoiding him. The last time we were together, I felt myself falling for him, and I panicked. Swiss swore that he was ready for me and a family, and that he'd tell my dad everything. He said he'd quit working for the family, get a regular job, and it'd be us. I was the one who got cold feet. I did what I had to do to move forward, and then I turned all my attention toward Javion, hoping he could erase Swiss's name off my heart. But Javion was only good for keeping my mind busy. All his kisses and caresses couldn't make my body stop yearning for Swiss. As long as Swiss was in the picture, my mind and my pussy would never align with the same guy.

I stared at the goose bumps rising along his chest. They matched the bumps that circled his dark nipples. "I'm kinda sort of in trouble," I told him.

He tilted my chin up with his thumb. The corner of his mouth quirked up into a half smile. "So I heard through the underground gossip line. Don't even worry about that bullshit. I'll handle it for you."

NOVIE

9

The Fairer Sex Never Plays Fair

Now that that was taken care of, I could focus on another pressing matter. I pressed my hand against Swiss's chest, urging him backward into the dark living room. The contact from his bare skin radiated through my fingertips, down my wrists, and through my elbows. He pinned me back against the front door the second it closed. His lips rained kisses down the side of my neck. We were getting a semicool breeze through the window, but it wasn't enough to keep me from breaking into a sweat.

He peeled me out of my T-shirt, covering my skin with kisses as he went.

"It's a li'l humid in here. My AC on the fritz. That's what I've been working on," he said while unzipping my jeans.

"I know you're still good with those hands."

He kneeled to tug my jeans down over my hips, past my thighs. "I had to keep myself busy since you weren't around for me to feel on."

I tangled my fingers in his soft locks, tugging them just a little. "Are you too tired to work on this, or no?" I asked.

My jeans hit the floor. Swiss wrapped one of his hands around my neck. It wasn't enough to choke me, but it was just enough to make me want more of him. He'd come close to kissing me before backing away in the sweetest form of torture I'd ever experienced. I let him know how much I liked it by dragging my nails along his back.

He had a way of taking complete control of me whenever I was with him; my mind, my body, and my senses. His finger blazed a ridiculously slow trail of heat up my inner thigh. The pressure building in between my thighs was so much it was almost painful. He was slowly parting my lips, teasing me at first, letting his finger explore the soft, sensitive skin around my already throbbing lips. I was already wet and ready. Swiss growled when he felt it, returning his finger to my mouth so I could taste myself. He licked my lips as he shoved two fingers deep inside me, and I swear I almost exploded right there on the spot. Before I could get too close, he kneeled between my legs. I squirmed underneath the hot slickness of his tongue running up my inner thigh.

"You know I ain't never too tired for you," he answered.

His hands were in all the right places at the right time. He palmed my ass, squeezing each cheek in alternating rough circles. My hips moved with him, circling toward him. Swiss buried his face in between my legs. He inhaled a long, deep breath, letting me feel his nose and the air he was taking in brush against my most sensitive parts. When he exhaled, he groaned. And it was a long, hoarse, deep sound that said, *I missed you, and I want you,* all at the same time. It rumbled against my clit and sent ripples of feel-good up my body that shot all the way up to the hairs on top of my head.

My panties dug into my skin before giving away with a loud rip. My legs were already feeling shaky, and the nigga hadn't even touched me for real yet. The last time I came good and hard it was by my own hand. Swiss closed his eyes, rolling his tongue across my skin slow and steady. His tongue dipped into the liquid heat between my legs and the world stopped. Swiss slurped and sucked up my juices until I couldn't hear anything except the sound of him enjoying his meal. I could feel electric points of light at the roots of my hair. They surged down my spine, arching my back, ending at my feet and shooting out of the tips of my toes. This nigga was my tour guide as I rode the tip of his tongue. He dragged me closer to the edge, sucking my clit slow and steady before flecking it with his tongue. Before I could dive off the edge, Swiss stood. The heat from his hands scorched my skin. He palmed my ass, sliding me roughly up the length of his body.

I wrapped my legs around his waist, locking my ankles together behind him. He crushed my lips with his, and I kissed him back with the same fierceness that he gave me. He was just as long and hard as I remembered. Before my mind went completely blank, I couldn't help thinking briefly about how he'd spoil me paying hundreds to get the best tables and the best seats whenever we'd go out. But this dick right here was the best seat in the world to me.

I don't remember falling asleep, but I drifted in and out through most of the night. It was muggy and Swiss's big-ass body was like a damn furnace. He had me tucked into his side with his arm draped across my bare hips, but as sweaty as I was, I was too comfortable to move. I'd had plenty of arms hold me, but none of them felt exactly right. Not like this did. *But* unlike every other time where I'd run back to Swiss with the hope that we'd work and be okay, I was coming to the realization that if I wanted to be happy with him, I'd have to do it in secret or lose my father's respect.

The bed shifted. Swiss leaned over me bracing himself on his elbow. He ran the tip of his finger over my eyebrows, tracing their shape. It was all good until he headed toward the tip of my nose, tickling me. I scrunched up my face, and we laughed as I tried to wiggle myself away. That got him growing hard and hot against the side of my thigh. I was trying to pick the perfect moment to ask him for help. Every minute I waited was a minute wasted. I'd gotten picked up when I was fourteen, so my prints were in the system. It wouldn't be long before I got found out. I reached down, giving him a soft good morning pat.

"Ahh, just because you're up, you think I wanna be up too?" I teased him.

"You the early bird. You know yo' ass was already up. Plus, I've got the best seat in the house right here waiting for you," he teased me back, placing kisses on my shoulders that led up to my lips.

I smiled at the nickname I'd given him from years ago. It was something I did with all of my boyfriends. In my opinion, naming a man's dick was like taking sole proprietor ownership of that bad-boy. Especially if he started calling it the name you gave it, you all but trademarked it.

Swiss leaned back, putting all his attention into plucking at a frayed thread on the sheet.

Something was on his mind. I didn't have to press him for details, though.

"How my sister been doin'? I mean, y'all really think she's gonna be all right with a . . . a . . ." Swiss was always hard to read. He was never one for showing his emotions. His face was blank, but the tone of his voice was distant and sincere.

My mouth opened and closed a few times. Loyalty to Shan made me clam up. She would have a fit if she knew where I was, let alone talking about her. But he'd never asked about them before. The least I could do was ease his mind.

"Shandy is gonna be fine. She has Momma to help her, so I'm guessing the two of them will make it work. Some chicks are made to be mommies." My voice caught in my throat. I turned away from him, focusing on the clumps of black dust piled along the edges of the ceiling fan blades. Yeah, Swiss and me always fell back into place, but not once had we ever talked about what displaced us to begin with. That was the bad part of the movie we both skipped over, because neither one of us wanted to watch it.

Swiss grabbed my hips, pulling me in close. His mango-lime-scented locks washed across my face, tickling my cheek. The fresh stubble on his chin was scratchy against my skin as he buried his face in my neck. My arms instinctively went around his broad back. I distracted myself, pretending my finger was a tattoo needle. I absentmindedly wrote my name over and over in his skin, hoping it would sink in and imprint on his heart the way his name was tagged all over mine.

"I am so sorry," Swiss's voice was muffled against the side of my neck.

My body stiffened, my finger stopped mid-O. I'd heard him, even though I didn't want to. Five years was a long time to wait for an apology. It never ceased to amaze me how my eyes could water just a little and drain every ounce of wetness from my mouth. He let me push him away from me. Tears that I didn't want to cry, that I shouldn't even have had, left, sliding down my cheeks. I dragged the sheet up toward my chin like a shield, glaring at him out of the corner of my eye.

Clenching my teeth against the tightness in my throat, I said what I'd practiced in my head over a million times for five years.

"Nigga, I was only eighteen, and you left me. I was pregnant and you—"

He reached for me, "I know what I—"

"Do not interrupt me!" I couldn't hold back anymore. I let go and reared up, slamming my fists into his chest, slapping his face. He could have stopped me, but he didn't. My nostrils flared wide, my eyes were glazed over from tears and years of things unsaid. I wore myself out and stopped to catch my breath. We both sat back on our knees, facing each other. Red handprints formed all over his chest and shoulders.

"You don't know *what* you did!" I screamed into his face, jabbing the tip of my nail into his stony cheek. "*I had to find somewhere to go to get an abortion where nobody would know who I was. I'm the one who stays up at night wondering if I did the right or the wrong thing all because I was too scared to do it without you.*" I hopped to my feet, standing no farther than a breath away from him.

Swiss was so sick with guilt he couldn't even look me in my eyes. He should have been weighed down with all the guilt—the one wearing all the emotional scars, not me.

I clapped my palms together circling him. "You should have manned up and taken care of us. Nobody else. *You!*" I screamed in his face. My throat was raw from yelling, and I wanted to—I *needed* to make sure my words sank into his dumb head. I took a breath to calm myself down.

Ever since I was thirteen, I'd been training at commanding Daddy's soldiers. Yelling was the attention getter, but quiet storms raised fear; they were memorable. Ignoring my nakedness, I got down in front of Swiss, planting my elbows on my knees. I gave him the same disgusted look Daddy gave dudes when their count was off or they got caught trying to skim off the supply. He shifted in place, his eyes drifted from mine to the floor and back uncomfortably. His hood ass understood that shit.

I let out an exhausted chuckle.

After all these years, it was finally out there, hanging in the air mixing with the dust, our sweat, and the lingering smell of sex. I hated him for being a coward, and I hated myself just as much for still loving him. The air mattress hissed as I dropped back onto it, tired from venting. Swiss's shoulders slumped forward. He moved like gravity was working against him as he dropped down next to me.

"Don't . . ." I started to argue when I thought he was leaning in for a hug. He laid his head on my stomach, facing away from me. I stared at the top of his head in disgust. I wanted to fight this out. I didn't want to feel bad for making him relive his lowest moment.

I could feel cold wet spots from his tears on my stomach, but I refused to acknowledge them. I'd cried an ocean and three rivers altogether. His fifteen crocodile tears wouldn't kill him.

"Now that we've finally aired out our issues, do you think we can do this for real this time?" he asked. "Sammie'll be good as new in a couple of days. He can get someone else to watch his back, and I can tell him that I'm in love with you."

My heart jumped up into my throat. I was still trying to process the whole list of shit we'd just thrown into the air. I wasn't ready for this kind of talk.

He finally turned to face me with this sad but hopeful look in his eyes. It made it hard for me to look at him.

"You know what I mean, Novie. Can we do *us*? Be together? All my boys got wives, and they on their first or second seed. I'm tired of these sometimes situations we stay having. I want this all the time. I want *us* all the time."

The sun filtered through the blinds, making long bright dashes across the shadowed parts of the room. Silvery flecks of dust whirled in the sunlight. I stopped staring off into space, turning my head toward him and angling my chin down. I was all of a sudden self-conscious about blowing my morning breath in his face. The man was a freak of nature. He never had dump-truck mouth in the morning, not even after a night of drinking. My breath would probably be like that too if I swore off red meat, junk food, and wine like he did. But none of that was happening, the same way I couldn't see us happening. Our past felt too cracked and too weird now.

We could never be like we were before. He'd admit it too, if he wasn't going through last-man-standing syndrome. All his friends were wifed up, so now he thinks he wants to be wifed up too. I tried to wrap my mind around the right words to say.

"Knock, knock, woman." He tapped his finger against my forehead. "All those thoughts you got goin' on up there right now, can you let me in on 'em because that face of yours don't hide a thing?"

I cracked all of my toes twice before stretching my limbs one by one. Swiss flopped back onto his pillow with a sound that could've been a chuckle or an irritated snort.

"Why can't we just do this like we're doin' right now? Like we usually do? And if it works, it works," I blurted out.

"And if it doesn't work, we fix shit and work on it until we get it right? *Right?* Is that what you're saying?"

That wasn't what I was saying at all. That meant we'd technically be together which I still wasn't sure about. Even though he was finally saying the right thing, he was saying it all the wrong way. I couldn't tell if this had anything to do with love or caring about me. I needed to know that he wasn't just tired of being the odd man out when it came to his friends. That I wasn't just his safety net.

I got up, making a big deal out of searching for my jeans to avoid his eyes.

"Yeah, something like that," I replied over my shoulder. I didn't want him to see the lie on my face as I gave him my walk-of-shame answer. I could only tell so much truth in one day. I'd have to find someone else to help me out. Swiss was too emotional and unpredictable. And here I thought I was the woman in the situation. Guess not.

I was walking toward the front door when it swung open so hard it bounced off the wall. A gloved hand reached in stopping it before it could bounce closed.

My mind instantly jumped to the one time where Shandy and Denise made me marathon *Police Women of Broward County* with them. We watched eighteen episodes of fools running from the police, and now I understood why they did it. My fight-or-flight instinct kicked in, and the only option my brain kept giving me was to run. I knew clear as day that I didn't want to go to jail or prison.

NOVIE

10

Woman to Woman

I knew that if I saw any part of the troop of officers that were outside waiting to swarm toward me, instinct would send me running for the hills. I, instead, went against everything I felt and waited with my eyes shut and my hands raised to show I didn't have any weapons. I didn't want to take any chances at having the cops think I was any more of a threat than necessary. These days, it didn't seem to take a whole lot to get killed instead of apprehended.

My eyes snapped open at the dull thudding pain that shot through my left cheek. I caught her out of the corner of my eye drawing back for number two, and I sidestepped just in the nick of time. It was the same bitch who'd gone off on Javion earlier.

"I knew it! I goddamn knew it. I'm out here carrying your fuckin' baby, and you playin' me like a fuckin' idiot. Who the fuck is—"

The pause only lasted for a split second, but it was long enough for me to see that she'd recognized me too, and long enough for Swiss to get ahold of her arms. He pinned them down to her sides while I swallowed the words I was so tempted to yell. They settled in my stomach like a big rotten potato. *Swiss,* my Swiss, was the homeboy Javion was talking about. My Swiss had been messing around on me the whole time I stayed away messing around on him.

If I decided to tell it, all the truth would fuck up this lie she was trying to keep up.

"Tinesha! Chill the fuck out. You are out of bounds right now," Swiss yelled down at her.

She was so short she had to be half midget or some shit. Javion, I could kind of sort of see dealing with her, but not Swiss. I rubbed my jaw. It wasn't broken, and all my teeth felt intact, but I could taste my own blood, and that pissed me off. If this bitch fucked up my face, I'd fuck up her little midget ass.

A shadow filled the doorway. "Get your hands off my sister, nigga."

I turned toward the front door ready to square up, if need be. A taller version of Tinesha stepped in. They had the same bad sew-ins. She was bigger and meaner looking than her little sister, but that didn't matter to me. What did matter was the sight of the toddler perched on her hip. I'd tried to imagine Swiss as a baby plenty of times, but there was nothing like seeing his mini-me with everything from his eyes down to his chubby fat feet. He couldn't deny that little boy if his life depended on it. His hair was braided in thick plaits that ended halfway down his back.

It felt like my lungs collapsed. Not only did he get this heffa pregnant, he already had a baby. And after all this time, he never bothered to tell me. Those were supposed to be our babies. I felt myself deflating as I stood there. The girl holding the baby gave me a disgruntled look with her nose scrunched up.

Swiss was still contending with his baby momma. "Tinesha, stop hittin' me. We ain't together, and you know it, so stop with all this bullshit," he growled down at her.

"So we wasn't together when you was in my bed on Wednesday or Thursday night? We wasn't together when you fucked me Friday morning before you left my house?" she yelled.

I couldn't believe my ears or my life. How do two completely different niggas fuck the same ho and let me down in less than two days? And in that same time frame, I find out my daddy ain't shit either. Men ain't shit, I swear they ain't. I didn't even see any point in bursting Swiss's bubble and telling him Javion might be the baby's daddy. He would figure all that out in due time.

"Tinesha, I'm gonna go get Brandon's diaper bag. Li'l nigga smellin' ripe as hell right now," the sister announced from the doorway.

Nobody heard her except for me, and I hoped she'd take as long as Swiss needed to get her sister calm. There was no way I'd be able to fight her off. She looked like a one-hitter quitter.

"Fuckin' don't mean we together, nigga. We was both horny, and we handled that. I been told you about getting all in your feelings," Swiss told her.

Tinesha glared from Swiss to me and back again. She propped her hand on her hip throwing her words around with as much venom and spite as she could.

"Okay, Mr. Tin-man. So this is the bitch who supposedly got your goddamn heart? All right. Let's see how bad she want that rinky-dink rusted motherfucka after I put that ass on child support. I'm gonna take all your fuckin' money," she spat at him before stomping toward the door. She gave me the ugliest, nastiest look. "Thank you for freein' me of this nigga," she spat at me. "You are more than welcome to wash his stank-ass boxers and clean the dirt from underneath his crusty-ass fingernails.

And he gave me trichomoniasis, but that probably came from you anyway. I am so over this bullshit."

Tinesha stomped to the door toward the sound of her baby crying from somewhere outside.

"On your knees with your hands up. We've got the place surrounded." The amplified voice crackled through the loudspeaker. It penetrated the walls, pinging my eardrums, turning my heart into a lump in my chest.

I exchanged glances with Swiss before shaking my head at myself with my tongue in my cheek. These niggas were gonna be the end of me.

11

Peter Piper Picked a Partner

Tinesha's sister stood by with a smug look on her face. It was fairly obvious that she'd gone outside to call the police. Who knows how many news stations my picture was probably broadcasted all over. An officer's hand roughly mashed the top of my head, shoving me down into the back of a squad car. The handcuffs cut into my wrists as I met Swiss's eyes through the window. He'd stopped arguing with Tinesha long enough to give me a pitiful look. His eyes said he was sorry, but I didn't need his apologies. It was pretty obvious who his loyalty was with.

One phone call home and my dad would have me out of this bullshit. The thought made me lift my chin ever so slightly. I was determined not to need him or anyone. They owed me for all the bullshit they'd put me through, and that would be a debt I'd never collect. They needed to regret their choices for the rest of their lives. I took slow, deep breaths to keep from crying. The back of the car smelled like Fritos, Claiborne for Men, and coffee breath. The smell turned my stomach. I hadn't killed anyone, but I knew this was the smell of my freedom slipping away.

The officers were huddled in front of the squad car. They were arguing over something. A few stomped away, arms swinging and all red in the face. It wasn't long before a Range Rover with dark-tinted windows rolled to a stop on the street a few feet away. Half the officers nodded respectfully, the other half spit at the feet of the man who climbed out of it. He said a few words to one of them. All eyes turned in my direction in the backseat. He casually walked over and opened the back door.

"You must be Novie," he said in a voice deeper and richer than hot caramel. "I hear you're in need of an attorney."

I couldn't believe my ears, but I didn't want to start thanking my lucky stars too soon. I eyeballed him up and down, taking in his tan flat-front slacks and the burnt-orange cashmere-silk vest peeking out from underneath his custom-tailored blazer.

"I might need one," I answered suspiciously. "The real question is whether I can afford one."

"They got you for a double homicide, right?" he asked casually, leaning with his foot propped up against the side of the car. He squinted up into the tiny bit of sun shining through the billowy clouds before turning his attention to Swiss and Tinesha arguing on the front porch. His cologne cut through the curry-scented hell I'd been sitting in. It was warm, peppery, and very masculine.

"A friend of mine called me and asked if I'd do this as a favor. I take it that you aren't the type to take handouts."

"I'm not. And I don't do that whole sex for favors mess, so you can keep it moving, if that's what you want." I made a big show out of sitting back hard against the seat. It hurt my wrists like all hell.

"Okay, Novie, one of my legal assistants hopped up and moved to New York without any notice. I've got a big workload and no time to go through the hiring process.

I will pay you and take a small percentage to cover my expenses if you'd like to do it that way. Sound like a fair trade?"

The cuffs on my wrists were cutting off my circulation, sending pins and needles dancing through my fingertips. That shit sounded too good to be true, but it sounded a hellafied lot better than working on the phones all day making cold calls to sell alarm systems. If all I had to do was sit in a stuffy office typing up memos to get myself out of this shit, then so be it.

"You have a deal," I stated in a firm voice.

"Looks like you picked a good day to start a new career," he announced with a grin.

I tried not to, but I couldn't help staring at him as he moved past me to address the officers. Attorneys didn't move like that, like predators. They thought like them all day, but Genesis seemed powerful and dangerous. He moved with purpose in confident, smooth strides. Like a tall, Guilty-by-Gucci-smelling panther. *Mmmmph.*

I was surprised when I was un-cuffed and released.

"Sorry for the confusion, ma'am. You're free to go," the officer stated.

The lawyer rocked back on his heels, clasping his hands behind his back. He flashed me a bright smug smile.

I rubbed my wrists to get my circulation back. My eyes traced the shape of his lips, curiously following the thin, jagged scar. It twisted the tip of his full upper lip into a tiny sneer that faded where his mustache ended beneath his aristocratic nose. Now *that* is a man. I tugged the tip of my tongue between my teeth. *Okay, Screw Face,* I thought, tilting my head to the side slightly interested. My stomach did high-speed somersaults at the idea of showing him my screw face. *Mmmph. Know my ass needs to stop. Javion would try to snap him into four pieces with one hand.*

"Okay, wait, hold on. Is that it?" I asked him quietly so the officers wouldn't overhear me. "You say a few words, and we're all done here?"

"Yeah, you are free and clear, and you'll need to be at work tomorrow. We start at 8:30."

He handed me a crisp white business card. Gold embossed letters spelled out Genesis Kane, Attorney-at-Law. It was the same card Momma had given me with the office address and his contact information listed beneath it. Well, shit, Momma must've had someone call in a serious favor because my luck was never this good. I blessed him with a bright smile. Let that nigga be jealous for a change. My ass was over being the caring one.

GENESIS

12

Girls, Girls, Girls, Girls

My steps were a little heavier as I walked into the office the next morning. No one knew exactly what went down at the Twenty-third Street Precinct, but the word was getting out about Javion and his boys. Even without his sister around, Javion was still making a name for himself, and for me as well. You can't have a station full of cops go down, and I be the only lawyer who walks out. It left a bitter taste in my mouth, not to mention the tension I was getting outside of the office. I went to help out this Novie girl, not knowing if I was going to get shot or locked up in the process. Hopefully, she'd be better in the office than the last assistant I'd hired on a lookout. If I said it once, I'd say it again . . . I hate favors.

Work was usually my personal sanctuary from the world outside. The entire building was made out of this sunglasses-dark tinted glass. You could never tell if it was sunny, gloomy, cloudy, or raining. It always smelled like the inside of an expensive car dealership. Like soft leather, Colombian coffee, and frigid, filtered air.

I stood in the hallway staring at the empty space beside the sleek black ampersand on the marble wall. When I signed those papers, it'd say "Schaefer, Brockman &

Kane." Brockman was a silent partner that I'm almost certain didn't exist. I gave myself a mental pat on the back as I shoved my hands deep into the pockets of my fireplace-ash-colored Van Heusen slacks. The key fob to my new company car sat heavy on the inside. It unlocked a fully loaded Audi A8 parked in my very own personal parking spot. Paula was slicker than I thought. She'd already had it delivered and waiting for me.

I was still excited despite the gloomy circumstances. Five years ago, a nigga like me would've needed a lawyer before I would've become one. I didn't care about shit like slacks or attorney meet-n-greet golf outings. And I for damn sure didn't know the difference between a fairway wood and a hybrid any more than I knew the difference between the Aventador and the Murciélago. None of that shit mattered to me back then, but the old me was dead.

"You should be proud. You've earned it." Paula came sailing toward me in a ruby-red pantsuit. Her Skippy-glow was on ten this morning. That's when a woman tans so much, her skin looks peanut butter brown all year-round. It always made me think of Skippy Peanut Butter, crave a PB&J.

I tilted my head in greeting to one of the legal assistants passing by as Paula gave me an awkward *we-not-fuckin'* pat on the back before nodding toward her own name on the wall.

"I can't believe you're young enough to be my son and I'm making you partner," she joked, displaying perfectly straight Chicklet-sized pearl-white teeth. She was ageist to the core. Paula broke out into hives if you put her in the same room with anyone over the age of fifty-five. And she'd slit you open, bathe in your blood, and eat your spleen without flinching if someone told her it'd take five years off her face.

"I don't know if that's a compliment or a complaint, but I'm a conceited man, so thank you," I answered.

"Ah . . . well, we've been soooo very . . . um . . . busy earlier that I forgot to say thank you for filling in at that symposium last month. As much as I hate going to Catalina with my husband, I hate speaking at those fucking things even more," Paula chuckled.

"Not a problem. *Anything for a partner*, right?" I asked, giving Paula a wink. Those were her exact words to me when she needed my help making a rape charge discreetly disappear from Kharter, her oldest son's, record a few months back. He was home from Harvard and didn't know how to handle rejection from a bagger at a grocery store he thought was gay. Kharter stalked him, followed him home from work. Broke both of his arms and the guy's nose before he raped him. A charge like that would've put a blemish on the family's smudge-proof image. As much as that gay-shit repulsed me, I fixed it, with Squatton's help.

Paula gave me an appreciative smile. She tapped the manila folder tucked under her arm. "I just need your Johnson . . . err, umm, your John Hancock. I need your signature—"

"Genesis Kane, my mothafuckin' ass!"

Paula and I both turned toward the sound of a woman screaming at the top of her lungs in the main lobby.

"Tell that fake-ass, dead-beat, lyin'-ass nigga to come out here!"

Not today of all the fucking days. The corners of my mouth turned down. I suddenly found myself preoccupied, straightening my Burberry cuff links as my mind zipped through a Rolodex of voices. As familiar as she sounded, I couldn't place that voice to any of my current sidepieces. No one in their right mind would come up in my place of business acting like that.

"I'm going to ask you to leave before I have you removed."

I could already hear Tangie, my no-nonsense body-guard-secretary corralling the woman out of the building.

Paula's finely arched pale yellow eyebrow made its way up to the top of her botoxed forehead. "Um, is there a problem, Genesis? I hope we haven't misgauged your fit here at Schaefer and Brockman?"

My nostrils flared. I'd worked too damn hard, put my dick at risk popping too many Viagra, and put in too many real labor hours for someone to unravel it all in seconds. Paula was the only decision maker, like most of that "we" shit that came out when the legion of voices in her estrogen-powered brain was irritated.

I cracked the stiff joints in my neck left, then right. The lobby had grown quiet, but there was a storm of unspoken tension beating up the air between us.

I blessed Paula with an award-winning, bullshit, fake-as-fuck smile. "Not at all, partner. Maybe, *I* misgauged some good cognac and bad company, but that was a long time ago. *Absence* makes the *heart* grow jealous . . . You know how that goes. It won't be happening again."

I straightened the lapels on my jacket, knowing good and well that I hadn't misgauged shit. My boy Foreign rounded the corner as I was about to make my way to the lobby. We stopped shoulder to shoulder. I checked the corridors to make sure none of the legal assistants or admins were out or within hearing distance before approaching him.

"Who the fuck was that?" I asked in an anxious whisper.

"Hell if I know. Tangie got her teeth into her before I got out there. But you been holding out on me, man?" he asked, punching me in the arm. "When did you build up the stable? But take a lesson from the master. You need to keep them in their place or *put them down* when they act like that."

Foreign gave me a serious, pointed stare. "Wait, did you get another one of those fucking bloody heart things?"

I looked away, disgusted with myself for telling him about it in the first place. Even though he was my boy, sometimes he didn't know when to let something go.

Foreign slapped his palms against his forehead. "Oh, fuck me. Do you think that was her?"

"Look, I'll take care of it, Foreign. It'll get it handled one way or another." I began making my way toward my office, signaling the end of the conversation. "Oh, and I've finally got a new legal assistant . . . to replace the last one. It's starting to get tedious retraining a girl every time we lose one, so this one is *off-limits*," I warned him.

Foreign grinned from ear to ear. "Off-limits to who? Me or *you*, playboy?" He aimed his index fingers at me like two pistols. "It's all good. I'm gonna be busy doing you a solid, taking care of your crazy lobby bitch problem. Tell Chief we about to go hunt us a wabbit."

I ran my teeth across my bottom lip. There's always somebody somewhere warning a nigga, telling him to watch what he does and who he brings up when he makes it. I put my boys Chief and Foreign on as private investigators. Now not only was I responsible for the trouble my dick got me into, but I had to account for their dicks too.

I had a better idea for a project to keep Foreign from terrorizing my staff.

"Foreign, find Chief. There's a missing girl I need you to find. Saniah Sutton. She'd mentioned something about Sammie Knox. You might want to see what you can find there first."

NOVIE

13

Mue Make Your Money

I dressed in the most legal-looking outfit I owned. High-waisted black slacks with some suspenders and a button-down blouse, completed with a pair of black heels made up my outfit. I arrived at Genesis's office on H Street. It was busy this time of morning, especially during the week. You had to keep it moving or get bum-rushed by homeless folk and con artists begging for money. I pushed my way through a group of guys in suits and sunglasses marching toward the Metro clutching their briefcases.

Both Swiss and Javion had been blowing my phone up all night, but my only focus right now was impressing Mr. Kane on this new job I'd landed. Every fifteen minutes or so, another text would come through. Javion had a million questions about where I was, what I was doing, and were we cool. Swiss was apologizing, begging for my forgiveness and understanding. The only thing they had in common is that they were both sorry as fuck.

I pulled my hair back into a tight bun, leaving a little out in the front for a small bang. I stopped to use the side mirror of a car on the street to check my face before I went in. Turning my head from side to side I admired my almond-brown skin. My hair framed my heart-shaped face, accenting my high cheekbones that were so much like Momma's. Lip gloss made my already full lips look a little too full, not a good look for the office, so I grabbed my Burt's Bees honey Chap Stick. My nerves had been all bunched up between my throat and my stomach all morning. I'd been doing everything from meditating to chanting. I even tried tantric breathing, and I think you're supposed to be having sex when you do that. It took a shot of Henny with a Listerine chaser and coffee before I was able to get myself dressed.

Aside from the one summer where I'd volunteered at the YMCA in high school, I'd never worked in an office. The few jobs I had worked were retail. Shandy was gonna stay at the house with Momma for a little while, so I had the apartment all to myself, and the silence I usually craved was driving me crazy. I'd googled, binged, pinged, and tinged every fact I could find about the legal business. I even watched every show on Netflix, Hulu, and Vudu that had a lawyer in it.

The office building was the only bronzed glass building on a street full of concrete giants. I was outside the front entrance trying to calm myself down. I went statue-still with my hand barely on the handle, watching the woman go off in the lobby. She was four-foot nothing, wearing a black pencil skirt and gold blouse that flared at the wrists. I had enough sense to step back out of the doorway. Sure enough, her little heated ass came tumbling out in a blast of cool air. She stood there facing the building with her mouth balled up and her hands folded in front of her like she was expecting Genesis to just come out to see her.

"What the fuck you staring at?" she snapped, without turning to look in my direction.

"Um, I'm not trying to get all up in your business, but did I hear you say Genesis Kane was a liar? I mean, he's lawyer, so, hey. But the thing is, I kind of work here now and I just wanted to know—"

"That sounds an awful lot like a question somebody trying to get all up in my business would ask," she replied with a smirk.

There were malicious flames in her eyes as she came toward me, jabbing the air, swinging some kind of gold medal.

"Look, *I'm* not crazy. *I know my husband.* He likes to play his little games, but I ain't playing. So you go up in there and you let that bitch-ass nigga know Tima said—" she slapped her open palm against her chest—"I will pull up every brick in this city to bury his ass. Eye for an eye, G for a G."

The look Tima gave me before she hopped in her illegally parked Hyundai Genesis was so spiteful and dead-ass serious, you'd have thought I did something to her little mean ass. Yeah, I'd give Genesis the message from LDYG4EV, according to her custom plates. She looked a little Genesis-crazy to me. *Who goes to work and almost gets beat down by the boss's psycho ex-whatever on the first day?* That's got to earn me some brownie points or something.

When I finally got the horse's hooves to stop pounding through my chest, I walked in and started my first day of work.

The double glass doors opened soundlessly as I walked into what looked more like a high-end boutique, rather than an attorney's office. If this nigga didn't tell me that he had a decorator come in, then he was definitely going on my gay list. The lobby consisted of two blocky, cream-colored sofas. In between them sat a rectangular glass table with yellow and white candles on glass stands. Earthy green eucalyptus trees were placed in different places throughout the lobby.

I followed the walkway that was lined on either side with crystal clear glass windows and drawn white blinds.

An older lady ran up on me from around a corner.

"You must be our newbie," she said. "Ms. Deleon, I presume?"

"Yes, but you can call me Novie."

Even though I was nervous as hell, I gave her a bright smile which the heffa didn't even bother returning. She actually rolled her eyes, spinning on her high goldfish-orange heels to go back in the direction she came from.

"I'm Tangie. Kane is expecting you. And you're late," she called out pointing up at a large glass clock on the wall that read 8:35. "Your attendance is tracked. It determines whether you will continue on with this firm. Eight occurrences means termination. One to fifteen minutes late and that is a quarter of an occurrence. A missed workday equals one full occurrence."

I pulled out my cell as the numbers changed from 8:29 to 8:30 on the screen. If this was what I had to look forward to, this job was already looking like bad news.

I was marched past a small open area with five desks, all with identical staplers, tape dispensers, and inboxes. Four of them were occupied. I assumed the one on the end was to be mine.

Tangie gave me a brief drive-by introduction. "That's Robert, Bobby, Beau, and Mavis."

No one looked up. They sat with their faces buried in their wireless monitors. Genesis's office was around the corner. The doorway was built into a large wall.

"Nice to see you again," Genesis announced with a genuine smile.

He looked just as good as I remembered and smelled even better. After Tangie was dismissed, I took a seat in front of his desk. He had an edgy but intelligently sophisticated look. Like he could roll a blunt, discuss world politics and investing, all while sipping Cognac over ice. His eyes roved over me a few times, making me squirm uneasily in my seat.

"The office gets a little stuffy. Let's take a quick walk," he said.

Genesis began walking in the direction of Chinatown. "You'll be helping me by going over my documents for cases and making sure my *I*s are dotted and my *t*'s are crossed," he said. "I give bonuses for every case we win, and most of my clients are people you'll recognize from television or movies."

My phone whistled from somewhere in my purse, but whoever it was would have to wait. Opportunities like this didn't just pop up every day for someone who was homeschooled by drug traffickers. I'd learned math measuring harvest bales. Daddy was so obsessed with knowing the laws just so he could break them, he had stacks of law books and encyclopedias worth thousands. He didn't believe in doing anything on the computer, so I studied those things old school with a pen, paper, and a dictionary.

I had to hit the sidewalk double time to keep up with Genesis.

The armpits of my button-down were getting damp. Trying to stay side by side with Genesis had me feeling like I could barely talk. "I was at that house, but I didn't kill anyone," I told him. "I'm just wondering if I'm qualified for the caliber of work that you do," I answered in between breaths.

Genesis's pace didn't change. Since I had on heels, it took me two, and sometimes three, steps to keep up with one of his. All the fucking and fighting I'd done with Swiss was probably the most cardio I'd gotten in at least two months. Just when I thought I was about to vomit or black out, Genesis slammed to a stop.

"Swiss is one of my best guys. When he said he had an old friend that needed my help, I didn't question him. But I need to know the particulars," he said in a perfectly normal I-jog-or-do-extreme-cardio speaking voice.

The comment he'd made caught me completely off guard. *Why would Swiss be some lawyer's best guy, when he was already Daddy's guy?*

"Were you sleeping with him?" he asked.

I probably gave myself away when I couldn't look him in the eye, but I wasn't about to own up to it.

"I don't know why that matters," I said breathlessly.

A small smile tugged at the corners of my lips. So, Swiss had actually helped me out this time. He hadn't left me out there to fend for myself like I'd thought. Maybe he was worth keeping. But if it wasn't for his aggravating baby momma and her sister, I wouldn't have needed Genesis's help to begin with.

"Novie, last year I kept Swiss out of prison at least a dozen times. But he kept it one hundred with me on all sides. I just need to know if my go-to guy has some conflicting drama that might affect his work here. His son's mother is already a handful; she'd send that nigga away for life if someone so much as offered to pay off her payday loans."

I shook my head, still trying to catch my breath. "No, I'm not messin' with him. But I don't think who I *do* or *don't* sleep with is any business of yours." My tone was a little snippier than I intended, but it was only because he was irritating me. It really wasn't any of his business what I or Swiss did, even if he was in the business of saving people's asses from prison.

Since he wanted to be all up in my personal business, I took it as a good time to share some of his.

"Tima, she said she was your wife. She said she's gonna kill you," I blurted out without warning.

Something flashed behind Genesis's bright golden-brown eyes. Distrust or maybe even anger. But it was there, and then it was gone.

"My *what?*" he asked like he'd suddenly forgotten how to speak English.

"I ran into her on my way in. Not sure what it's all about, but she was not happy with you. She actually said she'd pull up every brick in the city and bury you, G for a G. I think I got that right. I probably should've taken notes or something."

Genesis clasped his hands behind his back. I was certain that I'd let my damn mouth talk me out of a good thing.

"A good attorney always has a good argument." He admitted this with a smug smile curving his lips. "I can already see that you lose your mask when your feathers get ruffled. We'll have to work on that. But Tima was someone I dated who couldn't handle it when I didn't want to date anymore. That's it."

Before I could ask what that meant, he draped his arm across my shoulder in that macho way men do their homeboys when they agree to disagree and be cool. God, he smelled like cedar and spicy pink pepper, like he'd just gotten out of the shower.

"I honestly think you'd be an asset to any firm out here. You didn't break under pressure. I need a new source of inspiration. A new muse. I'd rather have someone like you on the team than working against it."

Relief surged through me. I even felt a little conceit coming on at being called a muse. That was a new one. I'd never considered myself a man's key to success, but I'd take it.

"Also, I prefer yellow Post-its. Fine-point pen in black when things can't be typed up, and you need better clothes. Attention to detail is one of my pet peeves.

C'mon," he directed, nodding toward the Macy's across the street. "We've got an eleven a.m. with Farrah Harper. You can't meet her dressed like that."

Well, damn, I knew my wardrobe needed a little updating, but was it that obvious? I thought I looked decent enough. Probably should've spent more time hitting it with the iron, but it still wasn't bad.

Genesis placed his hand at the small of my back, nudging me forward. *Damn, I didn't even get to sit behind my desk or ask if I had benefits, and this nigga was all in my business knocking my clothes? What's gonna be next?* All these specifications and minute stipulations were making me apprehensive. But it's not like he ran one of those dime-a-dozen e-businesses. It was time to step my game up. All of it.

After hauling out close to $3,000 in pencil skirts and button-down blouses, we were finally on our way to meet Farrah. Genesis had surprised and impressed me by picking out some of the hottest combinations in life. That man was more than welcome to dress me whenever and in whatever he wanted to, especially if he was footing the bill.

I'd changed into a Mediterranean Sea-colored skirt with a fitted sleeveless silk blouse in bright coral pink with blue splashes. Even my pumps were on point. They were covered in what looked like wet paint splatters in the same colors as my skirt and top. I don't know why I'd always been so scared to try something other than black or grey. If Shandy could've seen me, she would've oooh'd herself to death because I was "snatched to the gods," as I'd heard her say. I even got a nod of approval from Genesis with his overcritical self.

We pulled up in front of Farrah's office building ten minutes early. I checked my texts while we waited. Genesis synced his schedule with the office while listening to Drake's new album. It seemed out of place. He didn't come across to me as a hip-hop head, but who was I to judge.

Swiss called four times before he finally texted, saying it was over with Tinesha. He wanted to know if we could do dinner. Reluctantly, I agreed.

I massaged my fingers against my left temple in small circles. We weren't even a day into seeing each other again, and he came with what felt like five years' worth of drama. Call me a glutton for punishment, but now that Swiss was all *into me,* I really wasn't sure if I was feeling him. The *oomph* was gone. The thought of him didn't get me excited, scared, or nervous. Thinking about him actually felt draining. Before, it was like gambling. I never knew if I'd beat the house or lose everything. Now with it all laid out in front of me, I wanted to look at other options. I needed to make some side-by-side comparisons.

"You should wear blue and coral a lot more. Softer colors work with your skin."

I jumped at the sound of Genesis's voice. I was so lost in my head, I'd forgotten he was even in the car.

"They did a study," he went on. "Brighter colors are supposed to make you look friendlier, more likeable. It really works." He tugged at the orange and lavender bow tie around his neck as if he was proving a point.

He seemed so content and pleased with himself. I'd swear I was sitting next to my daddy if I didn't know better. Whenever he had to show me why his way worked better, he'd have that same, cocky, what-did-I-tell-you expression.

Worry lines creased my forehead as I picked at the hem of my skirt, like the material was suddenly not good enough for me. I wasn't even about to let Genesis feel like Father Superior. "I don't know if peacocking's for me. You know, looking bright and flashy so I'm likeable to all the other birds isn't really my style. Black is subtle, and it's always in. I'm gonna have to think about all this frilly, pinky, girly stuff," I teased him.

Genesis gave me a tight nod. "Whatever works for you, then. I'm just an ordinary nigga with an extraordinarily successful multimillion-dollar law firm who deals with successful women all day. What would I know about aesthetics or styling?" He turned to stare out the window.

And so we entered into the silent stare-out-the-window portion of the drive. *Wow, sensitive now, are we? Did this nigga just try to read me over what I wanna wear?* I silently argued with myself. *No, girl, Mr. Multimillion-Dollar Law Firm just read your ass over the reason why he's qualified to hand pick and pay for your new shit. Me and my damn mouth.*

The car rolled to a stop. Genesis rubbed his hands together, clapping as the chauffeur walked around to open the door.

"Game time, Novie. You ready to do the damn thing? I already know you are. Let's get it."

He didn't wait for an answer and was out of the car before I could blink. His sour or irritated mood at my comment about the clothes was gone just as fast.

And I could see why as a white silk-draped tornado spun out of the house before we could get to the first step. She pulled Genesis in for a tight intimate hug letting him know that her sister, Farrah, had to step out, but *he* was welcome to come inside and wait. I didn't miss her emphasis on the word *he* either. Genesis's rushed instructions for the driver to take me back to the office let me know exactly what was up with that.

14

Amu$ement$ Can Make That Money Too

I sat in bumper-to-bumper traffic with my new clothes piled high in the backseat. You can't tell me there isn't something in car exhaust that causes amnesia. I swear, every evening I'd see the reason why I should be taking the Metro, and then that shit would be long forgotten by the next morning. By the time I got to my overcrowded apartment complex, I was dead-ass tired.

Denise was standing behind her car in her parking spot next to mine as I pulled up. She yanked my door open before I even had a chance to put the car in park.

"Heather is gonna kill me, put me in a shallow grave, and dig me up so she can kill me all over again!"

"Aww, hell, what did you do?"

"I can't find Hennessey nowhere! I was counting when that nigga Stephen called to smooth shit over. I swear I was only on the phone for like five minutes. Maybe ten minutes, I don't know, but it wasn't that long."

She threw her hands up in frustration.

"Um, have you been day-drinking without me? And when did the liquor store stop selling Hennessey?"

Denise rolled her eyes and stomped her foot. "No, woman, I lost Heather's daughter!"

Both of my eyebrows shot up to the top of my forehead. I didn't know Heather had a daughter, and I know she couldn't have entrusted Denise with a live, little person. She could kill a fake plant. And, yes, fake plants can die. Try not dusting one for a whole year and you'll be burying it in your trash can.

I took a deep breath for both of us. "Okay, calm down. What's her name, and what does she look like?"

"Hennessey, um, she's short. She had on a pink tank top and shorts. Or, shit, I think it was a purple T-shirt and a jean skirt," Denise stammered. "Hell, I don't know. I've been babysitting a five-year-old blur. That little nigga don't stay still for shit. *Hennessey!*" she shouted through the parking lot.

I put my hands on her shoulders to get her focused attention.

"Dee, did you drink Hennessey today, or am I really about to look like a stoned up alchie walkin' around here yellin' for some Cognac?"

"Her name is Hennessey! She's a little yellow thing with funky-colored eyes. Lawd, I don't even remember what her hair is like. What if the police want me to do a little sketch with one of those murder artists? I've gotta call Heather. No, I can't. I cannot tell that girl I lost her baby. This is what happens when you pop molly with a white girl. You get fucked in the ass by your girlfriend's boy-boo and you lose kids and—"

"Y'all did *what?* You can tell me about that later. We've got to make moves. If she was snatched up, we need an Amber Alert, the police need to know, and so does her momma. You're 100 percent positive she isn't in the house?"

"She's not in there. We got locked out when I was going to check the mail. I left my keys somewhere in the house. We were just gonna play hide-and-seek until you or the maintenance man showed up."

I pulled out my phone. It was time to call in some help before we waited too long and lost all chances of finding Heather's daughter.

"Oh, shit, oh, shit!" Tears rolled down Denise's cheeks.

She held her phone up, shaking it extra close to my face. Heather's picture was bright on the screen. I snatched the phone from her hand.

"Hey, Heather, this is Novie. We're have little teensy tiny problem. We lost Hennessey playing hide-and-seek."

Denise was staring hard in my face, biting the tip of her fingernail. I put the phone on speaker so she could hear.

Heather sighed into the phone. "Novie, are you guys indoors or outdoors?" she asked. She didn't sound the least bit worried about the fact that we'd lost her little girl.

"We're outside in the parking lot right now," I answered.

"Is Dee's car there?" Heather asked impatiently.

Denise and I both turned to look at her little red Nissan Sentra parked beside us. Unless Hennessey could fit up under the seats, she wasn't in there.

"Yes, it's here," I answered her. "But—"

"I've told that little girl *a thousand* frickin' times . . ." Heather mumbled under her breath before answering. "Novie, go tap on the trunk of the car."

I raised my eyebrows at Dee and did as I was told. I walked to the back of her car, tapped three times with my ear near the trunk like I was thumping a damn watermelon. We both jumped back when the trunk flew open with a burst of giggles. Hennessey popped up, holding Denise's keys in her hand.

"Little girl!" Heather yelled through the phone. "You are getting the business when I get off work. You'll stand in the corner until your legs fall off. Do you hear me?"

Hennessey's June bug bright green eyes filled with tears. Her expression dropped. She let out a tiny, pitiful, "Yes."

I apologized to Heather. Denise helped Hennessey out of the trunk. I rolled my eyes to the sky and back. In the event we'd had to get the police involved, she would've had us all jacked up. This little girl had on a yellow shirt with blue jeans. How she got pink or blue from that beats me.

An hour later I was standing in the Denise's kitchen, me in my fuzzy house pants and my favorite Duke T-shirt, and Denise in a blue adult onesie with bunny ears, like the weirdo she was. Hennessey had gone to bed right after dinner as punishment. Denise poured overflowing shots of apple Crown Royal for us both. We were on our third round.

"I hope this whole babysitting thing isn't about to become a habit," I told her.

"Girl, my babysitting days *and* my Molly days are over. I'm not made for this kind of shit. I swear if Heather didn't lick me like a—"

I held my hand up for her to stop right there. "Eeew, too much information. I don't want to hear about any of that." I lowered my voice so the little ears in the other room wouldn't pick up on my convo. "Tell me about all this nasty shit that you're into all of a sudden."

Denise gave me a serious look. Well, as serious as she could in her onesie.

"Heather works hard for her paychecks, and she parties harder. Novie, she has niggas who will bow down and be our table while we eat. They be down there the whole time we're eatin' dinner or whatever. White, black, Asian. These niggas like that shit, and Novie." She put one hand over her heart and raised the other like she was swearing on a Bible. "Hand to the sky, no lie. They pay her money—money, TVs, she even gets that green crack. We got some medicinal shit called Padussy from this one nigga, and I swear the blunt fucked me because I was knocked out."

"You can officially never say a word about anything I do. Y'all some freaks."

Denise stuck her tongue out and bounced her shoulders. "We some paid freaks, though. You are more than welcome to come work with us. I'd cut you in at fifteen percent of my fifty. You don't smoke or pop pills, so you can help deflect dicks from goin' up my butt when I'm lit."

Laughing, I flung a grape across the kitchen table. It bounced right off that heffa's forehead.

"I will *pay you* fifteen percent if I can avoid having to see any part of what I just visualized in my head in real life," I choked out between chuckles.

"Novie, I swear if you could see some of the men and women we fuck with, you'd stop laughing and climb onboard the butt-hole bandit wagon. They be finer than sugar."

When we finally stopped talking about Denise's sexcapades, I gave her a rundown of my first day at work.

"Well, at least this Genesis Kane is startin' off on the right foot," Denise said with a satisfied nod. "Do we need to run him through the little daddy-database before you decide to hop all up in his bed? Heather can probably see some shit in the computer. You know the DMV got all kinds of records on niggas these days."

"Girl, no, I don't need y'all to look into or look up anything," I told her.

As tempting as it sounded, I wasn't about to be one of those women who damn near stalked every man that came into her life. Even though it did sound like it would save me a ton of time by weeding out the no-good idiots early.

"So, hypothetically, if she was gonna look, umm, what alls would she be able to see?" I asked before shaking my head. That was the liquor talking, not me. "See how you be tryin' to start shit? That right there's the reason why I don't tell you anything," I scolded her.

We took our shots while my phone almost buzzed itself off the table.

"Awww, is baby J callin' to apologize?" Denise asked, while reaching for my phone.

I snatched it up before she could get to it, taking off in the direction of the bathroom.

"Hello?" I answered as I eased the door closed.

"Novie?"

I leaned back against my bedroom door pissed that I'd even bothered to answer.

"Hey, Momma. What's up?" I asked.

"Look, some guys have been asking about your daddy. I already heard you're working in that office, so what have you found out?"

"Today was just my first day. There isn't much that I can do in a day."

"Well, I need you to hurry up. Something's going on, and it doesn't feel right." Her voice was whisper soft.

"When I have something, you will too. I can't rush in and mess up, or I'll get thrown out."

Not to mention I wouldn't get to hang around Genesis's fine ass either. I hung up before she could say anything else.

I was lost in my thoughts when the phone rang, flashing Genesis K.

What could he possibly want?

Bad enough I was a little tipsy. If he was about to give me some shit to do in the morning I'd need to focus.

"Novie, I'm on my way to pick you up. We need to head over to Farrah's," he ordered.

I giggled into the phone. "Good evening to you too, Mr. Boss Man. I thought I was off the clock, so I was doin' grown-up shit, like drinking. I can't go."

"Can you name any other job where you get paid to party?" he asked.

"Umm, party planner, club promoter, DJ, liquor repr—"

"That was a hypothetical question, Rainman. Get dressed. Put on that Rimondi cocktail dress we picked out, the red one. It'll be perfect."

15

Cinderella Dressed in Yella

Genesis gave me the evil eye while his chauffeur opened the door for me to get in. We needed to get one thing straight up front. My mother and father were not here. The last time I checked, I was very capable of dressing myself. To prove my point, I'd purposefully put on a canary-yellow dress with a low dipping neckline and plunging back. It was about a year old, but it still fit just right, hugging my hips, accenting my mermaid frame.

He chuckled as I adjusted myself in the seat beside him.

"Interesting choice," he stated dryly.

"Thank you. This felt like me, like it'd be more comfortable," I told him in a sarcastically chipper voice.

I knew I was doing too much. Trying to hide my nervousness made me feel even more clumsy and nervous. My clutch tipped over in the seat between Genesis and me. Lip gloss, loose change, and an emergency cigarette spilled over the leather seat. Genesis reached down and picked up the cigarette.

"You didn't strike me as a smoker. That shit's nasty."

He tossed it out the window without any thought. I considered diving out the back door and hitting the cement rolling at sixty miles per hour just to get it back. So what if he thought it was nasty. It wasn't his place to decide what I'd do with my body or my habits.

We made the rest of the drive from my place to Farrah's in silence. My eyes were glued to the window. I was silently pouting, pissed that he threw away my last smoke. *Who does that? Who the fuck does that?*

Now that I didn't have one, I was sure I'd need it. We rolled to a stop in front of a place called Fuerté. The building was made to look like a miniversion of the Roman Coliseum where the gladiators fought. It even had the crumbled part where half the upper wall on one side had fallen away. I'd seen it on E! and heard about it on TMZ. They had all these superstar chefs, and only the best of the best are there. Regular people had to spend at least a thousand just to get a table when celebrities and all the beautiful people got in and dined for damn near free.

Red carpets and paparazzi lined the walkway in front of the restaurant that also doubled as a lounge. Men and women stopped to pose flashing teeth almost as right as the cameras flashing around them. Others rushed toward the limo-black tinted doors to get in as quickly as possible without being photographed.

I noticed everyone walking in was dressed in various shades of red and burgundy. Genesis smirked down at me as he helped me out of the car.

"If you're colorblind, I can have a stylist come to you from now on if it'd help. Red seems to be the color of the year, so there will be more Red Parties. Otherwise, just go with my selections," Genesis said.

He adjusted the red vest underneath his tux and straightened the matching red bow tie at his neck. If I could choke him with that bow tie I would have. I stood out like a poorly dressed thumb in my dress that was the wrong color and several seasons too old. At least my face matched the theme of the night since I turned about thirty-five shades of red from embarrassment.

Genesis made introductions to a few of the people who were walking in with us. A few men stopped to watch me walk past while the guys with dates snuck peeks at me out of the corner of their eye. I plastered my best smile on my face, deciding to make the best of an embarrassing situation. All the nigga had to do was tell me that the party had a color theme. That would have made a lot more sense than just ordering me to wear a certain dress.

My irritation at Genesis slipped my mind once we got inside the building. The lights were so dim they might as well have been turned off. All of the booths lined up along the walls with silk red draperies that could be untied for privacy. Some of the booths had tables other had chaise lounges in front of cozy fireplaces with hot pink and purple electric flames.

Loud trancelike music thumped in my ears. I fought against the urge to reach out and touch a giant metal lotus blossom. It was almost as tall as me sitting in the middle of the room with real flames shooting out of the center. A naked man slowly walked past making me gasp when I realized he was covered in flames from the neck down. I could see other flaming men and women moving carefully through the crowd.

"He's covered in a special kind of gel," Genesis spoke into my ear. "We had to bring it in from Taiwan. It's illegal, but legalities don't stop us from getting whatever we want."

Someone mentioned how Farrah had gone in for tonight's party; she'd spent close to a million. Shit, the last thing I'd do with a million dollars was set some people on fire. I was staring hard, trying to figure out what the lotus flowers were made of when someone caught my eye through the flames on the other side of the room. *Swiss*. What the hell was he doing here? He winked at me through the flicker of the flames. He'd pulled his locks up on top of his head in a tight ball. He looked good enough to eat and ride.

I still hadn't forgotten that he'd gone and had a baby with another bitch, but it's not like we were together. Holding that against him would have been similar to him holding Javion against me. Life happened, and he just so happened to have made life in the process.

"Novie, this is Farrah Harper," Genesis interrupted.

I managed to pull my eyes away from Swiss to meet Farrah.

"Farrah, this is the newest addition to the team," Genesis introduced me cordially.

Farrah wasn't anything like I'd expected. The friendly faced stocky woman walked around me looking me up and down. When she finally stopped in front of me, she gave me an approving nod.

"They'll never see the likes of you coming," she said reaching around to smack my ass.

"Um, thank you . . . I think," I answered.

Genesis coughed under his breath, giving Farrah a wary look.

She waved his warning off. "I take it you haven't filled our little doll baby in, have you, Kane? Let me do the honor," she announced proudly. "Novie, that man beside you supplies half of the free world with every form of substantial sin you can think of."

I was beyond confused by what the hell she'd just said. Genesis was a lawyer, a really good and a really expensive one from my understanding.

Genesis's hand rested in the small of my back. He leaned close to my ear. "She's right. We aren't here to celebrate. We're here to pick up a shipment. Farrah supplies the stuff, and we move it. I need you, because I don't have a sexy smart-mouthed bombshell. Do you know how many ball players, rappers, and politicians we can lock down with you on the team?"

I looked at Genesis like he'd sprouted a second head. If I wasn't going to sell for my parents, there was no way in hell I'd sell for this nigga. He was out of his damn mind. I motioned for him to lean down so I could talk without yelling all my business.

"I'm not doing this shit. You can find somebody else," I said into his ear.

Genesis straightened up and stared down his nose at me.

"Novie, I can make those prints reappear faster than you can get through those doors. I told you that my service came with a price. This . . . and staying away from Swiss is all I ask."

My lips worked themselves into an angry thin line. *Stay away from Swiss? Staying away from Swiss wasn't an option, and it didn't have anything to do Genesis.*

Farrah sipped from the champagne flute in her hand. She tipped it back, emptying the glass in one gulp. As if Genesis could sense the fury welling up inside me, he grabbed a champagne flute from a passing server.

"Let's toast to our newest girl and her journey to becoming as successful as our best guy," he toasted with a smile.

I couldn't believe this shit was happening to me. This was some straight-up television entrapment-type shit, and there was nothing I could do to get out of it. I excused myself to the ladies' room. Maybe there was a window or something I could jump my black ass out of. I'd already run once, so doing it again wasn't impossible. It would just be harder this time around since I didn't have thousands stashed away in a locker at a bus station.

16

Model Millionaires Are Rare

I was too pissed off with Genesis to do more than throw the champagne back down my throat as quickly as possible while I searched for the ladies' room. It took everything I had not to bolt for the front doors. If I was going to get out of here, the bathroom or a back-door was my best bet. I'd figure out how to deal with Genesis once I was away from him.

A surge of jealous heat ran through my body when my eyes found Swiss again. He was smiling down into the face of a beautiful woman wearing a dress that didn't quite reach the middle of her muscular thighs. Jealousy should have been the last thing to hit me. Especially since he'd been dealing with her consistently, and I honestly didn't have anyone because I consistently compared everyone to him.

I'd moved into a less-crowded section of the building when a hand covered my mouth, yanking me behind a curtained wall. I screamed, but it was muffled behind somebody's hand.

"Shhhhh, I just wanted to see you."

Javion's voice brushed against my ear. He spun me around, slamming his dry lips against mine. I pushed against his chest, leaning away from him.

"What are you doing here? And you're the last moth-erfucka I want to see," I spat at him. "Surprised you ain't laid up with Catwoman right now. Nigga, you're the reason I'm in this shit to begin with."

"C'mon, girl. Ain't nobody checkin' for McKenzie. Why would you think I had anything to do with settin' you up? I wouldn't do no shit like that. Boss man gets whatever he wants, Novie. He been had his eye set on you. It was only a matter of time before he stopped watchin' the picture and tried to get in it. There ain't shit I could do to stop him."

"What do you mean set his eye on me? If you know what the fuck is goin' on, you need to help me, Javion!"

Despite my resistance, Javion pulled me toward him, holding me close against his chest. I would've kneed him in his nuts if my dress wasn't so damn tight.

"I've got to get out of town. I refuse to work for that nigga anymore. I sold off the last of my package, and I'm gonna use it to set up my own shit in L.A. Come with me. He won't look for you out there. Come with me, Novie. It'll be you, Mr. Weasel, and me. We can start over, live without anyone watching us," Javion pleaded pitifully.

Little did he know I honestly didn't have an affinity for Mr. Weasel anymore. I only gave him that name because he snuck into this pussy like a little weasel when I was emotionally distraught. Under normal circumstances, I would've never given Javion the time of day.

But for a split second, his offer did sound good. It sounded like a way to escape Genesis and his illegal drug bullshit. But I couldn't bail on Shandy, and even though I was being told not to, I couldn't stay away from Swiss. Now the thought of not having or seeing him was making me realize how bad I wanted him.

"I can't go, Javion."

"What do you mean, you can't go? You mean you can't go tonight? Yes, you can. You ain't gotta pack shit. I'll take care of everything." His voice cracked; he sounded like he was on the verge of an emotional meltdown.

I leaned in, giving him a soft peck on his chin. Yes, every kiss begins with "K" and sometimes "K" could stand for keep 'em coming, but right now, it stood for keep it moving. This way, I wouldn't have to come up with any flowery excuses or bullshit lies to cover up the truth behind the matter, which was, I didn't want to go. Apparently, still, that wasn't clear enough. Javion dipped his head lower toward mine. I put my finger up to his lips.

"What are you saying?" His words vibrated against my finger.

I stared at a point just behind his ear. I was trying to say everything without saying anything. And I think he was finally starting to hear me loud and clear.

Javion's face clouded over. His grip tightened painfully on my arms.

I looked down in disbelief at his whitening knuckles, his fingertips digging into my skin.

"I just gave up everything for you!" he hissed into my face, shaking me so hard my teeth knocked together.

"Nigga, you'd better let me go. I didn't tell you go and do that dumb shit," I lashed back when he finally stopped shaking me.

He shoved me away from him so hard I lost my balance. My arms flailed, searching for something to grab. Thankfully, the soft shag carpeting broke my fall. Javion was on top of me, straddling my waist, clawing at my throat before I could recover.

"You fuckin' bitch. Die, you stupid, fuckin' bitch! You ain't worth shit!" he hissed.

Flecks of frothy white spittle formed at the corners of his mouth. It sprayed from his lips. My fingers clawed at his hands around my throat. Nobody knew where I was, and I'm sure even if they did, with the curtains closed and the loud music, they wouldn't know I needed help. This was a different kind of feeling from when I jumped from the bridge. I'd chosen that ending, so I still felt in control, even though I was helpless. All I could feel now was this pitiful helplessness and anger over not being big enough to whoop this nigga's ass. His face was going in and out of focus as my lungs begged for air.

"Da fuck!" Javion yelled, falling back.

I coughed, rolling to my side to get away from him when I was scooped up into strong arms.

"You know you've got a thing for attracting the crazies, right?" Swiss whispered down into my ear.

I relaxed into his chest. "With my track record, that means you're crazy too."

"I'm the craziest out of all the crazies. *But* I'm crazy about you," he murmured.

As bad as I wanted to thank him, I wanted to get air past my raw throat and into my chest.

He pulled the drapes closed, sitting me down in the chaise lounge a few feet away from where I was attacked.

"Stay right there. I mean it," he ordered before disappearing through the red drapes.

I was massaging the tender spots on my throat when he returned. I don't know where the tears came from. One minute I was fine, and the next, I was just overwhelmed with the fact that I'd almost gotten killed. Swiss sat down behind me, positioning me so I could lay across his chest.

"Thank you," I told him in a watery voice.

"You know I have to go, right? I've got to get that body out of here before somebody finds it. Kane thinks I'm about to run a delivery across town."

I nodded against his chest, leaving big black smears on his red dress shirt from my mascara. Good thing I didn't have on a full face of makeup or he'd be walking out of here looking like he had a mask on his shirt.

There was a shaky hoarseness in my voice when I tried to talk.

"I'm not mad about your little boy or the fact that your side-ho is pregnant," I said quietly. "I am mad at all this bullshit I've been sucked into. And the fact that I've got this nigga suddenly controlling my life."

Sobs rocked me to my core, making my entire body shake. Swiss slid his fingers underneath my chin, nudging it upward so I could look him in the eye.

"Novie, it ain't as bad as you think. A nigga might see $60 or $70,000 a year out there sitting in a cubicle fuckin' with Excel five days a week. But that ain't for us; we ain't got university degrees, Novie. I got a master's in this street shit, and you got a Ph.D. I keep a low-profile crib and a low-profile life because my baby momma would cut off her own leg to get to my paper if she knew I had millions. I just want to see my li'l man grow up happy and healthy, I want you to be a part of that."

I would've scoffed at that last part if my throat didn't hurt. *He wanted me to be a part of his baby momma drama? Umm . . . no.* Tinesha would make both of our lives hell just for shits and giggles.

I shook my head against his chest. "Genesis said I'd distract you. He threatened to release my prints to the police if I don't cooperate."

"Novie, Genesis will only know what you want him to know. I make close to two-mill a year. This shit is superlow risk for that kind of dough. Imagine once you get in and see how shit operates. You'll probably figure out how to flip three times that."

I leaned back, giving Swiss an extra hard, extra thorough look. What he was saying sounded too good to be true. The only sour side of the deal was that I'd either have to cut all ties with Swiss or sneak to see him until we decided to cut all ties with Genesis.

"Okay, Swiss. I'll do this shit, but if that heffa hits me again, I'll break her face."

Swiss's face broke into a wide grin. The corners of his eyes crinkled while he laughed. He leaned forward, giving me a soft peck on the same cheek that his baby momma'd punched me in.

"Yeah, she snuck you with a good left jab, but you took it like a champ. You do know the two of us together are smarter than all the world combined, right? I say we do us, get this paper, and if you want to be done at any point, just say the word and we're out of it."

I bit the inside of my lip. Two against one sounded a helluva lot better than me against the world. If my daddy had never interfered in the beginning, Swiss wouldn't have abandoned me. He didn't abandon me when I showed up needing help, so I felt safe going into this with him as a secret ally.

"Let's do this shit," I announced with a smile matching his.

He was on the brink of giving me another one of his dangerously slow kisses when the red satin drapes billowed in toward us. I jumped, letting out a small surprised squeak. Genesis slammed through the drapes. He stood in the middle of the booth looking back and forth between Swiss and me.

I'd been so caught up in my conversation with Swiss that I hadn't even noticed that the music had stopped. The soft murmur of hundreds of hushed voices met my ears. My heart hiked across the inside of my chest in spiked cleats. *Oh, shit. How much has Genesis heard?* I knew I was gonna need that damn cigarette.

NOVIE

17

The Art of Allowing

I couldn't tell if Genesis was going to kill us on the spot or wait until later when he had some privacy. His face was dark and stony as he stood in the booth.

"Everyone's evacuating. Someone found a body in the men's bathroom," Genesis announced.

He gave Swiss what looked like a disgusted stare down before turning his eyes to me.

"Shit," Swiss cursed, pushing himself up off the chaise lounge. "I walked in on your boy Javion, roughin' her up. You know I black out a little when I get too worked up. One minute I was here, and then it was like I blanked out and snapped. Next thing I know, he was lying on the floor with a broken neck," Swiss told Genesis.

I looked at Swiss with different eyes. What happened to the man I used to know? The old Swiss would've knocked Javion out or cracked a few ribs. He wouldn't have killed him. Or maybe he would've done it, and I was just giving him too much credit.

Genesis's expression didn't change as he spoke to Swiss. "Get out of here before you get found out. I'll take her home," he said.

Swiss's eyes held an unspoken promise as he looked toward me before leaving. Once he was gone, I realized I was all alone with the intimidating Mr. Genesis Kane.

"Are you all right?" he asked with what sounded like concern in his voice.

"Mm-hmm, just shook up, but I'm good."

The tenderness in his voice caught me off guard. It was weird to see him acting like a normal, caring person. He helped me up from where I'd been sitting. A deep frown creased his forehead when he saw the bruises on my arms and my neck.

"I told you to stay away from him. Swiss can't focus on the mission in front of him when there are distractions. Now he has a body on his hands because you didn't listen."

I glared at Genesis. "*I* didn't listen? You'd be picking my body up off the floor right now if it weren't for Swiss. He saved me, and you weren't anywhere around to help."

"Novie, Swiss is not who you think he is. This isn't the first time I've said it, and I know I can't be the first person to tell you leave him alone. This time, I'm saying it because it's for your own good."

No, Genesis was actually third in the line of anti-Swiss conversation. My daddy had the number one spot, and Shandy followed him up behind in second. The conversation I'd just had with Swiss replayed in my head. Genesis's legal-beagle ass was probably superintimidated just being around a real dealer/hit man. If he knew half as much about Swiss as I did, he wouldn't be worried about anything.

I pasted a fake smile on my face. "All right, I got it, Genesis. No more Swiss. I understand."

It was close to two a.m. when I finally walked into our dark and empty apartment after yet another long, silent car ride with Genesis Kane. That man seemed next to impossible to peg down. One moment, he'd be cool, and the next minute, he could be obstinate and rude. I wonder if he treated his momma like that. That's if he actually even *had* a momma. If somebody told me he'd been raised by a pack of wild boars, I'd believe them.

I poured myself a shot, hoping I wasn't expected to actually get up, get dressed, and then roll into an office first thing in the morning. That shit was definitely not going to happen. Tangie could take that occurrence policy and shove it up her ass. I wasn't even in the mood to pick out my work clothes or log into Facebook. I kicked my shoes off into the living room, groaning as my toes stretched out into the carpet.

I was in the middle of a silent debate on exactly which details I could or should share with Shandy. She wasn't going to believe half of the shit that happened, but I needed to talk to someone. First things first, I needed a shower. I undressed, wincing when I saw the four long reddish purple bruises that wrapped around my neck. I couldn't believe Javion had really tried to kill me. I'd never seen him look like that before, not even on his worst day or when he was at his angriest.

Pushing away my thoughts of Javion and Swiss, I hopped into the shower, lathering up, letting the scent of vanilla orchids and blue coconut water ease into my pores.

Suddenly, the shower curtain peeled back—I dropped the bottle of soap.

"I got real dirty tonight fighting with my bare hands for the honor of this fine-ass chick I seen at the spot," Swiss announced.

I let out a relieved breath before throwing my loofah at his face.

"Y'all are gonna give me a heart attack with all this sneaking and popping up shit. How the hell did you get in here, Swiss?"

Our shower was big enough to fit one person comfortably, but if you put two people in there, it got crowded quick. Swiss's body swallowed up most of the space as he stepped in, grinning.

"You don't give me enough credit, Novie-star. I'm not the same nigga who ran off years ago. I learned a lot, and I'm better than what I used to be."

"Well, before you get all comfy, I guess I should tell you that Javion and Tinesha were fuckin' around behind your back."

Swiss kissed me so slow and deep I was dizzy when he finally stopped.

"I know. That's why I broke his neck." Swiss grinned like the cat that ate the canary.

"Nigga, you ain't got no shame! So you already knew she was cheatin' on you?"

"Yeah, me and her was talkin' until I found you again. I cut her off, and then you left, so I got her back. She kind of figured that I had someone on the side, so she started playing me. Guess I let it happen to keep the peace. So I could see my li'l man and see you. As long as she was busy stressin' Javion, she wasn't stressin' me."

"So you know the baby might be his, right?"

"Yeah, I know. But Brandon is here now, and he is mine. He's my only concern until she has the baby. I'll deal with that bridge when I get to it."

It felt conflicting to see Swiss stepping up to his responsibility after he'd abandoned me so many years ago. But he was right; he had changed, and that made him sexy as fuck.

"Let's go to bed," I suggested.

***

"Novie? I know you didn't get in your little bed with all this water all over the bathroom floor."

Shandy's voice dragged me out of the dream I was having. I groaned, blinking to focus my eyes. Bright light streamed in through the window. A baby cried from somewhere in the front of the apartment. Swiss snored in his sleep beside me. *Oh shit! I forgot he's here.*

"Bitch, what in the world did you do last ni—" Shandy stood in the doorway of my bedroom.

Her eyes were wide and round as she looked over at Swiss sleeping beside me, then back to my face.

I gave her a weak smile. "Hey, Shan. Look who I found. It's Kryptonite."

Swiss pulled himself up, tucking a pillow between his back and the headboard.

"Hey, little sister. You look like you're doin' all right."

Shan obviously didn't see the humor in the situation. She whirled around, stomping out of the room.

"So I'm your Kryptonite? And that's supposed to make you Superwoman or something," Swiss chuckled.

"Not now, boy, she's pissed. Shandy?" I hopped up, wrapping myself in the comforter.

Shandy was in the living room with her purse on her shoulder and her keys in her hand.

"You have lost your fucking mind bringing him here, Novie."

"Shan, it's not what you think. He isn't the same. He's nothing like he was back in the day," I reassured her.

"Whatever, Novie. I'm just mad that I rearranged my whole life to help you move forward, and you go right back."

18

Sex Kitten Vs. Sex Panther

I finally dragged myself into the office two hours late. With Shandy acting the way she was acting, it was best to leave her be until she decided to come around. Swiss, on the other hand, was not being cooperative at all. I had to insist that he not show up out of the blue like he did, but he wasn't trying to hear any of that. The only way I could keep him from showing up was by promising that'd I'd head over to his place after work.

The other paralegals who I'd decided to start to calling "Bobby" and the rockers were all surprisingly quiet as I passed. They were all guys, fresh out of college, and they could dress and party me under the table. Oh, and then there was Mavis; she didn't really talk much. She preferred to be called "Ron." Nobody asked why or thought it was weird; they just did it. But I'd take an office full of women over one with two and a half queens, a metro-sexual, and a mute.

My lip curled up in complete disgust as I stopped just short of my desk. Old, moldy, cobweb-covered cardboard boxes filled with folders had been stacked all across it. I threw my purse into the top drawer, scanning the neon green Post-it note attached to my chair. *Relabel and*

file by year and alphabet in the archive room ASAP—
Tangie.

As if she could hear me reading her note, she bobbed over, parking herself in front of my desk. "You're a little late getting in here this morning, aren't you?" she asked, nodding in the direction of the clock. Her shock-blond Afro wig bounced around on her head. I'd figured out the fact that Tangie was a twenty-three-year-old mean girl trapped in a sixty-five-year-old woman's body. She was petty, spiteful, and had a jealous streak from hell.

Her red, black, and green curled nails drummed across one of the boxes on my desk. I hated her nails and her nail polish. Why couldn't she pick one color instead of a different color for every finger?

I gave her a nonchalant shrug, pulling out some folders to work on. I didn't know I was supposed to work every hour on and around the clock. I almost got strangled to death, and I didn't get in until two a.m. That sounded like a legitimate reason to run late to me.

Tangie huffed and puffed before she hightailed it to her dungeon beside Genesis's office.

"Your hair looks really cute today, um, Novie, right?"

I looked up from the folders to see everyone staring expectantly. No, my hair actually looked like shit. I didn't have time to do anything to it except pull it back into a bun. Bobby complimenting me on it confirmed it, though. Those hating he-heffas probably wouldn't bat a fake eyelash my way on the days when I was on point. But let me look a little rough, and they were singing compliments my way.

I picked the Bobby closest to me to respond to.

"Thank you, Bobby. It was one of *those* kinds of weekends. I have been in la-la land ever since," I replied giving him a bright smile.

He ran his finger in slow circles around the lid of the Starbucks cup on his desk. "Oh. So, I guess you didn't hear about the client we have coming in today?" He ran his eyes up and down the length of my outfit.

I slow blinked from Bobby and his fashion bullshit back down to the stack files.

"It's Farrah Harper, honey, the wealth consultant. Who knows, that whole peasant look you got going on just might work in your favor," he blurted out, swirling his finger in the air in my direction.

Farrah's job title sounded like a bunch of bull to me. A wealth consultant, really? The way people just made up jobs these days was hilarious.

I couldn't help it. I had to ask. "What does a wealth consultant do?"

Bobby shook his bobble-head before exchanging looks with his underling bobble-heads. They were on the verge of a meltdown at the fact that I didn't know something that was obviously bobble-head common knowledge.

"She gives people these life-makeovers. And I mean *life*. They come out with better money, friends, social status—basically, turns shit to sugar. She was on *Oprah* and *Dr. Phil*."

They all nodded in unison. It was pretty obvious that none of them were associated with Genesis's illegal after-hours business. After the night I had, nothing about Farrah was impressive to me. She was just another boss who I had to contend with.

"Novie?" Tangie shouted down the aisle. "Genesis wants to see you in his office. *Now*."

I stiffly rose from my desk to go find out why I'd been summoned.

Genesis's office was an interestingly strange mixture of Japanese masks, legal books, and stuffy, old-man furniture. It even smelled like him with a hint of old library and leather books in the air.

"I think we got off to a rough start. I would like to take you to dinner after work, to get us on better ground."

It just seemed like it would've been weird if I was standing outside the boss's office waiting to go out, so I sat at my desk scrolling through different Twitter feeds. I let Swiss know I'd be a little late just to keep him from popping up at the house. Farrah had finally left Genesis's office after spending close to two hours, demanding copies of miscellaneous documents. Outside of our illegal partnership, she acted as if we didn't know each other, and that was fine by me.

No one was even slightly suspicious about why I wasn't on my way out. Even Tangie's militant behind barely glanced my way when five o'clock rolled in. She was probably just anxious to go climb back under whatever bridge she'd hobbled out from.

Genesis finally came by my desk. He looked surprisingly cheerful. I was getting used to the serious scowl he always had.

"How do you feel about sensory deprivation?" he asked.

"I have no idea that I even know what that is in regards to or how I'd feel," I told him with a puzzled look on my face.

"Doesn't matter." He rubbed his lips together. "We'll figure it out today. I'll pull the Porsche around."

Genesis driving himself anywhere was like hearing that Batman could put his draws on without Alfred.

He pulled up to the front of the building in a silver Porsche truck.

"Is the lady ready to step out of her comfort zone and figure out what she likes this evening?" he asked with a mischievous lift to his voice.

I chewed the inside of my mouth, anxious to find out why this place put him in such a good mood.

"Oh, wow, I always thought Porsches were these expensive little, eensy-weensy cars made extraspecial for dudes with little eensy-weensy tender-bits," I replied.

"Woman, you keep thinking like that, and you'll miss out on some of the biggest thangs life has to offer."

Well, damn. I can't argue with that.

We made small talk on our way to the restaurant. It was nice to have a decent conversation with someone. I was telling him about Heather's daughter and the whole trunk episode when he gave me a strange look.

"So, your best friend who you live with is a lesbian?"

"No, I mean, yes, but no. She likes a little bit of every-body," I told him.

Genesis got quiet. He seemed to be digesting that bit of information.

"So, has she ever tried to get at you?" he asked after several long, silent seconds.

"Who, Shandy? Hell no, not since high school."

The look he gave me made me feel like I needed to explain. "I mean, she was just figuring out that she liked women, and since we were besties, she tried to come at me. But no, that's my girl; that's it."

Genesis drove us to a restaurant called Dans Le Noir. We walked in through the front door into a small hallway decorated with abstract art and sculptures. Large black curtains with gold embroidery flowed from the ceiling to the floor at the end. I didn't know if I was going to step into a strip club, circus, or a pit of deadly vipers. Genesis grabbed my hand. His skin was comfortably warm. His long, smooth fingers gave mine a squeeze as we stepped through the curtains together.

I gasped as we stepped into complete and absolutely ear-shattering darkness. It was the kind of pitch black that made your ears instantly sensitive. Panic started to swell in my chest. I couldn't find a single point of light to focus on. No matter how hard I tried, I couldn't get my eyes to adjust. The only thing that kept me sane was Genesis's hand in mine. I knew nothing bad would happen as long as he was with me.

Slow footsteps approached us. They sounded too heavy to be a woman, with a shuffle and a lag in between each one. It's a damn shame that I could pick all of that up, but if you take away one sense, the rest really do get better. It was someone coming to greet us, and he was just in the nick of time because I was ready to drop to the ground and crawl for the curtains.

"Welcome, guests. My name is Louis. I'm your server this evening, and I am happy that you two have chosen to indulge your senses and dine with us tonight." The greeter's words were hinted with spearmint gum and what might have been vodka. It was hard to separate the smells coming from his mouth from the smells surrounding us. But I could definitely make out what I thought was vodka. Hell, if I worked in a pitch-black restaurant, I'd probably grab myself a shot or two from the bar.

Genesis tugged on my hand, and I shuffle-stepped in line behind him. I was scared I'd trip over the back of someone's chair and land on the floor. I couldn't tell where the rugs ended or began. They could've at least put in a little lighted walkway like the shit at the movies. I wonder how many lawsuits this place saw in any given week, because this shit was dangerous.

"How the hell can you see, Louis?" I asked the server.

"Ah, ma'am, most of the staff wears night vision goggles. Some of them are actually legally blind, so nothing extra is required."

There was a quiet hum from a thousand different conversations going on around us as we were led into the dark dining room. Not only were my ears extrasensitive, but my sense of smell was surprisingly keen all of a sudden too. I could smell everything from the red wine sloshing in glasses to the scallops being sautéed in white wine and rosemary somewhere nearby.

Louis took my hand from Genesis and pressed it onto a chair so I could sit without falling flat out onto the floor. He also showed us where our water glasses were sitting and the placement of our napkins and silverware. I listened to the soft tilt of his French accent as he read the menu to us. Everything sounded beautifully put together. I ordered pepper brined chicken with honey garlic sauce and sautéed greens with banana peppers. Genesis got the jerk chicken with pineapple salsa. Louis took our orders leaving us to the dark.

"What do you think so far?" Genesis asked.

Now his voice could ooze over me without the distraction of my other senses. It was like warmed-over salted caramel, smooth and rough but still very sweet to my ears.

"So far, I think this is one of the craziest things I've done since I've been in DC."

He laughed. It was a soft sound from somewhere beside me that sounded like genuine humor.

"Novie, I can think of over a hundred things crazier than this for you to do," he said with his voice barely above a whisper.

There was something so intimate about being in the dark that made it feel like we were alone, even though there were probably a dozen other couples within a few feet of us. We sat and sipped wine while we waited for our food. Mine was sweet and tangy. I could taste all of the blackberry accents, and even a little cinnamon.

"Novie, we have the same wine. I think your taste buds are shot, because I taste cherries, chocolate, and maybe a little black pepper."

I giggled at his description. "Sounds to me like you're tasting that cologne you wear. You should try to drink it without breathing in through your nose," I suggested.

"Or I can taste it right here," Genesis whispered.

He'd managed to slide his chair all the way over until he was sitting beside me in the dark. His lips were only inches away from mine. I could feel the air he exhaled on my chin and cheeks.

"Taste what, right where?" I asked in a whisper equal to his.

He answered by grabbing the back of my neck and melting his lips into mine. My heartbeat stutter-stepped in my chest. This was so not supposed to be happening, yet I wasn't doing a damn thing to stop it. Our tongues touched and entwined in a seductive, slow dance. He was right; his kisses tasted like cherries and chocolate with a little spicy pepper.

The pitch black of the restaurant made me feel daring and even a little raunchy. For all I knew, everyone around us were either tonguing each other down or fucking at their dinner tables. I could hear what sounded like a soft moan somewhere off to my left. To my right, forks clattered against a plate. And right in front of me, Genesis was keeping a calm, cool exterior, all while giving me searing hot kisses. I curiously slid my hand down into his lap. There was no way this couldn't be affecting him the same way he was affecting me.

I could feel him smile against my lips as I patted him, straining against his pants.

"Well, hello, to you, Citizen Kane," I murmured against Genesis's lips.

"Citizen Kane? I think I like the sound of that. Say it again and squeeze him a little."

This game we were playing had me melting into a puddle right where I sat. Good thing it was dark because my panties and the seat were going to be sopping wet whenever we got up to leave. Genesis pulled away, and I gasped when he came back. I closed my eyes, even though I didn't need to. He held an ice cube in between his lips, and he ran it across my shoulders, down the front of my neck. I let out a tiny yip when it dropped in between my breasts.

"Is everything okay?" Louis asked from somewhere over our heads.

That fool had probably been standing there the whole time, enjoying all the various freak shows that were going on.

Genesis squirmed in his seat beside me. "We are fine, thank you."

"Perfect. Your meal will be out shortly." And with that, Louis left.

I sighed, enjoying what smelled like white wine and rosemary over chicken. Everywhere I turned, there were smells to paint pictures in my head. Genesis leaned forward. It was amazing how well I could sense his body heat and hear him breathing. He poured wine into my mouth from his. It was shockingly cool compared to the heat of his mouth. A trail of wine ran down the corner of my mouth, and he caught it with his tongue. The heat from his fingers grazed my inner thigh as he slipped my soaking wet panties to the side. My teeth sank into his bottom lip as his finger dipped into the dripping honey pot between my legs.

Serving trays clanked nearby. I could hear the servers coming our way. I tried to close my legs, but Genesis wouldn't move his hand. Our food was set out and Louis explained what was what and where. Genesis strummed a steady rhythm with his finger. Spicy Jerk chicken, strum, pineapple and mango salsa, strum strum. I didn't hear a damn thing the man said after that. My mind was only on one thing.

When the servers disappeared, my senses were reeling from the exotic-smelling food heightened by the darkness and the slow lull of Genesis's hand. He pulled me toward the edge of my seat, dipping his fingers faster and harder into my pussy. A quiet moan slipped out of my mouth before he kissed me deep and hard, claiming the sounds of my moans as his.

Swiss had never done anything this exciting, and Javion had damn sure never gotten me anywhere close to the heights Genesis was taking me—and with a damn finger at that. He stroked until I could feel the walls closing in. I was standing right at the edge, ready to fall into oblivion—and he stopped.

"You didn't ask me if you could cum yet." His voice was dark with excitement.

I blinked several times, feeling empty and cold from his retreat.

"Okay, I'm sorry," I whispered leaning toward him. "I didn't know I was supposed to ask. Can I cum, please?" I fidgeted in my seat, crossed and uncrossed my legs. I settled on pressing my knees tight together.

"Well, I can't say no when you ask like that."

His hands were on my hips, quietly directing me to stand up. Cool air brushed against my bared ass as my skirt was cinched up around my waist. My knees almost gave out when he slipped my panties to the side, burying his tongue deep into my pussy. I found the back of my chair in the dark and held on to it for dear life. He licked, sucked, and lapped at my center until I could feel the dampness running down my legs.

I tasted myself on his lips when he rose up in front of me. He lifted my leg, wrapping it around his waist. I don't know when or how he freed himself from his slacks. But I felt every hard, hot inch of him as he pressed forward and upward, driving deep in one fluid motion. My arms wrapped themselves around his neck. I dug my nails into this back, burying my face in his shoulder to muffle my gasps and moans. We rocked together somewhere in the middle of the dark restaurant with people eating and chatting around us. Genesis stroked me over and over with the scent of red wine on our breath and the pineapple mango salsa on his dinner plate flavoring the air around us.

My legs started shaking. I wanted to scream his name. I pressed my lips against his ear, remembering the lesson he'd just given me a little while ago.

"Can I cum? Please, make me cum."

He answered me in strokes, going deeper and faster. I moved my hips in unison with his until we were both shaking and ready to explode. Pulses of light quaked from my pussy, sending beacons of light up throughout every nerve in my body. The lights danced in front of my eyelids and exploded in little flashes. As far as I knew, we were the only ones in the building. All my senses were dialed into the pulsing heat pressing upward between my legs. Genesis breathed against my neck, stroking my skin with his lips and sometimes his teeth. It sent me over the edge. I bit down into his shoulder—hard—getting a mouthful of suit jacket as our worlds exploded together. Genesis had to hold me up, else I would've hit the floor. That had to have been the hardest, longest climax I'd ever had in my life.

Afterward, I carefully eased down into my seat. Genesis handed me the handkerchief from his shirt pocket so I could wipe my legs. Never would I ever have guessed that his well-dressed, starched, and pressed legal ass could put it down like that and in a place like this. I had a lot to learn when it came down to judging people's characters.

Novie

19

Candy Kane

Genesis dropped me back off at the office two hours later. We exchanged a few good-bye kisses before he handed me a padded envelope.

"This is for a special client. I'll call you by ten with the drop-off info. We need to make sure he's still interested. Oh, and I would like it if you came by my place afterward."

Genesis winked and my blood was set on fire all over again. After the way he'd dicked me down in the middle of that restaurant I'd go or be wherever he wanted me to. Good food and an even better fuck had me ready to lay it down. Swiss was too unpredictable. The chance of him showing up if I canceled our dinner plans was too risky. When Shandy was in bitch-mode, nobody could be happy until she got out of her funk. Seeing Swiss would only make her extend that shit.

It was only seven thirty so I headed to Swiss's place while trying to come up with an excuse to roll out at ten when Genesis called. Worst-case scenario, I could make up something about Shandy babysitting and needing help because Hennessey was sick. Nothing short of Jesus' Second Coming was going to keep me from getting to Genesis and getting part two of my dick-down.

Swiss was already home and dressed when I got there.

"Hey, you." I slipped my arms around his waist.

He kissed my forehead and frowned down at me.

"You look different. Did you get your eyebrows done or something?" he asked. "You smell nice too. Is it something new?"

My heart paused. I'd forgotten about Genesis's cologne. I'd been smelling and resmelling it in my hair on my way to Swiss's.

"I had to ride with the Boss man to see Farrah. He freshened up his old-man funky cologne on the drive." I told my lie pulling away from him. The guilt I felt in my stomach was unexpected.

"This shit isn't gonna work," I complained to cover up my sudden lack of interest in doing anything with Swiss. "I can't work with that nigga all day, and then run and do all these crazy-ass jobs whenever he and Farrah snap their fingers. I'm tired, and I don't get any kind of rest."

Swiss, being Swiss, was sympathetic and understanding as usual. He ran his hands up and down my arms.

"We can stay in. I'll run you a bath, get you a drink. Take your mind off things."

Ugh, Swiss's way of taking my mind off things was not what I wanted. Genesis started this fire, and *he* needed to put it out.

I was pulled out of a good dream by my phone buzzing from somewhere in the bed. It never mattered what kind of grip I had on it when I fell asleep. It always wound up somewhere crazy, like under my leg or behind my neck. The buzzing stopped. With one eye open, I carefully peeled Swiss's arm from around my waist to feel around for my phone. It was tucked under his side.

I sighed and stared at the missed call. Genesis could really work a damn nerve when he wanted to. He was supposed to call me before ten, before I got stuck being the good girlfriend and playing house. Yet, here it was going on two in the morning, and he was blowing up my shit like he'd lost his damn mind after I'd just seen him at dinner.

Swiss groaned in his sleep. I froze, only moving again when I could make out the steady rhythm of his breathing. He was normally a lighter-than-light sleeper. I chuckled. He probably would have snapped to attention if I hadn't gotten him fucked up off shots of 1800. Desperate times called for desperate measures, and I just wasn't feeling the whole staring-into-each-other's-eyes, love-sex thing tonight. Not when I'd been promised an "a-cock-alyptic" dick-down, and that was the exact wording Genesis used. Half a bottle of tequila couldn't even get me in the mood for Swiss, not when I was thinking about Gen. So we had an hour-long drunk conversation about I can't remember what until Swiss passed out.

I slid the phone under the blanket to text Genesis back.

I was asleep. What happened to ten o'clock?

He texted me right back.

I'm sorry. I got caught up. You know Citizen Kane can't tell time, though. I won't tell him it's not ten o'clock if you don't. ☺ 125 Bloom Court.

A smug smile curved my lips. He'd used the name I came up with for his dick. Now I could officially say that I had myself a legal dick.

I glanced in Swiss's direction. He was out cold. I could probably leave and act like I'd gone into the office early.

He usually didn't question my work hours so long as I didn't get too crazy with it.

Okay. See you in thirty, I replied.

My phone buzzed again as I tiptoed to the bathroom. It was a video message of Genesis biting his lower lip, stroking Citizen Kane into all of his thick and long glory. It was prettier than I'd imagined.

> You better hurry up. I already started. Bring the envelope.

I made the twenty-minute drive to his loft near Union Market in a record time of eight minutes flat. I felt like a movie star from the moment I pulled up. There was free twenty-hour valet just for visitors, so I didn't have to worry about parking. And I'm sure Genesis kept them all content by tipping well whenever he had cash in his pocket. I handed my keys to the valet and stood in the heated roundabout so I could admire the fifteen-story glass-front building. A pudgy little doorman with greying hairs sticking out the sides of his red and blue hat held the door for me.

My heels clacked across the cream and gold marble floor. It was a maze of glass etched in green bamboo separating different seating areas. Floor-to-ceiling bubble tanks churned water and changed color with the electro-swing music playing in the background. They must have bought their lobby music from the same place as Forever 21 or Express because the music made me feel like I should've been shopping.

"Good morning, Ms. Deleon," the front deskman greeted me in a cheerful voice.

The fact that he already knew my name before I could say anything was creepy but very impressive.

"Mr. Kane has asked that you join him on the roof. I can have someone show you up if—"

"It's okay, thank you. I'll find the way."

Genesis texted me before I was even two feet away from the receptionist's desk.

Open the envelope in the elevator and follow the directions.

My face felt like it was on fire as I rushed toward the elevator. I didn't want everybody to know who or why I was coming to visit. And what was he doing on the roof I wondered as I stepped into the gold-mirrored elevator. I'd thrown on a simple pink and black medallion print wraparound dress. The only thing holding it in place was the belt tied around the waist. I squinted around the lightning-forked gold veins in the elevator's mirrored walls to check the wings of my eyeliner before opening the envelope. There was a small index card and a fancy pink and silver e-cigarette. The card read, *"This is better,"* in barely legible handwriting. Something told me it was Genesis's.

I had twenty-four floors to go, so I puffed on my new e-cig a few times. It was definitely different than my emergency cig. The lack of smoke was a plus, though.

Somewhere in my coat pocket my phone started vibrating. I pulled it out as the elevator stopped on the top floor. The picture I'd saved of Swiss smiled back at me. I hit the volume button to stop if from vibrating. Maybe he deserved something better than what I could give him, because I knew I deserved something better than all the grief he'd given me.

The doors swept aside, and I climbed off the elevator, making sure to tuck my new toy back into the envelope. When I looked up, my mouth damn near fell off my face.

Genesis stood naked, wearing nothing but the night air.

"Our client cancelled and Citizen Kane was starting to complain," he called out.

Either the roof was too high or I was in shock. I swayed where I stood at a sudden feeling of light-headedness. Purple lights lit up the pool behind Genesis. It made deep dark shadows that breathed and stretched across the roof. I was suddenly aware of every piece of fabric on my body. My dress felt like silk against my skin, and the breeze that flowed across the roof felt like angels' kisses.

As much as I wanted to turn around and get back on the elevator, something kept me swaying where I stood like a wild rose in a rainstorm. I couldn't take my eyes off of Genesis or the bizarre scene rolling out in front of me. This nigga knew I was coming, yet there he stood—with two naked hoes on their knees in front of him. The backs of their black weave brushed the ground behind their bobbing heads. They fought over his dick like two kids trying to lick the same candy cane. I giggled. I actually giggled. Technically, they *were* fighting over a "candy Kane."

A third girl was behind him running her nails down his back to his round ass, and even further downward to his calves. She'd go to the bottom and start all over again. The envelope fell out of my fingers. It hit the ground with a soft slap. Genesis reached back, smacking the girl behind him hard on her ass. Ironically, none of this was bothering me. I should've been back on that elevator as soon as I saw what was happening, but I was still there. Heat swirled between my thighs. Genesis motioned for me to come to him.

I shook my head no, watching the world turn into a hazy blur of crystal blue pool, purple lights, and brown shadows. Something was in that e-cigarette, and it wasn't nicotine, not with the way I was feeling.

"Come here," Genesis ordered. He pointed at the ground in front of him.

Jealousy crossed my mind, but so did something else. Competition. I walked toward him with the meanest look I could make, considering I couldn't feel my face. My fingers undid the belt at my waist. My dress slipped off my shoulders down my back, pooling into a colorful puddle behind me.

Genesis's hand wrapped around the back of my neck. He surprisingly found the spot that I never told anyone about in less than four seconds. A nigga could get me to do anything just by breathing on that spot. And now his fingers were swirling in the short hair that grew there. The feeling made my knees weak.

"You like your new e-cigarette?" he asked in a warm, slow voice. "It's better for you. Cannabinoids. Weed without the smoke; stronger and healthier."

Shit, my boss got me high. I would probably never be able to say that again in this lifetime. The chicks down in front of him didn't even acknowledge me. They slurped and sucked at what I considered to be my Citizen Kane. I was surprised but too fuzzy-headed to react to the tattoos covering Genesis from his collarbone all the way down to his thighs. He pulled my head toward his, taking a kiss and stealing my breath at the same time.

When he pulled away, he looked at me with proud eyes.

"I bought them for you, but you took too long," he said.

I wasn't worried about the other women anymore. I wasn't worried about anything except getting his full attention and his body to myself. My nails drifted down his chest to his navel. I let my fingers tangle in the hair of the girl closest to me. Genesis had better not get used to no shit like this, because this was going to be my first and last girl-girl-girl-guy get together.

Genesis groaned. It was deep and throaty, and it sent chills down the back of my neck. That was my groan. He needed to be making that sound for me. I moved to push myself in between the girls in front of him, taking the girl's wig with me. It must've tangled on the ring I always wore. She popped Gen's dick out of her mouth.

"Damn, bitch! It took me two hours to pin that shit just—" she stopped.

"Just so you can talk shit to me at home, and then sneak around, fuckin' my nigga?" I asked Shandy, poking my index finger hard into her forehead. The bitch beside her stopped what she was doing . . . and I wasn't even surprised to see Heather.

"Heather, you need to let that nigga's dick go. Now," I warned her.

Shandy was the last person I expected to see. Being high didn't help me focus, and it didn't help me stay calm. The more I reprocessed the sight of her sucking his dick, the more disgusted I got. The bitch behind him didn't even have the decency to stop what she was doing.

"Eh . . . hmmmm," I cleared my throat trying to catch her attention.

"Novie, if you don't calm the fuck down," Genesis interrupted. "I paid them to come out for a client. Me and you were gonna have us a peep show. He cancelled, and I figured we could have some fun."

"I can't believe y'all. This shit is what you consider *fun?*" I aimed all of my outrage at Genesis.

"Shit, we ain't even got to go through all of this," Shandy butt in before he could answer. "We can take what we've made and call it a night, sir, or Kane, or whatever your name is," she said to Genesis.

"Nah." Genesis shook his head with his lips turned down into an ugly frown. "I will give y'all five times your normal rate if you'll stay."

"Nigga, that's twenty thousand," Shandy sputtered.

I looked at him like he'd lost his ever-lovin' mind. I know this nigga wasn't about to pay Shandy and her crusty side chicks that much money. Shandy had the potential to do damn near anything for a dollar. Her mouth fell open at Genesis's offer; she didn't even need to ask Heather what was up. That bitch was already reassuming the dick-sucking position.

"Only thing missing is you." Genesis pointed at the ground in front of him.

I didn't need this shit, and I damn sure wasn't about to share. He must've sensed the hell I was thinking about raising. His face went hard and cold.

"I didn't know you knew them, Novie, and they weren't cheap to begin with. I want you to experience this. Being among friends should be a plus for you."

He pulled me toward him and held up his hand for me to open my mouth. I took whatever he was offering, letting it melt on the tip of my tongue. *Fuck it*. That was my last thought before I let myself be blindfolded. I felt weightless. There were hands and mouths all over me. The nigga didn't miss a beat. He held me up against him. Fingers and tongues ran up and down my back. Lips sucked on the back of my neck. I tightened my legs around his hips, wrapping my arms around his neck . . . the excitement, the thrill of having so many women around us when all he really wanted was me, fueled for a heat-seeking missile that was about to explode inside my pussy.

Kane palmed my ass in each hand. The heat from his long fingers seared my skin as he guided my pussy up and down the length of him. My head fell back, a soft moan leaving my lips. I was flying, floating, and about to cum, all at the same time. I could feel every inch of skin, every throb, and every muscle. This nigga was fucking me into some love. I chanted the words over and over; even though I was trying to stop myself, I couldn't keep from saying it.

Genesis groaned against my lips. "*Mmmm-hmmm,* you love this dick?" he asked.

I sighed, whirred my hips harder against him, trying to lock him inside me forever.

"*Ahhhhhh,* I love you. I love your dick. I love everything," I moaned back.

My walls contracted and closed in around him. It hit me like a flash flood that started in my pussy, working its way outward to my fingertips and toes. I couldn't breathe, couldn't hold myself up. Eyes closed, I let myself float on each wave as it came in.

NOVIE

20

Inspector Gidget and Inspector Gadget

Shandy and Heather were both sitting at the small bar that stretched across the kitchen cabinet. We normally used it as our dinner table, but it was currently covered with papers. A couple bottles of red wine and empty glasses sat between the two of them. I dropped my keys somewhere on the couch and kicked off my shoes.

I could tell they were up to something just by looking at them, but everything was still awkward after our night with Genesis. It was next to impossible for me to look Heather in the eye, considering I now knew what she tasted like. Shandy was the only one acting like everything was fine and dandy.

"I'm still mad at you, but now that I've got ten grand, I could care less what you do, girl. I'm keeping your fifteen percent, though," Shandy said. "That nigga is paid out the ass, and he love him some you. Go bat your eyes, he'll give it to you."

My eyes narrowed suspiciously. "What the hell is wrong with you two? That's the type of shit y'all be out there doing? I still don't know how I even feel about what went down or the way it went down last night."

"Well, we feel fine about everything we've done. Your little boo-thang is a freak. You better hold on to that. Good-looking, good sex, and he got paper. It ain't gonna get any better, Novie. If you don't stay with him, me and Heather already agreed on sharing him," Shandy joked.

They were still looking suspicious to me. Knowing them, they'd christened my bed or my bathroom. The two of them sitting there together just had this look like something nasty or sexually explicit transpired somewhere sacred, or where I eat maybe.

A slow grin spread across Shandy's face. The last time she got that look was when we worked together in this small office, and she'd started using the company card to stock our fridge.

"So, Heather and I have been doing a little investigating into your Genesis Kane. Even though he gave us a little fake name. He said he was Trent Santora when he booked us," she announced.

Heather nodded. "I had one of my girls run him through the database at work and—"

"You did *what?*" I snapped at her. My temper instantly went through the roof. "Shandy, I told you I didn't want to check into him or have you check into him," I reminded her. "Y'all get prostituted for one night, and now all of a sudden, you want to start running checks without anyone's permission?"

"Technically, I didn't do anything. Heather did all the work." She pointed her thumb in Heather's direction averting her eyes away from me.

"I didn't want anyone checking into anybody. How did I not make that shit clear?"

Silence filled the air as neither one of them could answer my question.

"Well, we did find something you might really want to know," Heather spoke up.

Even though I was miffed, my curiosity got the better of me.

"Okay, so what is it?"

Heather handed over a sheet of paper, and I waited for her to explain.

NOVIE

21

Home Sweet Home

Monday should've been an awkward part two day, but Genesis surprised me by calling in sick. I'd managed to avoid Swiss all weekend, but I could feel it in the air. He was bound to pop up sooner than later.

The office wasn't the same when Genesis wasn't there. Tangie seemed a lot more social than usual. The Bobbys were all on ten. They'd shown me every dance, cute shoe, and every outfit they came across, all while stalking their crush's Instagram. Mavis was the only one who was still quiet and all business as usual in her corner of the office. I was disappointed when I texted Genesis, and he didn't answer. I still felt some kind of way about sharing him with my friends, and then being ignored or avoided. Maybe he was feeling some of that "morning-after" shame too.

Genesis didn't come across as the type of man who would feel ashamed about anything, though. I flagged Tangie down during her coffee refill.

"Do you know where Mr. Kane is?" I asked her in as nonchalant of a voice as I could manage.

"Not sure; the boss doesn't have to let anyone know if he's going to come into work," was her snippy reply.

She softened it up a little when she saw the disheartened look on my face. "He probably has a bug or a meeting. I heard his voice mail in his office replaying messages. He normally calls and checks it when he's out and about working."

"I see." I tried to think of a quick lie to throw her off. I was too new to be checking for the boss like that. "He'd mentioned Farrah was coming by, and now I feel stupid for dressing up for the occasion."

Even though I was irritated, I'd dressed up just for him. Now I was irritated at him missing the chance to see me all dressed up.

"Well, if it'll make you feel special, you can entertain the auditor I'm expecting to arrive any minute now. I need to go make sure we shredded everything."

My eyebrows flew up at that.

Tangie cackled an old witchy sounding cackle. "Just messin' with you, baby girl. I'm going to touch up my lipstick. If it's the same auditor we had last time, I need all this," she ran her hands dramatically over her hips, "to be correct. The sight of that nucka' sent my menopause into remission."

Tangie tipped away in her leopard print pumps wiggling and giggling to herself. What in the world did she expect me to do to entertain this so-called auditor? What if he started asking questions, I was the wrong person for that considering the inside knowledge I had concerning Gen's finances.

"Hello?" someone called out from the small lobby at the front. Metro-Bobby popped up to escort her in. He came back moments later with a woman dressed like Agent Scully. She peered down at me over her glasses when they stopped in front of my desk.

"This is Novie. She'll be assisting you until the office manager Tangie is available," he announced, before going back to his desk.

"Hi, Novie." She said my name with so much attitude in her voice I did a double take.

Her hair was slicked back into a tight curly ponytail hanging halfway down her back. I couldn't place her face or her voice until I saw the rounded bump under the front of her suit jacket. My breath caught in my throat.

"Tinesha?" I asked in an unsure voice.

A slow smile spread across her face; it looked the same way the Grinch looked when he stole Christmas.

"The one and only. It seems like our world keeps gettin' smaller and smaller," she replied in a fake polite voice.

Lord, this can't be real. This has to be some kind of joke or some shit.

She eased down into the empty chair in front of my desk. Gone were the purple sprig-a-sprags and all the *ignance*, yes, *ignance* that she normally showed up with. Tinesha must've gotten a Ph.D. in chameleon business and life tactics. She had whoever had given her a real job completely fooled, because I'd seen how foolish she could get.

She looked around the office with her nose turned up, taking inventory and making assessments on the worth and value of everything Genesis had.

"So, this is where your nigga-thieving ass works?" she asked as she looked over the Bobbys who were all busy with trying to look busy. They weren't even fooling me.

When she was done with her visual assessment, she settled back in the chair and folded her hands in her lap. "I didn't take you for the type to hold down a real job. I figured you were more like a professional side chick."

This bitch has some nerve callin' me a side chick with all the dirt she has piled up in her yard.

I smiled at her so hard my cheeks burned. "Funny, and I was just thinking the same thing about—"

"Did you know, *Novie*, that when the IRS audits a business, we're just looking for hidden assets, misreported earnings, and fraud."

Oh no, this heffa is not going for the jugular and not on some play shit. Genesis's business doesn't have anything to do with the beef she has with me.

"All I need is one teeny-tiny mistake, and, by law, I have to make an *adverse opinion*." Her words sounded more like a threat than an explanation.

I prayed that Genesis had all of his shit in order. Swiss had said she didn't know about his dealings with Genesis. But if even one number didn't line up with another, I don't think she'd need to know anything about it. She'd raise enough hell in her own way.

The plush leather desk chair I was sitting in might as well have been a stack of heated cement blocks. I shifted uncomfortably. I had no idea exactly what an adverse opinion meant, but it sounded like something that would hurt Genesis more than it would hurt me.

"What do you want?" I asked.

Her top lip scrunched up toward her nose. She squinted at me through the lens of her glasses.

"Well, for starters, I want *you* to keep your damn mouth shut. You say a word to Swiss about Javion, and I'll make sure I find something to shut this bitch down."

Shit, it's way too late for that one. Hopefully, I could catch Swiss before he opened his fat mouth and told her anything I'd said.

"Second," she continued in a hushed voice, "I want to know where the *fuck* Javion is. The last time I talked to him, he said he was leaving with a bitch named Novie De-la-di-da. His phone is going straight to voice mail, and you're still here, so . . .?"

"So what if I don't know where Javion is? What if I haven't seen him since the day you stomped him down outside of his car?" It wasn't a lie . . . Well, half of what I'd said wasn't a lie. Last time I'd seen Javion, he was dead. It never crossed my mind to ask Genesis or Swiss what happened to the body or the cover story for the body.

"Then you'd better track him down or the IRS will make your life hell. People get audited all the time; they go to prison for tax evasion. Have you filed all of your prior year returns? Oh, wait, it doesn't matter. They will disappear if I need them to."

Tangie might be mean as hell, but I can say one thing . . . Tangie is no parts gangsta. On any given day, she kept the whole building on lockdown, and now her old rusty hind part's MIA when I need her to come to my rescue.

Tinesha wasn't done. "If Javion reaches out to you, make sure *you* reach out to *me*. I'll be in touch. And so you know how serious this is, I've already seen a glitch in Mr. Genesis Kane's information, and you are the deciding factor in what I do with that."

Tinesha wasn't even all the way out of the office before I started blowing up Gen's phone. He wasn't answering any of my calls or the texts I'd sent. Something was wrong. Something was definitely wrong.

After my visit with Tinesha, I was in panic mode. Initially, Tangie wasn't too enthusiastic about letting me leave early. Her mind changed real quick as soon as the word *flu* came out of my mouth. She shooed me out of the office in a lemon-scented cloud of Lysol, mumbling about a flu epidemic. I needed to get in contact with Genesis before Tinesha did something stupid. Hopefully, he'd be able to give me an idea of what I could tell her to throw her off. It would be nice if I knew what the fuck she'd found, though.

I'd started to make my way to Gen's loft, but Shandy and Heather's tip about this "mystery house" kept running through my mind. He'd never mentioned another house. It made me wonder if he lived there with some kind of secret family. If he was home, he could be gone by the time I left the loft and fought traffic to get out of the city. My best bet was to head out of the city first and work my way back in.

An hour later, I was standing in one of the richest neighborhoods in the city with my heels glued to the rust-colored cobblestones underneath 'em. I'd parked a few blocks away so I could take a minute to get my mind right without having my car spotted. Since I wasn't supposed to know about Gen's place out here, I didn't want to risk him recognizing my car and not answering the door.

All the gusto I'd felt earlier shrank away as I stared at houses lined up as high as mountains. Each one bigger and badder than the next, like I'd stepped into my own episode of *Real Housewives*. Even the sidewalks looked expensive as hell with cobblestones instead of cement and fancy silver lamps lining the streets. Their tiny flames flickered, getting brighter as the sun started to set. I definitely wasn't in Norfolk, Virginia, anymore. But that was the last place I wanted to be anyway.

My insides were shaking like Jell-O shots at a sorority party. It didn't make sense for me to be feeling this kind of nervousness mixed with anger. But considering how many times we'd been together, Genesis had only taken me to his loft once or twice. *Yes, that's it.* Shit, and even then, it was late as hell, and I was too damn tipsy and too busy trying to get some ass to take in the details. He'd never felt the need to mention his house.

This was all Shandy's and Heather's fault. If they hadn't run his name through the system, I wouldn't have been dying to figure out why he had so many addresses. And since he wasn't at the office or taking my calls, this felt like my only option. What he was hiding? Nobody hides something like a house unless they've got somebody up in that bitch.

I shook my head at myself and took a shaky pull from my stress Newport twisting my lips as I exhaled so the smoke would blow into the wind. I should've borrowed one of Shandy's wigs, just in case he was outside and I chickened out; then, I could make a quick escape unnoticed.

I dropped my half-smoked cigarette, crushing it under my heel as I marched toward my man's house. The oversized gift bag I'd made for him was balanced in the nook of my arm as I dug through my much-hated purse. I had this thing down packed. Sanitize the hands, follow it up with the fresh lotion, and pop a stick of gum. It all must've worked because not once did anyone ever complain.

I stopped in front of the address I'd memorized forward and backward. There were a few lights on inside, but I couldn't tell if he was home. My fingers locked around the handles of the gift bag in a sweaty grip as I marched up the circular driveway toward the Swiss archway of the front door. Now, we'd finally see about Genesis and this so-called *flu bug*. In my defense, it was only right that I check in to make sure he was really suffering . . . and really alone.

My plan was to peek in, and if all looked good, I'd just make that ass some chicken soup and hot toddies until he was too full and drunk to complain. Yes, this was probably all parts of wrong, depending on how you looked at it, but he *was* my man, and as Genesis liked to say, *if ain't sneaky, it ain't freaky.*

I propped my ear toward the door listening for the TV, or movement, or some bitch whose ass I'd have to whoop in case he was, after all, lying about everything. It was dead silent. *Girl, if this ain't the craziest shit you've ever done.*

After a few quick glances up and down the street, I pressed the doorbell. It let out a deep, loud dong, like a church bell. *You are wrong for this; he's probably sick as a dog, and you done popped yo' ass up over here. Mmmph mmmph mmph. Bet not get me sick, I know that much.* I held my breath, praying he'd appreciate this and not be mad. That he wasn't laid up with another bitch, cheating.

The sound of the lock turning sent my heart slamming into my chest. The door opened slow as all hell. Yo, my nerves and the excitement had me hopping from foot to foot, running in place like a jogger on a street corner. As soon as there was a gap big enough for me to fit through, I slid in without invitation, smelling and looking at everything I could see from the front door. It was warm cinnamon and apples, black forest oak wood flooring, and from what I could see, bulky, masculine furniture.

Genesis was standing to the side, one hand still on the door handle with the other holding up the *New York Times*. His face was plastered to the paper as he focused on whatever he was reading. He was wearing a long red robe like the ones boxers wear before they step into the ring. The hood hung low over his head, nearly covering his eyes. I tried to hone in on his face under the shadowy hood. The corners of his mouth were turned down in an ugly frown. I knew that look. It meant something was wrong; either he'd lost money on his retirement account, or a stock had dropped. There was no telling with him, but whatever it was, he wasn't going to be in a good mood behind it.

Suddenly, I realized how stupid this whole idea was. I should have at least called first. Now, here I was uninvited and invading his space. My eyes shot around the foyer looking for a place to hide while I tried to figure out if I could run my grown ass back out the door before he saw me.

"Where's your key, baby?" Genesis murmured in a low, distracted voice. "Guess you changed your mind about going to the—"

He looked up from his paper with confusion flashing across his face as we locked eyes.

My face scrunched into a wince, smile, and a cringe at being caught red-handed snoop checking up on my man.

"Hey, you," I whispered back.

"Novie? How did you know where to find me?" he asked, sliding the hood of his robe back off his head. This made the front of the robe fall open, showing off the grey and black tattoos covering his smooth brown skin from his collarbone on down.

I stared up at him, momentarily speechless. That's how it felt when I saw him after any kind of hiatus. Our silent stare down came to a stop when his words finally registered in my brain. *Wait, did he say "baby" when he didn't even know I was at the door?*

All of the love, care, and attention I'd put into his gift bag was out the window. I let his gift bag hit the floor.

I marched right at him shooting electric sparks from my eyes. My index finger was already raised in accusation.

"Who were you calling *baby* if you didn't know it was me?" My voice was surprisingly calm, even to me, as my finger made invisible quotation marks in the air. "And what . . . *What* did she forget? Humph, I know how y'all DC niggas do. Is it even a *she*? I know for *damn sure* the word *key* won't about to come up outta your mouth," I snapped with my voice going up three octaves.

I was so pissed I could feel the pistivity rising up off of me like heat waves.

Genesis snapped the newspaper he'd been holding shut, methodically folding it in half before tucking it under his arm. He was probably trying to bide his time while he worked up a lie.

He let out an irritated sigh. "Are you done?" he asked calmly.

My eyes narrowed on him like a target. *No, this nigga did not have the nerve to look and sound perfectly healthy.*

"Kane!" An irritated woman's voice ricocheted through the house. "Kane? If that's my pizza, check and make sure it got extra sauce on it. Last time, it was burnt *and* there won't no sauce," she screeched from somewhere upstairs.

My eyes widened and my head went on swivel. I looked from Genesis to the stairs and back. Shit, hopefully, I'd give myself whiplash so I could sue his ass. I ain't know exactly where that ho was, but she was about to catch it. *I know this nigga ain't got another bitch up in here.* I closed my eyes trying to find the words that would drop a man dead. He must have seen what was coming.

Genesis shook his head at me. "Calm down, Novie. There's a logical explanation for all of this."

"*Psht*," I hissed at him. "Logical, my ass." At this point even his calm demeanor was pissing me off. "You must logically think I'm an idiot."

"Kane? I'm gonna drink the last Naked juice. I don't feel like driving to get ginger ale . . ." her voice trailed off.

My gaze shifted slowly from Genesis's blank face up the winding staircase. They stopped dead center on this light-bright heffa standing on the balcony. She was wearing a black boxing robe similar to his, and it didn't look like much else underneath it. My blood ran so hot I got a headache and started sweating, all while picturing my hands around her throat.

"Dang," she talked like she didn't have a care in the world. "Why didn't you say you were having company? I hope you ordered enough pizza for everybody, because I ain't sharing my shit." With that, she turned and walked off.

My jaw dropped. I launched myself toward the stairs with tears blurring my vision. This couldn't be happening. Genesis's arms snaked around my waist, yanking me back against his chest. He became a human straitjacket, wrapping his arms around mine, pinning them to my heaving chest.

"Let go of me! You *smell* like you been fuckin'. Got that bitch's scent all over you. I swear on my life I'll—"

"You swear what?" Genesis barked down at the top of my head.

I was let go for the quickest second before his fingers dug into my shoulders. He whirled me around to face him. I was eye to eye with the tattoo of a sugar skull painted over a woman's face. She was beautiful and eerie at the same time. In the beginning, I didn't really think about it when he said sugar skulls honored someone who's passed. But the fact that he wouldn't tell me about this woman who meant so much to him he'd put her face on his body starting making me jealous little by little.

I refused to look up at him. I didn't want him to see my tears or how much he'd hurt me. My jaw was clenched so hard my teeth hurt as I settled in for a staring contest with his tattooed lady. She stared out at me from the middle of his chest; her empty eyes laughed at me.

"Well?" Genesis asked quietly.

My nose was running, and I couldn't remember the question.

He used the sleeve of his robe to dry my face, and he even wiped my nose.

"Novie, you might as well come on in, sit down, and have a drink with me. I was trying to wait for the best time to talk to you. There are a few things I was scared to tell you about myself . . . about my life."

GENESIS

22

You'll Never Lose Women Chasing Money

Novie was a piece of fucking work, and that was an understatement. She had all her five feet of nothing squared up like she was ready to battle. She didn't even consider the fact that she'd just invaded my space and my privacy. She was the one who'd spied, gotten my address, and then showed up uninvited. It amazed me how women could go looking for some shit, and then have the nerve to be hurt when they step in it.

Kenisha was still watching from the balcony. I avoided looking in her direction altogether. She was either getting a kick out of this or building up her own arsenal of shit to come at me with later. Even if I asked nicely, Kenisha wasn't about to budge an inch so long as Novie was acting hostile. My home protects home first, and in the event I needed to get dealt with, she'd do that when it was just the two of us. I ran my fingers across the hairs on my chin and nodded toward the living room.

"Why don't we go sit down and talk about all this?" I asked in as calm of a voice as I could manage.

I didn't keep up nor did I put up with drama or dramatic episodes. Novie gave me a slow nod. I led her into the other room with the sound of Kenisha sucking her teeth from above. We sat across from each other, and her big brown eyes were shimmery with tears and hurt. She angrily crossed her arms over her chest while she glared at me. I seriously debated on just cutting this shit off completely. I'd never had a woman physically track me down, show up at my house uninvited, and invade my space like she just did. If I'd wanted all my cards on the table, I would have put them all out there. I operated the way I did to fend off the charity cases and chameleons. Once someone knows your worth, it gets harder and harder to figure out if they're down for you versus your assets.

"Who is that woman, Kane?" Novie asked in a small angry voice.

I was momentarily at a loss for words. My own name sounded strange to my ears. She never called me Kane. I was always Genesis or Gen. She was still sexy as fuck, though. Even when she was mad as hell with her nostrils flaring and her hair swinging everywhere all wild. It was rare to see honest, raw emotion. Everyone in my world from the police, to the other attorneys, to the clients were all so calculating and manipulative. I rarely saw *real* feelings. The realization made me bite the inside of my lip and fake an ear scratch so I could look away to hide my smile. When I turned back, I was composed and ready for whatever.

23

What Had Happened Was

"Kenisha, come down here for a minute, please." Genesis hollered through the house.

I didn't want to meet no damn Kenisha or hear any bullshit excuses. I wanted the black-and-white honest-to-God truth.

The girl lazily waddled into the living room like she'd just been summoned to a hearing.

Genesis introduced us. "Novie, this is my niece, Kenisha. My brother got himself locked up, and as her next of kin, I stepped up and took her in. We've been getting along pretty well. Kenisha, this is Novie."

Kenisha looked me over curiously with her nose turned up like a little pug. She pointed between the two of us. "Y'all got a thing or somethin'?" she asked Genesis.

"Yeah, somethin'. I just wanted the two of you to meet face-to-face. That's all."

Kenisha rubbed the side of what I could now see was a belly underneath the huge boxing robe. "Okay, well, this baby's foot is in my ribs, so I'm gonna go lie down and wait on that pizza."

When she was upstairs and out of hearing distance I turned to Genesis. "She's pregnant? How old is she? How far along is she?"

His face looked older than usual; worry lines creased his usually smooth forehead as he ran his hand back and forth across his chin.

"She's sixteen. Been staying with me since she was fourteen, and I don't know shit about raising girls. I stayed home today because she's been having early contractions, gas, or Lord knows what. But she said pizza would make her feel better. I never know when to do what with her. She isn't even supposed to be pregnant, not on my watch, but all the lying and sneaking around, the attitudes, and know-it-all-ness. She's like a miniature version of you."

I punched his arm, forgetting how angry and embarrassed I was just seconds ago.

"Nigga, I am *none* of those things. Don't be mad because I have my own opinions and need justification for bullshit."

I wanted to punch Shandy and Heather in their nosy faces for this one. I'd gone and run up in this man's house looking like a lunatic. What if Kenisha would've answered the door, or if Genesis hadn't stopped me before I could get my hands on her?

Genesis eyed the goody bag sitting in the middle of the floor. "Did you bring me a surprise or is that where you keep your gun, Inspector Gidget?"

"I brought you some get well soon rations, but now I can see that you don't need them."

Genesis smiled as though he appreciated the gesture. He offered me a tour of his house, showing me everything from an indoor heated pool, to a full gym and sauna. We stopped on the third floor in a room that could've been a home office or a library. I followed Genesis out through white, billowy curtains onto a large balcony made of blinding white stones. Big bottle-shaped vases were carved into the sides of the walls made out of the same white stones as the railing and floor. They were piled with tropical orange and red hibiscus. A hummingbird zoomed by, taking my breath away. I'd never seen one in real life before, only on TV.

Genesis sat down at an all-white patio table. Deposition papers, his laptop, and cell were all strewn about across the table. I had to keep reminding myself that he was still a smart and very reputable attorney. Outside of work, in his element, he could've passed for anything. An actor, a rapper. I looked at him wondering if I'd ever get to know the man behind all of the masks.

"I was downstairs with Kenisha all morning. Glad it didn't rain, or I'd be out shopping for new electronics."

I used that opportunity to fill him in on Tinesha's visit to the office, as well as her threats.

Genesis didn't even seem slightly fazed by that information. He stared out into the woods that surrounded the edge of his backyard. Dirt trails split in at least five different directions through the trees. They were either hiking or dirt bike trails.

"Tinesha isn't going to be a problem. I'll send a little birdie her way just to make sure we've got all of our bases covered. Thank you for keeping an eye on things. I'll be back as soon as I know Kenisha's good."

My phone rang. I dug it out of my purse, but not before Genesis could see Swiss's face flashing across the screen. I wasn't fast enough.

Genesis's face went stormy. "I thought I told you to stay away from that."

His voice was so low and quiet I could barely hear him over the sounds of the birds chirping in the trees around us. I silenced Swiss's call, giving Genesis my undivided attention.

"And I told you that it's *not* what you think. *He's* not whatever it is you're thinking. You fucked my friends, yet you have the biggest problem with even the thought of me fucking one of yours?"

"Swiss is no friend of mine!" Genesis roared, jumping to his feet, flipping the table.

I jumped, sidestepping his phone as it slid across the ground. This was not the type of reaction I'd expect from someone who did regular business with another dude. There had to be something more behind Genesis not liking Swiss than he was telling me. If Genesis wasn't going to tell me what I needed to know, that only left one other person for me to talk to.

"I need to talk to you," Swiss blurted out as soon as I answered the phone.

"Okay. I'm leaving the office now. I just need to run home and freshen up and then I'll head over. Your women better not touch me or my car, Swiss."

NOVIE

24

Step Up Or Get Stepped On

I rushed home and after a quick shower I was finally ready to relax and let myself breathe. Swiss was waiting for me to come scoop him up so we could have a "talk." We'd been so hit or miss lately. Well, I'd actually been missing him on purpose. Genesis was always on my mind, taking over my thoughts. It was time for me to let Swiss go, and I wasn't sure how he was going to take it.

I almost didn't make it out of the house on time since it took me close to forever to remember where I'd put my keys. I needed to start laying them in one specific spot when I got home. They were in the dish by the front door where I normally never put them. But with Heather and Denise and Shandy all planning a weekend in, it should have crossed my mind to ask one of them where they were instead of searching for an hour. They all seemed to share some kind of extreme OCD that involved moving and rearranging things that did not belong to them.

Whoooo hooo! I swung my hair, loving the way it felt as it brushed across my shoulders. One hand was up through the moon roof with my fingers snapping on beat to the stars and the streetlights. I whipped Genesis's Jag through the streets, swerving around taxis and traffic like

I was in the Daytona 500. Swiss reclined in the passenger's seat with a bottle of champagne in one hand and a bottle of Hennessey White in the other. He'd said Genesis had picked them up for him.

For Genesis to be as hell-bent against Swiss as he was, he sure did a lot of nice things for the man.

Swiss tapped my shoulder. "Girl, slow this bitch down. You weren't that late scooping me up. Damn, we can still make the movie. We comin' up on a red light. Here." He held out the Henny.

I took the bottle with a smirk, lifting it to my lips. He was trying his best to get me fucked up, but I'd just wind up dropping him off and go see my babe. Every red light brought another round of shots as we hooted at the parade of women crossing over the crosswalks. I was getting further from sober and closer to having to pee.

"What is this grudge Genesis has against you?"

Swiss took another long, deep swig from the bottle. "Novie, why does it feel like this nigga's name keeps popping up every time I'm around you? Can we leave work at work for once?"

"I need to know, Swiss. I want to make sure he doesn't try to do anything to hurt you. It's not some kind of regular shit; it's like a full-out raging *I hate that nigga* grudge."

"He has more to worry about what I would do to him. It's a pheromone thing, or fuck if I know; maybe he's trying to get at you and it's just some plain old nigga bullshit."

"It's deeper than that, Swiss. He acts like he can't stand you."

"If that nigga feelin' some kind of way, he'd better to step up before he gets stepped on. He's always cool as cream when I deal with him. As long as my pockets stay right, I'm fine with it."

Giggling, I watched Swiss fumble, trying to put the cap back on the bottle.

"Nigga, you really can't drink, can—"

Bam! Thoomp! Thuddump!

The words were knocked loose from my brain before they could leave my mouth. Droplets of rain sprayed me in the face as I jerked forward before slamming back into my seat.

Oh, fuck, I've been shot.

Dazed with my head spinning, I looked over for Swiss. It was either dead silent or I couldn't hear anything over the ringing in my ears. The passenger-side door was sitting wide open. He was gone. He'd actually bailed on me again.

Everything slowly came into as much focus as it could with all the shots I'd taken. People were running around the car. They reminded me of silent movies or mimes the way they were pointing, gesturing hysterically, and pulling out their phones to take pictures. Cameras flashed by the dozens. I was hit so hard the trunk had popped open, slamming into and breaking the back windshield. My door was yanked open. A little Filipino man looked me over with an anxious expression.

"Somebody called an ambulance. I saw everything, but I couldn't get the plate off the car that rear-ended you," he said in a shaky voice. "Just hold on. You're gonna be okay. You were wearing your seat belt but . . ."

He looked away from me, staring off and down the street at something. I followed his line of vision. It was then that I saw streetlight folded into the hood of the Jag. It wasn't even raining. Blood ran into my eye. Swiss was lying half on the sidewalk and half in the street. I could see him clear as day without the windshield. His leg was bent at an unnatural angle. I slammed my eyes shut at the big jagged bone that had torn through his jeans sticking out of his thigh.

My Bluetooth announced Denise was calling.

"Answer," I called out in a weak voice. "Dee, me and Swiss were just in a car accident," I blurted out before she could say anything.

An ambulance pulled up in a blur of deafening sirens and red lights.

"Novie? What happened? Are y'all okay? Where are you at? I'll come out there," Denise asked a frenzy of questions through the speakers.

"Somebody hit me, they pushed me into a—"

Suddenly I couldn't be heard over all the police officers and firefighters swarming around the car. They even got up to run over from where they'd been huddled around Swiss in the street.

"We've got a Code 4 back here! Code 4 on a kid in the trunk," one of the EMTs shouted over all the chaos.

"Novie? Did he just say a kid?" Denise screamed, her voice echoed through the speakers, bouncing around the inside of the car.

"Oh my God, is Hennessey with her? Is she okay? Did you tell her we looked everywhere for her?" Heather was chanting and panicking in the background.

I lay my head back against the headrest, wishing I was the one lying in the street instead of Swiss. Tears slid down my face. Hennessey's little body dangled lifelessly from a paramedic's arms.

"Novie! We've been looking for Hennessey for the last hour! She wasn't hiding in the car, was she? Answer me, Novie!" Shandy begged over and over for an answer.

My throat constricted until I couldn't speak. It all made sense now. Why I couldn't find my keys. Why I'd heard three thumps . . . one when I was hit, another when I hit the post, and the last thump was a tiny person being thrown around in the trunk of my car.

"Get out of the fucking car now," officers started shouting.

Lights were put on me. They were so bright they made my head spin. Guns were drawn, and the officers posted up around my car like I was some kind of criminal.

"I don't think I can move," I cried out the driver's side door with my hand shielding the light from my eyes.

It felt like my arm was being pulled out of the socket when I got yanked out of the car and thrown down onto the ground, right there in the middle of the street. Glossy golden motor oil ran down the pavement. It puddled where I lay. It was sticky and hot against the side of my cheek as someone's knee went into my back, pressing my face into the cracked black asphalt. Broken glass scraped my cheek and poked into my chest through my dress as my arms were cuffed behind me. A lonely blue and white shoe sat on the ground underneath my car. Blue laces draped across the face of one of the princesses from *Frozen*. I'd never figured out who was who, but the movie would be on repeat whenever Hennessey was in the house.

Tears slid down my cheeks, burning the scratches on my face. I should've never been drinking and driving in the first place. There was nobody to blame for any of this except myself.

There was only one person I knew of who could get me out of this, and I had no idea if making that call would save me or sign my death certificate. First Javion, now Swiss. I'd singlehandedly disposed of Genesis's number one and his number two guys. He'd probably let me rot in jail, or he'd make my life so hellish, jail would seem like a walk in the park.

25

Alpha Dog

To the chagrin and dismay of more than a few officers, it was easier for Genesis to get me out of jail than I thought. The DUI and double homicide charges all but disappeared before my hand could put the crusty phone in the station down onto the receiver. Genesis gave me his word that everything would be taken care of, and from what I could tell, he'd kept it.

A few hours later, I was climbing into the back of the Lincoln Town Car that'd arrived outside the jail. My eyes were red and sore. I hadn't stopped crying since the police had put me into the car.

"Novie, I swear you could put CIA operatives and hired hit men to shame if you ever decided to expand your résumé," Farrah chimed from the backseat.

I jumped in surprise. I wasn't expecting her. Genesis had given me the impression that he'd be coming to pick me up. Disappointed, I climbed in, giving Farrah a weak smile. Talking wasn't at the top of my list right now.

"It wasn't what I'd intended, I promise," I assured her.

She handed me a miniature bottle of Perrier. I accepted it, even though I hated that mess. It tasted like carbonated yuck. I'd rather just drink regular water.

"Well, now with this tragic turn of events, I've found myself in need of a new captain. A new number one. I've looked into your family, Novie. The Deleons have a solid reputation. You come from good stock."

I frowned, trying to see Farrah's eyes through the oversized shades on her face.

"My family and I had a falling out. But I'm sorry, Farrah; blame the concussion. I'm kind of confused," I admitted. "I, um, I thought Genesis was your go-to person. The boss, or your number one guy, I guess I should say."

Farrah scoffed at me. "Who, Genesis? Oh, how that control freak would love to be the man in charge." She laughed. "That's a good one. Genesis Kane as a boss? Not hardly. He's my legal muscle, the reason we all stay damn near untouchable. Genesis has helped cover up dirt on behalf of the police department, city council, even the mayor. If they ever decided to be uncooperative, well, I'd pretty much own the city. But no, Genesis has never been in charge. Swiss was my burly Alpha warrior. He was my number one, my go-to man." Farrah let out a sad sigh. "And my go-to fuck. God, sex with that man was better for my body than Pilates and water aerobics combined."

Fizzy lemon-lime water went down the wrong pipe, making me choke and sputter.

I dabbed my watery eyes with the back of my hand. "Sorry, wrong pipe," I muttered after I'd gotten my composure.

Swiss and Farrah . . . What the fuck? Well, damn, who wasn't Swiss fucking?

Yes, Swiss always had aspirations of being the leader of a cartel, but since when did Swiss actually become the head of anything? And as high and mighty as Genesis acted, his ass wasn't even in charge. I'd have never guessed that, not with the way he carried himself like he was Father Superior, the all-knowing and all-important one. I almost punched the seat in front of me. This shit was more than I was ready to face or process right now.

"So, Novie, back to my question. Do I trust an outside source to come in and pick up where Swiss left off, or do I give you that position?"

Okay, this was definitely way too much for me to process. I'd just killed a man and the daughter of my best friend's girlfriend. Those two deaths hanging over my head were making my stomach reel. By now, Heather and Shandy had been contacted, and I still had them to deal with. How do I apologize for accidentally killing someone's child? How could I make that up to someone? All I really wanted to do was crawl into a hole and never crawl back out.

"Farrah, can I have some time to think. It's just that all of this was kind of traumatic. I just need to get my bearings."

"Sure. As bad as Genesis wants the title for himself, I'm giving you forty-eight hours to come to grips with reality. You've taken out my two best guys. If you don't take this offer I can't say that I will have much further use for you." The lines around Farrah's lips wrinkled as she pursed her lips together. It made it look like she had a little pink-sour asshole poking out of her face.

I nodded my understanding.

It was pretty clear that my only option was to accept her offer or she'd renege on one of my get out of jail free cards. I'd never been good at ultimatums. The last time I was faced with one, I tried to kill myself. But this time, the thought of being in charge, running things, hell, even running Genesis, didn't seem as bad as it sounded.

The car rolled to a stop in front of an Enterprise Car Rental.

"We have an account here. Genesis has already set you up with a car," she stated.

Half an hour later, I was leaving the rental office in a compact blue Prius. This had to be Genesis's way of punishing me for Swiss's death. It still felt too soon for me to go home and face the aftermath that I knew was waiting so I called the devil himself.

"How many times had I told you to *stay away* from that nigga?" Genesis growled in the phone without saying hello.

"Now you don't have to worry about that ever again, Genesis. It's been handled permanently!" My voice broke.

I'd been holding in guilt on top of resentment on top of anger at myself. Saying the words out loud made me feel the impact of what had happened. Swiss's sons would have to grow up without a father, and Heather would have to go on without her baby girl. I pulled over to the side of the road. None of this felt right. Why did God let me live over and over again?

"Where are you at, Novie?" Genesis asked.

"Somewhere near Enterprise," I sniffled into the phone. "I pulled over."

"Well, stay there. I'm coming to get you. We can go get your mind off of things."

An hour later, Genesis and I were going shot for shot at a brewery not far from where I lived. Genesis had gotten us a cozy corner table away from the crowded bar so we could talk. Even though I didn't have any kind of an appetite, I ordered steak fries since he insisted I put something in my stomach with all the alcohol. The waitress brought out my fries, hovering over Genesis for a moment or two longer than necessary to make sure he was good. When she finally left, I turned to him juggling a bite of the piping hot fried potato between my teeth and my tongue.

"Why did you lie to me? You let me think you were running everything," I asked once I finished wrestling with my food.

He didn't even look shocked or caught off guard by my question. Genesis stopped twirling the toothpick that he'd been tossing from side to side in his mouth. He laid it neatly on the side of his napkin.

"If you know what's what, then I'm guessing Farrah has already spoken to you," he said.

"Yes, and she wants me to take Swiss's place."

Genesis scooped up his shot glass. "Let's take another shot, and then I'll tell you everything."

Tequila burned its way down my throat and chest. I almost gagged the shot back up. It reminded me of why I hated it in the first place. It was Genesis's choice, so I didn't complain when he ordered it, but boy, my head and stomach were surely gonna complain in the morning.

"I didn't lie. I never said I ran anything. You assumed that part. I've worked with Farrah for a good number of years. I was only twenty-five and fresh out of law school. She was my first client, and I lost her case because I was inexperienced. When she got out and wanted to start over, I helped her because I owed her one, and I saw her vision."

"What? Let me find out the wealth consultant was on her Martha Stewart back in the day," I blurted out in shock.

"Yeah, and she brought your boy Swiss in a couple of years ago. He made shit happen, and he did it fast. Got territory covered, mapped out who we could deal with, who we could work for, and . . ." Genesis pointed in my direction. "He figured out who could be useful to us."

"Useful?" I gawked at Genesis. "Useful, like how? This was all a bullshit fluke. If that shit hadn't went down with Javion—"

"Novie, if it wasn't the shit that went down with Javion that made you cross our paths, it would've been something else. Swiss's mind had been made up about pulling you in way before you ever knew what you were being pulled into."

And just like that, what little appetite I had was gone. I threw a half-eaten fry back into the basket, rubbing my fingers together to dust off the salt.

"No. Genesis, I'm telling you that you must have misunderstood something somewhere. Swiss was—"

"Novie, Farrah wants to tap into the medicinal marijuana industry. Swiss insisted that he knew a woman who could do more than all of our efforts combined. Said he had *intimate knowledge* of you." Genesis scowled saying the words *intimate knowledge* like they left a bitter taste in his mouth. "Swiss had guys watching you and your apartment for . . . I don't know . . . a year, maybe longer. You even got a few phones he had preloaded with spyware. He knew where you went, who you saw, and what you were doing. Javion was originally one of the guys gathering info on you. He didn't know why he was doing it, but he fucked up when he crossed the line and used what he knew to get in your panties."

Genesis stopped to tell the waitress who'd wandered back over we were good. I too declined her offer for water and another shot. I was still in shock. This was all way too much to process in one day. *Javion had been watching me?* Now it all made sense, why he knew so much about me and how he seemed to remember it all so effortlessly.

"I know this sounds crazy, and it's probably too much to tell you considering what you've been through, but you deserve to know the truth."

"Did Swiss tell Javion to shove the broom up the daughter's ass too, or was that all Javion?"

Genesis shrugged. "Either way it goes, if you hadn't left your prints on the front door, Swiss was going to plant them when he went back to slit Beau and his daughter's throats."

"Would he have let me go to prison if I told you no when you approached me that day?"

The grim look on Genesis's face made my stomach turn.

"I had enough cash on me to buy the entire Eastern shore if that's what was needed to get you out. I was told to take the money to a field and burn all of it if you declined."

I slumped back in the hard wooden chair with my mind whirring. I ran from Swiss and the drug game, just to get sucked back into it all over again. There was no way I could work for Farrah. Too many people had already died because of me, and I wasn't about to get any deeper into this shit than I already had.

Genesis touched my hand across the table. "That's why I kept telling you to stay away from him."

"So that's the reason why you were doing things for him? You were his errand boy? Hell, the champagne and Hennessey we'd drunk were—"

"They were items he requested. You can't find Hennessey White in the States, but I know a guy. The same goes for the de Brignac. For a hood-ass nigga, Swiss had good taste. Look at his choice in booze, to cars . . . women."

I ignored his little suggestion at the end. There were still too many unanswered questions, and my heart was still too heavy for me to get distracted that easily. "So what happens if I tell Farrah that my answer is no? Do you turn into the bad attorney and go out planting seeds all across town to get me locked back up?"

"Turning Farrah down isn't an option, Novie. I'll protect you for as long as I can, but you know a lot of damaging details. She won't trust you not to talk. Bottom line, you need to choose between working with us . . . or disappearing. Forever."

NOVIE

26

The Only Thing Stronger
Than Another's Love
Is Another's Hate

I tripped over something as I walked in the front door of my apartment. Something was always out of place, or laid down and forgotten about. The extra key to the Prius Genesis rented for me clanged loudly onto the coffee table in the living room. Hearing them clank onto the table brought fresh tears to my eyes. Hennessey probably stood at the window by the front door, popped the trunk, and then ran to get in, dropping my keys into the dish by the front door. I didn't even know to look or listen for her in there.

It was almost three a.m. Genesis and I drank until the bar stopped serving liquor. Both of us had an early morning to get ready for, so he'd dropped me off horny and drunk. I left him the valet key so he could have someone drop off my rental. I was really hoping he'd take me to his place and fuck the sadness out of me.

I regained my balance while trying to focus my blurry spinning vision on whatever was lying on the floor trying to kill me. Suddenly, the corner lamp came on with a loud click. I jumped so hard it's a wonder I didn't get scared sober. I whirled in the direction of the light, blinking against the bright light.

"I didn't sign up for this bullshit, Novie."

Shandy was sitting on the couch balancing a vodka bottle on her thigh.

"Hey, Shan," I whispered.

She stood up almost nose to nose with me, forcing me to look into her eyes flashing with pain and fury. Her hair was pulled back into a loose ponytail, giving her more of an angry teenager look versus a grown woman.

"Nah, Novie, don't 'hey' me. I told you to leave well enough alone. I told your ass not to get mixed up with my brother again."

She slammed the bottle down on the wooden coffee table, like a judge slamming a gavel. "You didn't listen, and Denise doesn't have anything because of you. Heather can't stand the sight of her. My brother and Hennessey are gone. I'm tired of living my life as Novie's crutch. You have to go. Tonight."

A confused frown creased my forehead.

"Go? Are you putting me out?" I sputtered. "Where am I supposed to go, Shandy? Girl, you know I don't have anywhere or anyone else."

"There are mad shelters out there. Pick one! You can sleep under the little desk in your office for all I care. I'm done giving a fuck about you!" Shandy stomped her foot. She flung the vodka bottle at the wall behind me. It left a big gaping hole before hitting the floor and rolling. "I had to call and explain to my momma that her son is dead because of you. She won't even take my calls anymore. I know my momma wasn't shit, but she and Swiss were all the family I had, Novie. You've still got all your family *and* your side nigga. Just go. Somebody will feel sorry for you and try to take care of you like I did."

My drunken mind jumped from plan to plan, explanations to lies, to the absolute truth behind her words.

"Shan, you don't mean that shit. You can't even afford the lease on this place by yourself—"

"Since when has someone else's ability to do or not do been a concern to you?" she hissed at me.

My eyes dropped to the points of my silver studded pumps. I was doing my best to hide the anger building up inside me. I'd lost. I'd been hurt in all this too, and she was putting me out on the street like I wasn't shit. After everything we'd been through, this is how she was treating me?

"Shandy, I am so very, very sorry about—"

Her hand flew up cutting me off.

"Do you lie to fool *you*? Because you ain't fooling me. Sorry, yes—yes, you are a sorry excuse for a woman, but you ain't contrite." Her voice was shaky and low, but her words were acidic. "I moved, I started over. I didn't have to, Novie. I *really* gave up everything to help you."

She circled around me, stopping just behind my right shoulder.

"And you couldn't give up one thing for me. Your selfish ass just couldn't leave my brother alone, and now he's dead because of you! I fucking hate you, and I hope you get everything you deserve!" Her argument ended with her screaming in my ear.

She stepped back in front of me with her hands clenched into tight fists. Tears ran down her splotchy red cheeks. Everything she'd said was true, but I couldn't admit that to her, and I couldn't be stuck out on the streets either. She brushed past me toward the dark bedroom.

This wasn't the plan. I was so mad I could barely breathe. My breath was ragged and choppy. I should've died in that crash, nobody else but me. Genesis should've let me go to prison and serve time as punishment. I didn't deserve to be out. But it's not like I did it on purpose. Shan couldn't stand Swiss, and she barely like Hennessey, and knew it. Her anger was inexcusable.

I marched toward the door where my things were sitting in sloppily organized little piles. She didn't even have the decency to let me get my stuff together myself. I snatched up as much as I could carry in one trip. One of Genesis's flunkies had gotten my car to the apartment in one piece. If I put my shit in the rental I wouldn't have to deal with her neighbors staring at me.

It was quiet outside as I rushed to get my things in the car as fast as I could. Three trips later, I was down to my last few items. I'd just finished putting my suitcase and laundry basket in the backseat, and all I had left was my favorite perfume and a few toiletries. I was almost at the car when the toe of my pump caught a crack in the pavement. My eyes went wide, and it was either going to be the perfume or me, so I let that shit go. The black bottle hit the ground, shattering to pieces. I teetered, reaching for anything to catch me and getting nothing. Before I could brace myself, I flopped forward, hitting the ground hard as hell.

White-hot pain seared through my chin. My right wrist felt like it was broken or sprained. I sat up slowly trying to see if anything else was hurt. It felt like water was soaking through the front of my turtleneck. *Great, I fell in sewer water. I'll probably grow a third nipple now.*

I'd barely gotten my shaky, wobbly legs to hold my weight when I noticed the red stain on the front of my sweater. Blood was dripping from a big open gash in my chin. I pulled out my cell and dialed 9-1-1.

"Nine-one-one, what's your emergency?" the operator asked in calm, mechanical voice.

"Yes, ma'am. I, um, I need some help. I'm bleeding really bad."

The throbbing in my chin fell in sync with my heart. Every throb sent blood dripping and pain shooting through my face.

"Ma'am, where are you and what happened?" the operator asked.

My voice was shaky and breathy. "I just . . . um."

My mind went blank. Maybe the fall knocked something loose. I probably had a concussion. I stared at the thin white clouds that my breath made in the air. Each one disappeared like the thoughts in my head.

"I got in a fight with my roommate." The words spilled out before I could stop them. Once they hit the air, I knew it was too late to take them back.

"She hit me. I fell, cut my chin." My voice was shaky from the cold and from the pain in my chin, but it made me sound scared and desperate.

"What's the address, ma'am? I have officers and an ambulance on the way."

I gave the operator my address and moved to sit on the stoop in front of our unit. Back home, I might have bled to death before help showed up. Shit, I'd just started arguing with myself over whether the red and blue lights flashing in front of me were real because they got to me so fast. An EMT rushed toward me with three police officers trailing not far behind. I was moved into the back of the ambulance, where I told them the same thing I told the operator. The officers gave each other a look before going toward the apartment.

The third officer stood just outside the ambulance. "Ma'am, one of your neighbors had called in a noise complaint not more than ten minutes ago. They heard some yelling and whatnot. One of you is gonna have to leave here tonight. Just say the word, and we can press charges, file a protective order, do whatever we need so you're safe."

On the outside I was dazed and frazzled, but inside, I smiled.

I nodded to the officer. "Yes, I want to press charges. She'll probably try to kill me since I called you. I don't feel safe."

The officer hoisted his pants up, giving me a stern nod. I could hear Shandy's voice as they dragged her outside toward a car. She sounded furious. The EMTs gave me a shot of something to dull the pain. The world moved in slow motion after that, and I tuned everything out and drifted to sleep.

NOVIE

27

When Love Is a Hustle

After the night I had it's a wonder I woke up at all. I was in the emergency room, two hours late for work. The cut in my chin wasn't as bad as it looked. I didn't even need stitches. It was just a meaty spot, and according to the EMT, I was a gusher.

Genesis left me the longest, most drawn out voice mail.

Sorry for getting you drunk and being the bearer of sour news. They won't be checking for you in the office today. I know what the deal is, so you've got the next two weeks off with pay if your answer is yes. Just make sure you call before your forty-eight hours is up; there's a lot of work to get done. A lot to fill you in on. I'll be in a consultation all morning, so don't call me unless it's an emergency. Talk to you later.

I skipped over a message from Officer Whoever who took my statement last night and called myself a cab. I'd deal with the police and last night's drama later. Right now, I just needed to figure out how I'd get a new car and work my way into a new place.

***

I smirked to myself as I inched down an empty alley off of H Street, making sure to go slow past the overflowing green Dumpsters. I needed to make sure there weren't any crazy bums hiding up, in, or around those things. Not that I was scared or anything like that. But I put a lot of planning and work into the moves I made, and I ain't do surprises.

It was almost ninety degrees out, and the sky looked like we were about to get a good thunderstorm. Both of those issues worked in my favor. The Prius's engine rumbled and puttered in complete disagreement with the temperature outside. I gave the shiny leather dashboard an understanding pat. "I know, baby. You too wacked for this shit. And that's exactly why Momma has to retire you so she can get a new baby," I cooed to the car.

The breeze whipped through the alley kicking me in the face, tossing around my shoulder-length spiral curls as I climbed out of the car. The ground was covered in dirty puddles and potholes. The first few drops of rain fell down from the sky. They clung to my feathered lashes. This was not the day for me to have my hips cinched into a pencil skirt and five-inch heels. But in the words of my momma, "It was a woman's job to look and smell amazing at all times, and a man's job to make sure she got whatever's necessary to keep that shit up."

The thought made my shimmer-glossed lips curve into a small, devilish smile. I took a deep breath, leaned down, and counted. *VS2, VS1, VVS2.* Yes, I used diamond clarities to amp myself up. Going from very small inclusions to very, very small inclusions built up my courage. When I got to *FL*, flawless with no imperfections, I rammed my pocketknife into the driver-side tire wall, twisting the blade until there was a huge open gash. After doing the same to the back tire I hopped back inside, cranking the heat up as high as it'd go.

Semiwarm exhaust-scented air gusted back at me. I didn't even bother with turning the AC up any higher. This Prius acted finicky as hell if it was set colder than seventy when it was hotter than eighty degrees outside. It even had a little digital thermometer in the display panel so it literally *knew* when to act a fool and say, *"Bitch, we shouldn't be out here."*

I fumbled through my purse for my phone. *Ugh, I hate purses.* Digging and hunting for my own shit annoyed the hell out of me. I hated having all my stuff clumped together, and I hated carrying it to clubs or parties because everybody and they momma without a purse always wanted to throw their shit in mine. I paused to breathe in through my nose and out through my mouth. That bag was a hair away from getting dumped out of the damn window. It was one of the more recent gifts Javion had given me, with a fancy name I'd never even heard of.

In all of his logic, he thought that hardly ever seeing me with a purse meant I didn't have any nice purses. To the contrary, if you could find any nigga with even a teeny bit of paper to his name, you'd find every purse you've ever wanted. Or didn't want, as was my case. There was a box in my trunk full of nothing but purses and clutches. But at least I *knew* who made those.

Slamming the purse down on the seat, I made a mini eye-roll. My phone hadn't gotten lost in my tote-along black hole. As soon I could do away with it without Genesis noticing, that pink python, "stuff-trap" would go right in the bag box, or I'd sell it online.

I was having a silent auction in my head over how much it'd go for as I pressed the word "Gen" on my phone. I'd planned out just about everything except for what I'd do if he didn't answer. But, Genesis could be so predictably logical that him not answering might have made this a little more fun.

He answered just as I predicted, placing me on hold in place of saying hello.

"Novie," Genesis sighed into the phone, "you didn't check your voice mail? I told you not to call unless it's an emergency. This better be important. I'm in a consultation with a client," he whispered in a rushed voice.

"I know. I'm sorry. I didn't know what else to do. The car started driving funky so I turned down this street and *bam* . . . two flats. So now I'm stuck in this alley behind some old abandoned hotel. I'm scared it might have been some kind of bum trap or something. Maybe they strand tourists so they can break into their cars. I'm scared one might run out of nowhere and—"

"I'll send out a driver and tow truck. It has insurance, and I think we even got you the roadside assistance."

His tone was a lot softer, even though he still sounded a little short to me.

I turned on my damsel-in-distress charm to kick things up a notch.

"Can't you just leave real quick and come get me? I've got this thing when it comes to riding with men I don't know. What if I get one of the crazies?" I spoke slowly, choosing my words carefully since I wanted something.

Every word had to be deliberate and precise. I was a chameleon, changing and adapting to whatever he wanted.

I could hear low voices and papers shuffling on the other end before the line went completely silent. I checked to make sure the call hadn't dropped. His name was still there, and the call counter was still going. See, that kind of rude buffoonery right there is what had made me exercise my most extreme levels of patience. Genesis was always good for randomly muting the phone at any point during our convo. It was always to *uphold his lawyer-client confidentiality,* or so he'd say. As far as I know, he could be laid up, trying to make a quick escape to carry on the call so I or whoever else wouldn't hear anything. Even if it was business, he was still rude and inconsiderate by the way he went about doing it, and that habit was one he'd need to break out of.

He unmuted the phone, making a sound that was somewhere between a groan and a conceding sigh.

"All right, I'm on my way. Send me the address of whatever's nearby."

I did as I was told with a knowing smirk on my face. Just like I thought, he would answer, and he would come get me. *Don't call unless blah blah blah, my ass.* He might run it in the courtroom, but I ran my relationships, no matter who I was with.

No more than thirty minutes had gone by before my stomach was growling. It was a little after eleven, and the bagel I'd had for breakfast was long gone. Genesis and the tow truck driver both showed up before I could make up my mind about whether or not Slim Jims get old. I'd found one crammed in the back of my glove compartment, but Lord knows how long it had been in there.

Genesis came over to open my car door, sending all my doubts and love requirements swirling away. Seeing him felt like a mixture of waking up on Christmas morning and opening a box of Ferrero Rocher chocolates. His dark brown blazer was open, showing off his gold, tan, and yellow vest. It tapered at the waist, flaring over his broad shoulders, and all I could think about was unwrapping and nibbling at all the chocolate that I knew was underneath.

He glanced into the backseat. "Why does it look like you're moving your—"

"Oh, it's nothing. A pipe burst in the apartment above mine and flooded me out." I didn't want to sound like a charity case or make him think I was trying to beg my way into his life. A lie just seemed to sit better with me than telling him Swiss's sister put me out on my ass.

"I see. Well, I had to reschedule the Morelli consultation. I'm billing seven seventy-five an hour for that one. I think somebody owes me a little face time." Genesis winked down at me with a slick grin.

The mention of "face time" would've normally made me melt on the spot. But I was under more stress than any normal person should have to handle.

Genesis checked to make sure the tow truck driver was out of hearing distance. "I think you should stay at my loft. Let me take your mind off of things. Get you wet while your apartment dries out."

"Really, Genesis, why do you always have to be so nasty?" I gave him a sour look for being so inconsiderate to my emotional state. I wasn't made for or used to this type of shit.

"You'll get used to this business, and when you do, you'll realize that there are casualties. There will always be casualties in our line of work, and you have to know when to let go and get on with shit."

At the end of the day, I needed to live and make a living. Who would it really matter to if what I did was legal or not? Swiss said he was sitting on top of millions, and if I was the girl that they'd wanted from the beginning, then maybe it was all worth a shot.

"Okay," I gave Genesis a tight nod. "I'll do it. I'll take Swiss's place. And for starters, no one works under me who I don't personally choose and approve of."

Genesis started to question my request. This wasn't something that could be argued over; it wasn't a bargaining unit. If my ass was gonna be on the line, I didn't want any weak links or weak niggas on my team. Javion never would've made the cut, and Swiss never would've been in charge of any unit I was overseeing. I needed loyal and reliable people in my corner who would take a fall for me, rather than let me fall.

28

Road Runner

I tossed and turned all night. The penthouse didn't feel the same as my apartment with Shandy. I didn't have the sounds of city traffic to put me to sleep at night; the walls were supersoundproofed to the point where I couldn't even hear the neighbors.

Genesis had gone home to make sure his niece was okay. His absence gave me time to busy myself organizing my things and putting my stuff away. In less than forty-eight hours, I'd gone from a woman torn between two lovers to a murderer set free, and now I was a boss.

I was trying to figure out what to eat when Gen called.

"You have work to do for Farrah. Meet her at M Street and Fifty-eighth. Don't be late."

My work was never done, and the days always felt crammed with stuff to do or someone to follow up with. I did as I was instructed, meeting Farrah at one p.m. on the nose. She handed me a small box with specific instructions.

"They're a bunch of Swedish filmmakers. Weird fuckers, if you ask me, but they buy a fuck ton of coke whenever they're in town. Cosimo, Constantinus, and Eckhardt are going to pick you up. Get into the backseat on the passenger's side and hand the passenger this box. He'll hand you $50,000. Take ten off of that and bring me back forty."

I sat in my car listening to the radio, watching the space where the Swedes were supposed to pull into. Not even a full hour had passed before a black-on-black Jeep pulled in with blacked out windows. The license plate read "Direct4You." If that wasn't the film producers, I didn't know who else it could be. The driver-side window rolled down, letting dense weed smoke filter through the gap.

"You Farrah's girrrrl?" he asked with a hard roll on his *r*'s. If I had to imagine what Swedish men would sound like, that was definitely it.

"I am." I smiled holding up the small white box. It was about the size of a shoe box, but it felt like an eight-pound bag of sugar.

"Climb in, will you? We can't have you out there in the broad daylight and such."

I did as Farrah had instructed, making sure to get in on the back passenger side. No sooner had the door closed before one of the guys snatched the box out of my hand. I was thrown back against the seat as we took off with the tires squealing. The guy beside me smelled like two-day-old beer and blue cheese. He smiled, flashing me with a wide gap between his front teeth.

"Farrah didn't say this was part of the exchange," I told him.

"Eh, we're going to get your dollops. I don't keep thousands on me for carrying-around money. It's right up this way, not far," the driver called back.

He stared at me through the rearview. I was momentarily taken aback by his eyes. They crinkled at the corners like he was always laughing at a funny story or a joke. Farrah was going to be missing twenty thousand if I survived this joyride. Boss or no boss, she wasn't going to be sending me on shit without a proper heads-up.

The Jeep bumped and bustled through the streets as the guys passed around the box of cocaine. They'd snorted so much I'd started worrying that maybe this was a setup. A few more twists and turns and we veered off a side street into a wooded area. This wasn't part of the tour. I inched my hand up to the door handle and pulled. Either the child lock was on, or it was rigged to only open from the outside because it didn't budge.

The guy beside me who I'd figured out was Cosimo leaned toward me with a creepy leer on his face. I screamed as he grabbed both my wrists. This was it. This was my time. I was going to die in a car in the middle of nowhere, and nobody would know where to find my body. Constantinus leaned over the passenger seat throwing a dark hood over my head. It smelled like rotten potatoes and mildew.

I squirmed and fought until something sharp pricked my leg and my world went black.

My nose was itching, but I couldn't scratch it. I moaned. There was the worst throbbing pain in my head. It felt like I'd been out drinking all night. I opened my eyes, trying to remember what the hell had happened. Straw, real live straw, was strewn across the ground all around me. To my horror my clothes were gone. I was shivering on the ground, suddenly realizing how cold it was, and my arms were tied behind my back and my feet were tied at the ankles.

Either Cosimo or Eckhardt started talking to me from somewhere in the dark.

"Hello, my little mermaid."

"You mean Sleeping Beauty, idiot. My little mermaid was half fish," Constantinus answered.

"And she looks like a half fish with her legs tied like that. Hose her down again."

I snapped my eyes shut against the feeling of the water spraying over me. It was so cold I'd started to scream, but the water went into my nose and mouth, making me regret that decision. The ground underneath me was turning into a muddy pool. Long dark earthworms began to slide up from the dirt. They thought it was raining and time to come out. I tried squirming away from them, but they were everywhere. As I struggled to sit up, I was yanked into a sitting position. Cosimo pulled me by my shoulders, forcing me to stand.

He whipped a knife out of his back pocket and cut my hands free.

"Now we will hunt you. Whichever one of us catches you gets to fuck you first." He winked before whispering, "Let Daddy Cosimo catch you. I'm hung like a stallion. You won't feel nothing else after I get through ripping you apart."

The other two men called to him from outside. The sun was setting, casting an orange glow cross the sky. The trees all around us were shadowed and dark. Nobody was going to catch me. I'd chew out his jugular if I could get it.

My hands were untied. I stood in front of them shaking, naked, and filthy, with the barn off to the side, and the woods at my back. They did more coke off the hood of the car before turning on the headlights. I held up my hand to block out the lights.

"Run, rabbit! Run!" one of them shouted. "We'll even give you a head start."

I turned, running toward the woods behind me. Their laughter was getting further and further away. When I passed the barn, I acted like I was going into the woods but I ran around the side, watching them do more hits of coke off of the hood of the Jeep. They gave each other high fives before they each broke off into the woods in different directions. Once they were out of sight, I sprinted with everything I had toward the Jeep. My hands were shaking so bad I could barely get the door open. Once inside, I frowned at the video camera sitting on the dashboard. It had been recording for the last two hours.

There wasn't any time for me to figure out who was who or what was what. I turned the key in the ignition and peeled backward down the dirt road, throwing mud and rocks spraying. My clothes were in a ripped pile in the backseat, so I was forced to drive naked. When I was closer to the city I slowed down enough to grab my phone. I called Genesis.

"I was just kidnapped and tortured and—"

"Let me guess, was it three Swedish guys?"

"Yes, and I'm driving to your place right now. I don't have any clothes. I'm naked."

"Hold on, hold on, Novie. They didn't give you your clothes back?"

"Give me my clothes? Nigga, they just threatened to rape me in the woods if I got caught. I'm sorry if I didn't wait around to see if they'd politely hand me my shit."

Genesis chuckled in the phone, and I wished he was in front of me so I could ram the truck into his smug face.

"Novie, there should be a video camera on the dashboard. They're film directors. They like to do these dumb-ass gag reels with retarded scenarios. Constantinus, I think, is the one who likes to dress up like a zombie or an alien and go running out into the woods after you. They might have switched it up so that just as you think you're about to get raped or killed, he comes crashing up on your assailant. These things sell big overseas."

"What? They do what?"

"Yeah, I thought Farrah explained all of that."

"Farrah didn't explain a damn thing. And I was naked, completely, fucking naked. I'm still naked, and now I'm driving a stolen Jeep with God only knows what kind of contraband in it."

"Just come here. I'll handle it. Everything will be fine. I know it's not funny, but I think you're probably the first person to get out of the woods. I'm sure I'll be getting a call from Farrah when the guys hike themselves to the nearest gas station."

"If this is the type of shit I have to look forward to working with you two, I quit. It's not worth my sanity."

29

First Response

I was starting to get that lightheaded, queasy feeling that had been hitting me on and off for the last few weeks. Something in my gut told me to pick up a pregnancy test on my way back to the house. I grabbed a four-pack just to be on the safe side. Whichever result I got, I wanted to be certain of. Genesis had said several times that he didn't want a baby. If that was the case, I needed him to be just as adamant about wearing a damn condom.

The house was empty when I walked in. Genesis wouldn't be home from work until later and Kenisha was staying at a friend's or a boyfriend's, I wasn't sure which one anymore. I threw my jacket on a chaise lounge in the front sitting room and kicked off my shoes. My eyes rolled at the filth Kenisha had left in the kitchen. The black granite countertops were covered in random empty cookie containers and halfway closed chip bags. The juice and half a rotisserie chicken was left sitting out. She even left the damn mayonnaise sitting out on the counter without the lid.

I know this heffa hasn't made a sandwich or whatever and left this shit like this. It didn't make any sense for me to be on a constantly shortening leash when Genesis let that girl get away with murder.

Grabbing a cucumber and tomato out of the fridge, I sliced them up into a bowl with a splash of vinegar. This is all I'd been thinking about all day. I cleaned up whatever I used, leaving the rest of that mess exactly as I found it. Let Genesis clean up after her. My behind was ready for a hot shower and a good hour-long nap. Since neither of them liked anything I cooked, I wasn't even going to waste my time trying to find a recipe to impress their fucked-up taste buds. They could order a pizza or get something from that new service that delivered damn near everything under the sun.

I'd started toward my bathroom when an idea stopped my feet. Genesis always spent so much time in the bathroom with the door shut tight. I could stare under the door and see him pacing back and forth, or he'd be in one place for what would seem like forever. I tiptoed into his immaculate bathroom. Everything was in its place. The floor and mirrors were spotless. I looked in the medicine cabinet, disappointed to find nothing but Motrin and allergy pills. The linen closet was actually in the bathroom. I opened the doors wide and stared at his pristine, perfectly folded white sheets. All except for one at the very top. I had to use the second step as a foothold, but after I pulled myself up, I found it. It was a poetry book, or a journal of some kind sitting on the top shelf underneath a crooked towel.

I turned to page one. Genesis's handwriting immediately leapt off the page.

GENESIS KANE'S JOURNAL

30

In the movies, the nigga always dies first. Those were my exact thoughts as I stood on the upper level of the parking garage beneath the downtown hospital. Ladybug, my tactical exploration robot, had run herself into a dead spot. I couldn't remote control her from the surveillance van, so, of course, me and myself aka the only nigga, had to step in for a closer look. Technically, I wasn't the only nigga. There was my boy who was out sick, Warren, the blue-eyed bandit who we called Foreign. His moms looked like Weezy Jefferson, and his pops looked like Red Foxx. We swore up and down that nigga was the milkman's baby. If I was thinking, I would've stayed home and called in sick too. A day at home with a whining woman and an even whinier baby didn't seem so bad compared to the day I was having.

The garage was silent as a tomb and hot as an oven. There were eight of us working the FBI Explosives Ordinance field office in Norfolk, Virginia. Overtime was becoming a popular subject with all the work we'd been getting thrown our way lately. Let's just say, it takes a real special motherfucker to run in and finger fuck an explosive when everyone else is running away. No one could do what we did or understand the rush you feel from death hissing down the back of your neck.

My hand wandered aimlessly to my left side, to where I kept the five-pointed Gold Medal of Valor in my pants pocket. They give it to agents as recognition for extreme acts of heroism. It was awarded to my pops when I was nine. He was one of the best too, before he got killed in the line of duty. Now his medal went with me on all my bomb-runs. It was a good-luck thing. Morbid, I know. But it made me feel like he was watching over me, bringing me some guidance.

It had to have been working because I was still alive. Earlier, the calls had started coming in one by one. Protocol required us to send at least two techs out to oversee bomb disposal, but we had all been dispatched to different locations. So far, all the other locations had come back as false alarms. I sure as hell hoped this was one as well. Sweat stung my eyes, forcing me to squint through the hazy visor of my blast suit. It was ninety pounds of fire-resistant Nomex and Kevlar.

"Jarryd, what do you see, son? My neck been bothering me all morning." Peterson's voice crackled through the two-way com in my headgear.

He called everyone son. Even though most of us were in our late twenties, and he wasn't any older than forty-five. He'd been through more than any of us, even did a short stint in Kuwait until he got caught in some crossfire. The only thing holding that nigga together was metal pins and grit; 148 of them ran up his spine. He always complained about his neck hurting right before some shit popped off. Hell, I trusted Peterson's neck better than any bomb-sniffing dog.

I squinted through one eye, keeping the other closed. I always forgot how hot it got inside these suits until my black ass was back inside one, cursing because we didn't have the newer air-conditioned ones.

"One minute, sir. Right now, I can't see shit for my own sweat."

My heart was karate-kicking the inside of my chest, making my breath come in short, garlic-scented spurts. Lunch had consisted of garlic-knots from a little hole-in-the-wall Italian spot that we went to every Friday called Feldecci's. They were always on point, but I don't think there was anything on the menu that wouldn't leave your breath humming for the rest of the day. That wasn't the worst of it; the real problem was me. I was shaky and unfocused from slamming back Monster energy drinks to compensate for lack of sleep. This wasn't the kind of job that allowed for a nigga to not be well rested, but try explaining that to a crab-assy bundle of constant tears and shit.

My new baby boy, Jarryd Junior, was eleven or thirteen weeks; hell if I know. I can't keep track of that shit. Tima'd been celebrating everything from his first shit to his first sneeze. Let me know when that little nigga hits one aka twelve months so I can crack a beer or something. Since the day he was born, I hadn't eaten, fucked, or slept the same. How was having a baby supposed to be this big joyous occasion when all it did was managed to erase all the joy out of my life? Now there was just constant pressure to earn more and buy the best of everything. When I wasn't working or stressing about work, you'd think I'd get to relax, but, nah, I was expected to spend every free minute with that little nigga.

We had the biggest house in one of the best neighborhoods, and now she had this grand delusion of getting an even bigger house in a neighborhood the director of the FBI probably couldn't even afford. All that shit was starting to make me bitter and cynical. I'd even googled whether it was normal for a man to hate his own baby. It didn't feel natural. All the sites said I was most likely suffering from some kind of male-postpartum depression. Fuck that, I'm a damn man. Men don't get depressed or upset. Only a woman would write some bullshit like that. Men get angry; we get mad, and if I was feeling any kind of way, I was pissed the fuck off. Not fucking depressed.

Tima used to draw a nigga baths at night with candles and wine. She used to cook four-course dinners, and now she be on this four-day dinner routine. That's what I call it when she makes some shit and stretches it out so we have it every day except Friday. Back in the day, a nigga was taken care of. I ain't mind handing over a paycheck or buying her anything under the sun when I wasn't eating spaghetti four days a week. I wasn't mentally prepared for this life of baby talk, baby proofing, and baby bullshit.

"Son, are okay in there?" Peterson sounded on edge. "Akins is on his way back since his call was a false alarm. We can bring him in if you aren't up to snuff. I'm sure the new baby is wearing you down."

My mind was all over the place. I'd started to tell Peterson I wasn't on my A-game, but I manned up. Nah, there was no way I'd admit to getting mind-fucked by an infant. Unlike parenting, I'd been doing this type of stuff my whole career. Everybody can't do what the fuck I do. Niggas run screaming out of the places I voluntarily walk into.

"I'm solid, sir, just hot as fuck in here. This ninety-degree weather ain't helpin'."

I flexed my fingers, hyping myself up as I maneuvered through rows of cars toward the crumbling column in the center. Ladybug sat waiting in a puddle nearby. I removed my ID badge from the utility holster on my side and inserted it into her driver. "Don't worry, Lady, you just sit here and watch me work. I'll be right back." Yeah, I talked to her like she was a real person. I talked to anything with artificial intelligence. If there was ever a robot uprising, your boy would be safe. I'd tried to explain that shit to Tima, but she'd just get pissed off. Let her tell it, I talked to my machines more than I talked to her or my own son. You damn right; my machines had enough sense not to talk back.

Ladybug's system recalibrated with a series of loud clicks and whirrs. NASA held the original patents for her design. She was made for exploring planets and collecting samples. We kept a lot of the original specifications so she could run on autopilot or remote control. After her reboot, she'd automatically trek back to the recon van.

"All right, Ladybug, you watch my back." I gave the metallic claw on top of her canister a fist-bump before moving on.

I checked the numbers on each column until I got to the one with D8 stenciled in faded red letters. The red paint flaked off the side. Someone had made a 9-1-1 call saying there was a suspicious object sitting in front of it. I squashed the fear gripping at my insides and cleared my dry, scratchy throat as I laid eyes on it.

"Sir, this is some devilish but beautiful shit. Are y'all getting this?" I angled my head to make sure the camera mounted on the side of my visor could pick everything up. "The detonator has a bilateral release trigger. One side is an explosive, and I'm talkin' citywide radius. But the other one is some kind of haz canister, and I don't know what the fuck's inside it," I replied, anxious to either get out of there or get to work.

Peterson made a deep, gravely sound in the back of his throat. It was a cross between a grunt and groan. I'd heard it before. A year ago, I'd been awarded a Congressional Gold Medal for diffusing a similar situation near the Federal Building downtown. It was a lot *bigger and nastier than this one; anything could have set that shit off.*

"Well, all right, Jarhead."

Peterson called me by my old nickname, making me feel more like my old self and less like the old man I was being forced to become. Before I joined this bomb squad that my wife wanted me to quit, I was a marine specializing in explosives. My ace back then was a goofy nigga named Chief. He saved my ass so many times and vice versa, we swore if one of us ever hit the lottery or got rich, we'd come back for the other one.

"Don't stand there clutchin' your nuts, split some wires," Peterson ordered. "I don't know about your house, but it's wet-mouf-Wednesday up in mine. I've got to get my ass home before the old lady has too many mojitos. She's sloppy and slobby after three. My balls don't take too kindly to cold drool," he barked in what was an obvious attempt to lighten up the tension in the air.

Everyone was holed up in the surveillance van topside watching the feed from the camera mounted to my head on a closed-circuit network. Every time I diffused a bomb, I'd fast-forward to afterward in my head. I imagined myself celebrating in some big old encouraging titties. I didn't celebrate at strip clubs anymore; you get a wife and a kid and somehow, everything that was once a reality became fantasy. But the sooner I got this over with, the sooner I could throw back a cold beer and maybe talk Tima into giving me some head.

The headgear was making it too hard for me to focus. I'd sent my spare drones out for repair. Budget cuts had everything stuck in a holding pattern somewhere. Ladybug being out of commission meant I was the damn drone today.

Even though it was a stupid move, I removed my headgear, placing it on the ground beside me. Peterson's voice was a muffled string of what I could only imagine to be f-bombs and curse words. He could string together words that'd make you feel lower than dirt and more useless than shit.

The air was still and thick with the smell of exhaust and concrete. Sweat poured down the back of my neck. Normally, adrenaline rushes would send me into a calm, methodical trance. But that wasn't happening today. I sucked in a few shaky lungfuls of air, hoping it'd squelch my nerves.

I knelt as carefully as I could in front of the white tank with death flashing all over it. The device wasn't wired like anything I'd ever seen before. A sinking panicky feeling started to roll itself around in my gut. My brain was processing everything at warp speed, connecting lines and wires to switches. This wasn't your normal, everyday device. The orange-tinted lights of the garage reflected off the flawless chrome valves. Every piece of metal was perfectly polished. There wasn't a fleck of dust or an oily fingerprint anywhere on it. It was finely detailed all the way down to the wooden crate it sat on top of. I tried to get a look underneath it for a fail-switch.

If I didn't have perfect 20/20 vision, I might've missed the clear wire running along the underside of the device. It was thinner than fishing line and slightly shaking, which was weird because there was no breeze in the parking garage. A hundred questions drifted through my mind as I rose on shaky legs. Peterson needed to know about this. I was reaching for my helmet when I saw something out of the corner of my eye. My eyes locked with his; dread filled me to the core of my being.

"Don't move," I said in a calm, quiet voice.

The man standing across the garage stared back at me. His yellow Polo shirt was dirty and ripped around the collar. Blood ran from his nose, and his left eyelid was swollen to about the size of an egg. What the fuck is he doin' in here? They said the garage was all clear.

I edged toward him, trying to figure out if he was a victim or the perp. I followed the line from where it started to where it rested in his bloody hand. His eyes were panicky and glazed with pain, but he didn't make a sound. If he yanked or dropped that string we were done.

I decided to skip protocol and reason with him. There wasn't going to be any time for me to call this in.

"You don't have to do this, man. I'm sure we can solve whatever the problem is reasonably."

Sweat gleamed on his forehead. A nasty purplish-blue knot was forming at the right side of his temple. His lips barely moved. "Run."

In antiterrorism training, they teach you to remain calm and give whoever it is whatever they want.

I held up my hands. "All right, man, in a minute. Tell me what you need and I'll go get someone to help."

"I didn't do this. I . . . I woke up in the trunk of a car. They busted my hand up and made me hold this wire . . . I can't keep holdin' this."

His Adam's apple bobbed in his throat. There wasn't going to be enough time for me to get topside and bring down help. Ladybug was still sitting where I left her booting up. She weighted eight hundred pounds; there was no way I'd be able to get her over here fast enough.

"Okay, okay. Just stay calm. I'm gonna make sure that both of us will walk out of here." *My words sounded way more confident than I felt.*

I inched my way closer, mentally running down the odds. Can't cut the wire, can't remove it from his hand. Can't guarantee there'll be enough time to diffuse the device before he drops the wire. This is a lose-lose situation.

"Evacuate the hospital. Let me die." His words were breathless urgent gasps.

"We've already done that, my dude. Everybody's gone except you and me. I got this, I'm not about to let you die."

I was finally close enough to see his hands. How he managed to hold anything was an act of God himself. His fingers looked like they'd been run through a sausage grinder. I made an effort not to wince or make a face at the white bone sticking out where his index finger should have been. Every nerve, every cell in my being was screaming for me to get the fuck out of there.

Blood-splattered papers littered the ground, indicating some kind of a scuffle had gone down. A wallet laid open at my feet. I picked it up, scanning over his driver's license. His name was Genesis Kane. I gave him a friendly, encouraging smile. Hopefully, I could bring him around, give him a sense of security by using his name. Maybe it would rehumanize him if he heard it. Maybe it would give him some hope.

"I'm Jarryd," I introduced myself. "How about we work on getting you out of this mess, Mr. Kane. Can I—"

A blinding yellow flash lit up the garage. It shook the ground and the concrete pillars. The sound of the blast pounded against my eardrums. It felt like an oven had opened behind me as heat rushed against the back of my neck and head. Something told my brain they were flames, but it all happened in a frame of time too short for me to react to. I felt searing heat, jarring pain, and weightlessness, and then I didn't feel a thing.

When I finally managed to open my eyes, I thought I was dead. Dust tickled the hairs in my nose. It felt like there were layers of it crammed up there. My ears wouldn't stop ringing, and my eyes burned like I'd dipped my head into a pool of saltwater. I drifted in and out of the darkness, waking up in small enough stretches to feel a new painful sensation in a different part of my body. I couldn't tell if I'd been asleep for a few minutes or a few months. It took several minutes for me to realize I was lying down in a hospital.

The television was the first thing to break through the dull ringing in my ears. "The FBI have recovered the body of one of their own from the blast zone. Investigators have now identified the human remains uncovered not far from where investigators say the device detonated. Special Agent Bomb Technician Jarryd Keening's ID was found close to the center of the blast radius. There were no other casualties, although several bystanders on the street were injured."

I stared blindly at the TV, barely able to make out the face of the woman reporting the news. What looked like Peterson's ugly mug darkened the screen. He recited a prewritten speech about how good of a man I was. How I was a fallen hero who'd made him proud.

What the fuck? Why would everyone think I was dead? I wasn't fucking dead! *I tried to sit up and fell back from the pain that shot through my shoulder.*

A cheerful nurse breezed into the room in a blur of pink scrubs and caramel skin.

"Good morning, Mr. Kane. It is so good to see you're finally awake. Now I'm gonna need you to behave and be still."

Wincing at the pain now shooting from my shoulder to my forehead I sat still so she could tend to me.

"What happened to me, how did I get here?"

"Genesis, sweetie, you were caught up in an explosion and found by some volunteer search and rescue workers

who found you outside of a parking garage. They flew you in from Norfolk. You're in DC, sweetie."

Did she just call me Genesis? What the fuck? *Why was she calling me by that other guy's name? I opened my mouth to correct her. My name was Jarryd Keening. I had a wife and a new son I couldn't stand. They were home waiting for me in my house with the mortgage that I was struggling to pay. Tima was probably beside herself crazy, grieving over this mix-up, planning my funeral.*

My thoughts stunned me into stupefied silence as the nurse tended to my wounds. She examined my collarbone, nodding to herself before tending to a bandage that I didn't even know was wrapped around my head. As the gauze unraveled, I tried to do the same with my hazy memories. Seconds before the explosion, I'd picked up Genesis Kane's ID. The force of the explosion must've thrown me out of the garage. Without my helmet latched on, it most likely knocked me out of my blast suit. Since I was supposed to be the only man in the garage, when they found the other man's remains inside, they must've assumed it was me. Everyone had just assumed that I'd died, and why wouldn't they? They had a body, my ID, and since I was the idiot who went against protocol, they didn't know anyone else was there.

That little slip on my part could cost me my career if I contacted my command now. I'd lose everything and probably get blamed for the death of a civilian too, all because I was trying to be the hero.

The nurse leaned across me chatting away with her titties not more than an inch away from my face. "You should know that you've been very well tended to these last few days. You won our finest patient award." She giggled flirtatiously. "It's been hell keeping all the other nurses from trying to steal my best patient."

Inhaling, I hid an amused smile. She smelled like ripe, juicy peaches drizzled in honey. It'd been a minute since I'd gotten a compliment from a woman other than Tima. We bomb technicians stayed tucked away at the office or out in the field. We didn't get to "flex on 'em" like the boys in the penguin suits did. I mumbled a low thank-you for the compliment.

"Not that I was snooping or anything. But your IDs and stuff were all charred up. The only way we could identify you was by your Bar Association card. Um, may I ask what kind of lawyer are you exactly? Because I've got all these damn speeding tickets, and I probably can't afford you, but I really need a good stiff *lawyer to help me out."*

Her hands left the bandage wrapped around my head, making their way down my chest toward my lap. I'd dated Tima faithfully for three years before we'd gotten married. Five years of fucking the same pussy had my Johnson leaping to attention at the thought of getting rubbed up and possibly falling into some new pussy.

"You keep doin' what you're doing, and I'll be any kind of lawyer you want me to be." The lie slipped out of my mouth so easily I couldn't believe I'd said it. But she was sliding her fingernails up my bare thighs, getting closer and closer to the tent-pole sticking up in the middle of my hospital gown. Her fingers felt like heaven warmed over when they finally wrapped around me.

I had to keep that shit going. "But to be completely honest. I practice tort law, and I do the whole trial thing too. You know, I've never lost a case," I ground out through some shit I'd heard on a commercial through clenched teeth. I probably wasn't even saying it right or using it in the right order.

But shit, it was the truth . . . granted I ain't never had a case, let alone stepped foot into a courtroom. She ain't need to know all that.

This would be the day Jarryd Keening would officially die and Genesis Kane would be reborn. I just needed to let Foreign and Chief know where I was. We were about to initiate a DC takeover.

31

Discovery Channel

I dropped the journal. It hit the floor with a loud slap. A picture of a little girl named Janay with a snaggletoothed smile floated out of it. HAVE YOU SEEN ME was plastered along the bottom in faded yellow letters. Genesis, I mean Jarryd, or whatever he wanted to call himself, wasn't even a real attorney. No, no, no. I backed away from the book like it was on fire. What kind of man would just leave his wife and son? I was shaking my head in disbelief. He was probably just writing some kind of fictional short story and was too embarrassed to be seen doing it by the light of day. But Tima was real. She was at his office my first day on the job.

I picked up the journal and the picture with unsteady fingers. *That nigga probably had an entire harem of women and kids that he'd just wipe out whenever it was convenient.*

The lights automatically clicked on, offering me dim guidance up the stairs toward the bedroom I slept in when I wasn't sleeping with Gen. I still wasn't used to it or all these fancy features that Gen's house had. Probably never would be. Once inside my room, I decided to take some quick action. I reluctantly stopped eating long enough to take my pregnancy tests into the bathroom. They all needed three minutes, and if this wasn't the longest three minutes of my life . . . While I waited, I grabbed a Post-it note from the box of things I'd brought home from my desk. At least Kenisha would know from me personally that the way she left this house was unacceptable. The note I scribbled out for her was straight to the point. *Clean up after yourself.*

It was short and simple, and it would probably send her little spoiled ass through the roof. Kenisha's bedroom was the size of a small palace, complete with vaulted ceilings and a balcony that stretched the length of the back of the house. Unlike Genesis's balcony, hers had two reclining lawn chairs with a large multicolored umbrella set up above them. *I really got the short straw on the room selection. My shit doesn't even have a bay window, and it's half the size of this shit.*

My nose turned up at the clothes strewn all across the floor and bed. Half-eaten cereal bowls littered her vanity. Her closet and drawers were half open with clothes and underclothes hanging half in and half out. How did she ever find anything in here? I wandered over to her closet, stepping over candy wrappers and empty Twinkie boxes. It was like a Forever 21 bomb went off, and all of the clothes landed in and all over her room.

This was ridiculous. My momma would've taken every piece of clothing I owned. She would've held them all hostage or given them away until I learned to keep my shit neat. There wasn't even a clear place to put a note. Not one where she'd see it. There was so much shit everywhere it would just get lost. And then I had an aha! moment. Her little conceited ass stayed in the bathroom. I'd just slap this bad-boy up on her bathroom mirror right at eye level. She wouldn't miss that.

A noise from downstairs made me pause. Panicky and suddenly nervous about getting caught I waited, listening to see if it was a door closing or maybe just a car on the street. Genesis usually headed straight for his office when he came in. He'd put his stuff down, shuffle through the mail, and finally make his way upstairs. Kenisha was a different story. Sometimes she'd fly into whichever bathroom was closest. She'd sit in there, peeing like a baby pony with the door wide open. Then there were times when she'd come directly to her room with an attitude from hell.

I rushed around a pile of shopping bags and empty shoe boxes stacked near the foot of her bed heading toward her bathroom. It usually took her an eternity to climb those stairs. They'd slow her down, giving me just enough time to get my note in place. My toes dug into the plush carpet; even the carpet in here felt softer than the rest of the house. It was like walking across cotton ball fluff. Thankfully, the door to her bathroom was cracked. I'd be able to slip in and out faster this way.

I'd started to just stick the note on the door itself when I saw them in the mirror. The lights were off but there was enough late-evening light coming through the bathroom window to illuminate them in grey and blue shadows. Genesis's hand was pressed over Kenisha's mouth. His face was hidden in the side of her neck. They looked like some kind of silent, horrifying painting standing against the far wall of her bathroom. Genesis's pants were around his ankles, his dress shirt strained against the muscles in this back. Kenesha's turquoise sundress was up around her waist, her eyes were shut tight. One of her legs was thrown over his arm as he maneuvered himself around her swollen belly, pumping in and out of her quietly.

Half-eaten tomatoes and cucumbers rose in my throat. The horror of what I was seeing made me shake all over with disgust and outrage. The note fluttered from my fingers, landing beside maternity panties on the floor. They looked torn, like he'd ripped them off of her. What was he doing home when he told me he was staying in the office late?

My brain fired a thousand different courses of actions in a matter of seconds. All of them led me to the same blocked wall. Genesis had too much power. He could make me disappear for what I'd just seen. That wouldn't give me any time to help Kenisha. It wouldn't give me a chance to get her, and myself, away from this monster. He'd be outraged; he'd deny what I'd seen, or worse, he'd kill me on the spot.

The only direction my feet would move me in was backward out of the door. My vision was too blurry for me to see my way. I sagged against the walls, using them to guide me as I staggered back toward my room. That poor girl, that poor, poor girl. I couldn't get the image out of my head. It twisted my stomach into bubbly knots until I ran into my own bathroom heaving vomit on the way. The spasms were so hard it felt like the veins were going to break through the skin in my neck. The sides of the toilet were icy cold against my fingers while I prayed this shit would hurry up and be over. When there was nothing left in my stomach, I fell back exhausted, sitting on the floor with my back up against the bathroom.

Too weak to do more than lean forward, I snatched the edge of the hand towel hanging off the counter. Pregnancy tests clinked onto the hard tile floor all around me. My stomach lurched again, but there wasn't anything left in it. Each and every single one of those tests was positive.

32

Stockholm Syndrome

It was dark when I finally opened my eyes. I'd either fallen asleep or passed out on the bathroom floor. My body was stiff and sore after being on the floor for so long. My knees were wobbly as I tried to stand. I turned on the cold water, watching it rush down the drain with my life and my faith. How did I let myself get fooled into caring about a man like that? There were so many questions running through my head. I rinsed my mouth out with cold water from the sink before splashing it over my face. This felt like a nightmare I couldn't wake up from.

The sun had finally set, and the bedroom was dark as I walked out. It was somewhere near ten. There were no missed calls or texts on my cell. Even though I was avoiding him, I don't know why it bothered me to know that Genesis hadn't bothered to check on me, nor had he asked me to come sleep with him last night. I know if he'd gone downstairs, he'd had to have seen my coat or *the note!* The note I'd written had fallen and landed on the floor. He must've seen it, or maybe Kenisha saw it. He probably knew that I'd seen him. Hiding in the dark security of my bedroom felt like the best answer after I tipped over to quietly lock my bedroom door. I used my phone's flashlight to find the letter opener I'd packed in my workbox.

The bed creaked as I climbed onto it fully clothed with my letter opener clutched tightly in my hand. I didn't know what to expect or what to do. All of this worrying could have been for nothing. But, now I had a new problem. I had a baby to protect, and Kenisha was somebody's baby too. Now it was up to me to get all of us away from Genesis. My pillow was soaked with tears by the time exhaustion sank in. I crashed into a restless sleep filled with running shadows fucking and Genesis yelling.

I jerked awake with the sun streaming through the blinds smacking me in the face, feeling like I hadn't slept at all. A wave of nausea sent me scrambling to the bathroom. I dry heaved until my throat was raw and my stomach muscles felt sore and strained. This was a whole new experience. I didn't have a single day of morning sickness when I'd gotten pregnant with Swiss's baby. That shit felt like it was a whole lifetime ago. All the old chapters of my life combined didn't have anything on the pages I was writing with Genesis. *How the hell can I even approach him about a baby after seeing what he's done to Kenisha? What if we had a daughter? What if something happened to me and she was left with him?*

There was no way I could get rid of my baby, not again. But now, I'd have to live, knowing I'd made a child with a monster. He didn't even seem real to me after what I'd seen. Nothing about Genesis felt real or genuine. I stared at myself in the mirror with unseeing eyes. Where was Shandy when I really needed her? I hadn't heard from her at all since the night I packed my shit and left. Revenge felt good in the moment, but now a million questions came up whenever I thought about her. Aris hadn't even crossed my mind when I did what I did. And I had way too much pride to call and ask her if they were okay. Without Shandy, without Denise, there was no one for me to confide in; there was nowhere for me to run and hide until things felt safe.

A knock at my bedroom door scared the devil out of me.

"I'm in the bathroom," I called out in a shaky voice.

"I hope you slept as well as I did. I'm making us all breakfast, so come on before Hungry Jack eats everything in the house," Genesis yelled back.

I didn't have the strength or the will to respond. There was no way I'd be able to face them both together at the table. Let alone eat anything. I dawdled for as long as I possibly could, taking an extralong shower, washing my hair, and scrubbing my body over and over. I dabbed foundation under my eyes to hide the dark circles. There was no erasing what I'd seen; there wasn't going to be any looking past it. I'd have to find a way to address this, and then I'd have to deal with the outcome.

Genesis was still bare chested, wearing nothing but blue sweatpants when I walked in. He was just setting down plates stacked high with blueberry pancakes, next to a bowl full of fried potatoes, scrambled eggs, and another dish of grits. All of it made my stomach turn. If I could eat, I'd have settled for a salad, maybe with strawberries and balsamic vinaigrette. He gave me a big bright grin as he walked over to kiss me on my lips. I turned, giving him my cheek.

"Think I might be coming down with something," I blurted out.

"Well, I've got plenty of juice and vitamin me to help you get over that."

The look of disgust that wanted to spread across my face almost broke through giving me away. Thank God he'd turned to tend to a pan full of strips of bacon on the stove. Kenisha waddled in holding the small of her back.

I looked her over from the top of her head down to her bare feet. Nothing on her looked out of place, bruised, or roughed up. She was wearing a sunny-yellow and green Mumu wrap. It pushed the tops of her swollen breasts up until they looked like they were about to spill all out of the damn thing.

"Thank you for cooking because I'm about to fuck up everything on this table," she announced just before trying to ease down into a seat.

Genesis dropped the pan of bacon he was tending to rush over to help her ease down into the chair. I watched them closely from where I stood by the fridge. There were no signs of awkwardness, disgust, or even shame as Genesis touched the small of her back. My eyes were waiting to see if she'd flinch or shy away, if he'd react sexually and try to hide it. But they were all business as usual. I probably had more jealousy and disgust to hide than either of them did. Kenisha even smiled sweetly at him, thanking him for helping her with her chair.

I excused myself to my room, claiming I didn't want to get Kenisha or anyone sick. The poor girl was probably suffering from Stockholm syndrome or he'd brainwashed her into thinking what he'd done was normal.

The sooner I could be alone with her, one on one, the sooner she could answer my questions so I could help get us out of here. How we'd leave and where we'd go I didn't know yet, but I would do something. I sat in my room staring a hole in the wall. When I heard Genesis go into his bedroom, I ran to find Kenisha. She was still in the kitchen with a half-eaten strip of bacon in one hand and massaging her boob with the other.

"I can't wait to get my body back. These thangs right here hurt like all hell, and it's worse if I try to put on any kind of bra."

I scooted into the chair beside her and gave her a polite but timid smile.

"I saw you two in the bathroom yesterday," I rushed into my speech before I lost the nerve. "Kenisha, no matter what happens, I want you to know that you have somebody on your side. Genesis is the adult, and you're the child. He will be punished for what he did. I'll make sure of it."

The bacon fell out of her hand, clattering to the table as her eyes glazed over. Her bottom lip quivered.

"What are you gonna do?" she asked in a little voice.

"Whatever I need to do. So long as you're safe, I don't care. He's going to go away for a long time. Okay?"

She nodded quietly with tears slipping down her cheeks.

"After I figure out a few things I'm going to get us away from here. I need you to go upstairs and get your hospital delivery bag. Make sure you have everything you need. We're leaving tonight."

Genesis whistled as he made his way downstairs. I gave her hand a gentle, reassuring squeeze before I slipped out through the dining room toward the stairs. Genesis had no idea what he was in for. I waited by the stairs listening, trying to figure out which part of the house he was in. There was no way I could face him and not give myself away.

"She knows, and she said she'll send you away," Kenisha's voice was a rushed pleading whisper. "You said having her here would make our lives easier, that we wouldn't have to worry about anyone figuring us out, and she knows, Kane."

"Don't even worry about that shit, babe. You go wherever she tries to take you; act like everything is fine. Nobody's gonna hurt you or my baby. I'll handle it," Genesis answered in a dry, emotionless voice.

I almost fell out right where I stood. I was wrong. I was so *very, very* wrong, and now it might cost me my life.

NOVIE

33

Going Home

I took the stairs two at a time, locking my door behind me. My heart was beating so fast I felt light-headed. As bad as I wanted to break down, throw shit, hell, throw both Genesis *and* Kenisha, this wasn't the time. There was an old gym bag underneath my bed. I grabbed it and began slinging clothes into it as fast as I could. There was still time for me to save myself. Genesis was waiting for me to run with Kenisha, but if I left without her, it bettered my chances of getting away.

Genesis shouted through the house that he was leaving for work. He was trying to keep up appearances, which was fine with me. It gave me time to get my shit together and get out. Kenisha thumped up the stairs.

"I'm going to pack and get my stuff together, Novie," she shouted through my bedroom door.

I didn't respond back. I waited until I heard her bedroom door slam shut before I grabbed my bag and crept down the stairs. There was only one place I could think to go. Hopefully, my presence was still welcomed. My heart hurt, my spirit felt crushed. That nigga played me with his sixteen-year-old niece, right under the same roof as me. If this wasn't the most shameful, disrespectful shit I'd ever dealt with I don't know what was.

Thankfully, Kenisha's bedroom was on the backside of the house. I put my car in neutral, letting it roll down the driveway quietly. I didn't put it into drive or crank the engine until I was safely in the street. Genesis's house loomed above me. It didn't look like home anymore. It looked like a cage of lies, a stronghold of secrets and insecurities. I started driving home, to my real home. It was the only place I had left to go.

It was almost dark when I pulled up. But the house still looked almost identical to how it did the day the last time I was home. Momma had gotten the shutters painted in a soft cornflower blue. They stood like beacons out against the red bricks. Lights were on in all the rooms.

After a deep breath and several Visine drops in my eyes, I climbed out and walked up the cement steps onto the front porch from my childhood. The doorbell was loud enough for me to hear it chime outside as I pressed the button. Chairs scraped against hardwood flooring, followed by heavy steps in the direction of the door. The front porch light flickered on. I squinted against its brightness, waving at whoever was looking through the peephole with a fake smile glued to my lips.

"You finally decided to climb up out of Genesis Kane's ass. You must be in trouble." Daddy opened the door slowly with a sour scowl on his face.

I wrung my fingers together, feeling how it felt when I was eight all over again.

Momma walked up behind him. "Who the hell's at the door at this hour . . . ?"

Her face lit up when she saw me through the storm door. She pushed Daddy out of the way and launched herself through the door.

"My baby girl is back! Oh my God, look at you, baby. Hug your mother, girl."

She pulled me into a hug so tight I could barely breathe. Happy tears welled up in my eyes as I hugged her back while staring at Daddy over her shoulder. It seemed like no matter how right I thought I was, I was still choosing to side with the people who were the worst for me. I'd done it consistently from day one with Swiss, and I was still doing it now. Genesis was just another notch on my bad call list.

It was time for me to learn how to forgive. I owed my parents the mother of all apologies. They'd only been trying to protect me, and now I could see it for what it was, because I would do the same thing for the little girl or boy that I had growing inside of me right now. I stepped out of my momma's arms, giving my daddy a cautious glance. One side of his lip slowly cracked into a lopsided smile. His eyes were sparkling with tears that he wouldn't shed because he was a rock, and rocks didn't cry.

He hugged me, picking me up off the ground, swinging me back and forth in his arms before he set me down with a kiss on my forehead. He knew something was wrong, and he also knew that he'd given me the tools and the mind-set to deal with just about anything.

"Doesn't matter what it is. You know it'll get handled, baby girl," he said in a gruff voice.

I nodded in agreement before shuffling past him into the living room. Egyptian musk hit me square in the nose before I even had both of my feet in the door.

"Hi, Tariq."

He was sitting on the couch in the semidark living room with the remote in one hand and a blunt in the other.

"Welcome back, Nono," he called out, using the nickname I went by as a kid.

I shuffled in the direction of my bedroom, suddenly anxious to get some real food and some much-needed rest. It was safe here. If Genesis tried to send anyone out this way, Daddy would respond with an army of niggas.

Everything was laid out almost exactly as I remembered it. Momma had changed the color scheme of the kitchen from peach and blue to black and red. All of the carpets were now a blended light oatmeal color instead of the deep navy blue that used to run through the whole house. Momma was going a mile a minute about everything from the day she realized I was gone up until the day she'd called me. I was so tired I couldn't hone in on a single word. My mind was ready to recharge.

"Okay, Momma. In the morning, Momma, I'll tell you and Daddy everything, I promise. I just need to get some sleep, okay?"

I smiled at the collection of stickers I'd stuck all over the outside of my bedroom door back in the day. Momma had obviously thought against redecorating it. I recanted that thought as soon as my hand turned the knob.

"Baby, before you get upset or whatever, let me explain." Momma walked into the room and stood with her arms spread wide.

Gone was my queen-size bed and armoire, a small red Corvette-looking thing with a mattress on top sat in its place. My armoire was replaced with a tiny red and blue desk. The baseball glove-shaped lamp sitting on top of it cast shadows across the whole room. I couldn't step inside until I knew what was going on.

Momma walked over and held my face between her warm hands. "We named him Justus. You kept saying it over and over when they first dragged you out of the water. It seemed like the right thing to do."

My eyes ran back and forth over hers. I was trying to make sense out of what she was saying and what I was feeling. The questions all lodged themselves somewhere in between my brain and my mouth. They fought their way through my subconscious mind. *Is she saying what I think she's saying? Did my son survive, and then die, or did they make him a room and give him a funeral?*

"Please, Momma, just tell me what this is."

"Come here, Novie," Daddy spoke from behind me.

My legs felt like they weighed a ton as I moved toward him, questioning him with my eyes.

"Bryan Novellus Deleon just turned four not too long ago. They saved him, Novie, they saved your son."

I always thought the women who fainted or hand-to-forehead swooned in those old-school romance novels were always full of shit. That was up until I'd gotten the most shocking surprise of my life, and my world went black.

When I came to I was laid out on a bed in the guest room. One of Grandma's old brown and burgundy quilts was pulled up to my chin. The house was so small that the acoustics were damn near perfect for eavesdropping. I stared at the light coming from underneath my bedroom door, listening to everyone arguing over and about me in the kitchen. It was obvious that I wasn't the only one with mixed emotions about being back home. And I had a son. He'd lived all these years without me even knowing he was alive. I'd been beating myself up and mourning a loss that never happened. They should've told me.

On the one hand, I could feel hatred swell up in my heart toward them. They knew the guilt ate me alive, but they let me stay in that state of mental purgatory. All it would have taken was a word, a phone call. I was robbed. My baby was robbed. There were so many parts of his life that I'd missed and would never get back. I buried my nose in his pillow and inhaled. He smelled like Swiss, or maybe that's how I wanted him to smell. I curled into a ball, and I cried for the baby I had who I didn't even get to name.

"You need to tell her when she wakes up," Momma said in quick whisper.

I sniffled into my baby's pillow and calmed myself down so I could listen. The clink of a bottle let me know that the men were taking shots. Momma was most likely having a glass of wine since she never drank hard liquor.

Tariq cleared his throat loud. "I don't think we should say anything just yet. She's obviously been through a lot. Might need a minute just to adjust to all this."

"And when she starts asking for him, what do we say?" Daddy asked.

"You'll say whatever's true," I announced as I walked into their argument about me. "So who is the 'he' you're talking about? And where is my baby boy?"

Their eyes all dropped in unison. I got an unsettling feeling in the pit of my stomach. I know they hadn't made a fit out of telling me Justus was alive, only to finally admit that something had happened to him.

"Tell me what happened!" I slammed the side of my fist against the wall.

Momma set down the glass of wine she'd been sipping. "Novie, sweetheart, you might want to sit down."

"I'm fine, just tell me whatever it is that y'all are trippin' over."

"A month ago we were celebrating Bryan's birthday. I invited all the neighborhood kids over. We even had a few extra ones crash the party, but there was plenty of ice cream and junk food to go around so I didn't even—"

"Ma, just tell me what the hell is wrong."

She wrung her hands in front of her. "I tried to tell you when I called awhile back. See, the thing is, his daddy came asking for him a while ago. We couldn't deny him the right to see his son. He'd visit off and on, but something wasn't ever right with that nigga. Then he stopped visiting altogether. Shandy brings this little boy named Aris to Justus's birthday party. They were playing and getting along, and next time I looked, they were gone," she ended with a teary sob. "That bitch stole my grandbaby. We got guys looking everywhere, and nobody knows anything."

For the second time in one day I almost fainted, but anger kept me standing my ground. Swiss knew! He knew about Bryan the whole time, and that's probably what he wanted to tell me too. I never in a million years would've expected the person who I called sister, who I loved like a sister, to play me to the left.

I looked at my parents and Tariq sitting at the table.

"We will get Bryan back. He has to be here, so he can meet his little brother or sister." I patted my still flat belly with a small sad smile on my face.

This time, the chair slid across the floor and a glass hit the ground at the same time as my momma.

34

No Justus, No Peace

One thing at a time. A woman can only deal with one thing at a time. Genesis was still in the forefront of my mind, but now I also had to deal with the issue of my snake-in-the-grass ex-best-friend. Shandy was crazy. She had to be. She had the nerve to take my child. We didn't judge her or pass her off to the next person. All we'd ever done was treated her like family. What happened between me and Swiss, and what happened to us was our business, not hers. But she wasn't going to make me feel guilty for the rest of my life about an accident that took the same person away from me too. Family forgave each other, but bitches did bitch-ass shit. They'd clap and run for cover when you clapped back.

I waited until Momma was back to herself an hour later. Daddy and Tariq had gone to check on the latest harvest. They needed to stay on top of this new crop of guys or they'd take too many breaks and take twice as long to bundle up the product.

"Momma, you know Tariq helped me escape, right?" I asked her.

She shifted the icepack on her forehead, giving me a confused look. "No, he said he was jumped when he stepped out to go to the grocery store. That you had some guys waiting to rescue you."

I laughed. "Shandy might be as loud as a group of guys, and she might even eat like that. But no, he wanted to holla at her so bad she distracted him so I could get away."

Realization set in on her face before the words were fully out of my mouth.

"We've had a few guys watching her momma's place. They were trying to find Swiss just in case the story his momma got was fake."

"No, Ma, he really did pass away. I was driving the car when it happened. But Shandy, she was pissed at me for a whole 'nother reason. If she didn't go to her momma's house, there's only one other place where I'd look for her."

"Your daddy and Tariq are gonna be gone for at least another hour."

I climbed into the passenger side of my momma's Chevy Blazer.

"When are you gonna upgrade this thing?"

She smirked at me. "That's why all those young fools get caught up. Nobody looks for somebody who does what we do driving this," she pointed out.

Momma was right. The reason they'd stayed under the radar for so long was because they worked smart, and they weren't flashy. I knew all that shit too, but being around niggas who made flashy dumb moves made me forget all my training.

"What is he like?" I asked after a few minutes to break up the silence.

Momma smiled at nothing in particular. "He reminds me of you when you were that age. He's extremely smart; he knows how to work his iPad and pick the movies he likes. One time, I told him not to go out the gate and to stay in the backyard and play. When I came back, not even ten minutes later, he was on the other side messing with the roly polies. That boy has a smile that makes my heart melt. When I asked him what he was doing out in the yard, he said he didn't go through the gate. He climbed the fence."

I couldn't wait to meet this little person who sounded like he was the best parts of me and Swiss all rolled into one little being. A part of me was worried about how I'd get him from Shandy and whether he'd like me once we met. I didn't even know if I'd be a good mommy or where we'd go after this. We wouldn't be staying at my parents' forever. In the space of a night, I'd gone from no babies to having a toddler and a baby. My life had a crazy way of never going the way I expected.

It didn't look like anyone was home when we pulled up at Tariq's place. There weren't any cars in the driveway, and no lights were on inside. Genesis called my phone, making us both jump.

"Girl, you still got that damn thing?" Momma grabbed my phone slamming it onto the dashboard before snatching the battery out of the back and throwing it out the window.

"If whoever you're running from has even a lick of sense, they can track you. Get a new phone and a new number."

I hadn't even thought about it. But knowing Genesis, if he was calling now, it was only because he'd realized I'd left him and his precious Kenisha. The reality of my life was slowly starting to sink in. I was about to be a real full-time single mom with two kids. But I'd also been kidnapped, shot at, beat up, and I survived a jump from a bridge. As scary as being a single mommy sounded, it was nowhere near as scary as all of the other shit I'd survived. For the first time ever, I could honestly say that I was ready to take on the world. And Shandy was my first stop.

The plan we came up with really wasn't much of a plan. Momma was gonna go up on the porch and ring the bell and knock like she had an emergency and was looking for Tariq. We only hoped that Shandy would answer the door. I pulled the blazer off, parking down in front of a house a few doors down. I made sure I had the keys and all before creeping around the side of Tariq's place. There weren't any lights on at the front of the house, but there were plenty on around back. The doorbell echoed through the house, and I stood on my tippy-toes to peek in between the small crack between the blinds.

It was the room from my nightmares. The one I'd laid in for months while Tariq watched over me. Shandy's silhouette was all of what I could see at first. She climbed off the bed, taking the sheets with her, leaving some dude naked on the bed. I squinted to see where she was going . . . but not before I saw my daddy sit up on the bed. I dropped into the bushes beside the house with my heart in my throat. I could hear movement from the window on the other side, and I eased up. Tariq had a handful of wheat-colored hair wrapped around his fist. Sweat poured down his back, pooling in the dip above his ass. Heather's head was tossed back; her eyes were closed in ecstasy. There were two identical cribs in the room with them, and my heart stopped in my chest. I know these niggas were not fucking in the same room the babies were sleeping in!

Momma was on the porch knocking and ringing the hell out of the doorbell. I slid around the side of the house and caught her attention.

"Abort mission," I whispered, scared that she'd spook Shandy into running with the kids.

"Huh?"

"Shhhhh. Abort mission." I pointed in the direction of the Chevy.

The woman had the nerve to shake her damn head at me.

"Yo' daddy will bring Tariq out here so we can handle this shit," she hissed at me in a sassy whisper. She pulled out her phone dialing Daddy's number.

I cringed.

"What the fuckin' fuck," Momma blurted out from the front porch.

Daddy's phone had started ringing from inside the house. He had the ringer set really loud, always had it that way because he'd never feel it when it vibrated and he wouldn't hear it if it wasn't turned up super loud. "Footsteps in the Dark," by the Isley Brothers played loud and long in the house.

Momma hung up, and the song stopped. I leaned against the side of the house. Shandy was the worst kind of friend a bitch could ever have. I probably wouldn't even get the chance to kill her for all the bullshit she'd done. Not if Momma got her hands on her first. I didn't know what to do with myself. If I walked around to the front door there was a chance Shandy wouldn't open it at all once I was spotted. The humidity and my nerves made sweat bead on my forehead. I inhaled, smelling the rain that was coming and the rosebushes on the side of the house that'd just started to bloom. The sky was dark from the clouds gathering in the distance. Lightning flashed every so often, lighting up the sky. I stood waiting but was completely unsure of what I was waiting for.

NOVIE

35

Allow Me to Reintroduce Myself

My blood turned to ice water in my veins. A hand closed over my mouth and something was thrown over my head, handcuffs were tight around my wrists. Rough carpet scraped up my arms and elbows. I hit whatever it was so hard it hurt my ribs.

Metal slammed shut, and I was rocked into motion. I lay still and listened, trying to figure out who'd grabbed me and where they were taking me. Whoever it was stayed quiet, but I could hear someone nose-breathing from the passenger seat so I knew if I tried to do anything, there would be two people to contend with instead of one. The tires rumbled across the road. We were moving fast from the sound of it. I rolled across the back on a sharp turn. The darkness of the hood over my head and the motion of the van or car was starting to make my stomach turn. When we finally stopped, someone grabbed me by my ankles, sliding me out of the vehicle. I kicked and fought back until I thought I'd pass out from doing so much.

"Are you finally gonna put in some work, or do I have to do this job too?"

I knew that voice. The question came from Genesis's number one dick rider, a nigga everybody called Foreign.

We already had enough bad blood between us. He
yanked the hood off my head. I wasn't trying to catch
anymore so I buried my chin in my chest, avoiding his
gaze. He walked over to post up near his partner Chief
standing beside me. We both knew that this *"job"* Foreign
was asking about really meant me.

I almost laughed out loud at how stupid I'd been.

Chief shifted his weight from foot to foot hesitating. He
either had to piss some kind of bad, or he was avoiding
the question.

Foreign rolled his eyes and hissed through his teeth.
"Move out of the way with your old soft ass. I got this, just
like everything else. But you buying me a cheddar bacon
burger from Five Guys when we get done."

Foreign looked *foreign,* like his name, with dark
autumn-brown skin, pretty, naturally curly hair that he
kept cut low on the sides, and vacant ice-blue eyes. They
were glassy, empty points on his face that would've fit
better on something without a conscience, like a snake
or a cat. Permanent dark circles under his eyes made him
look half man, half raccoon. Something about him had
always made me uneasy. He just came off as shady, the
type that'd steal from his boys and ask you to hide that
shit when they came looking for it type of shady.

Chief backed up so Foreign could take over.

Foreign's dirty nails dug into my elbow. It didn't make
any sense for a man as pretty as he was to come off so
dusty and unpolished, but he did. Maybe he thought
his good looks exempted him from maintaining good
hygiene.

Foreign reached into the back of his waistband. *Don't
cry. You better not fucking cry,* I chanted over and over
to myself. They weren't about to run back and tell that
nigga how I cried and begged for my life or for him to
have a change of heart. The tears still marched down my
cheeks, even though I told them not to.

Dread was tearing me up inside as I watched him go for his pistol. He waved it, motioning for me to turn and face the other direction. The nigga slid in, pressing himself up against my body until the short prickly hairs on his cheek brushed against the side of my face.

"You know how baaad I been wanting to put something up in you? Just to see what made you *sooooo* fuckin' special," he admitted in a deep, ragged whisper. "Damn shame it's gotta be this hot lead instead of this hot pipe."

I exhaled the air I'd been holding, relieved when he stepped back, pressing the heavy barrel of the gun between my shoulder blades. "Don't be scared, heaven or hell awaits," he cooed.

I almost turned around to laugh in his face. I'd spent so much time playing hide-and-seek with the devil that I wasn't even scared of hell anymore. Hell was empty. All those devils and demons had been right here the whole time.

"I'm gonna make this as painless as possible, but I don't want brains on my van. So walk," he demanded.

His orders were accented with the poke of the barrel into my back.

Daddy had taught me more about guns by the time I was five than most people learned in their entire lives. Between the DEA's drug raids and other dealers, he was so paranoid that he kept guns hidden all over the house. It was safer to show me how to use one, than to have me find one that he'd forgotten about and accidentally shot myself or someone else. I'd never been scared of a pistol, just scared of being at the wrong end.

Daddy would always tell me take a deep breath to steady my aim before sliding my finger onto the trigger. So now I waited, listening for that breath that meant a bullet was on its way. All I could hear was the swooshing of waves underneath me; they crashed against the rocks as my heart pounded against my ribcage. Air shot through my nostrils in quick, erratic spurts. It seemed like I could hear everything except Foreign. I could barely make out Chief, eerily reciting what sounded like the Lord's Prayer. And that's when I heard it. The shift in the air as the pistol rose from the middle of my back toward the back of my head. Foreign inhaled a slow, shaky breath through his mouth. His calloused finger was steady as it slid across steel.

It wasn't supposed to be this way. But my dumb ass had to be a part of Genesis Kane's world, a world he manipulated to get what he wanted, no different than the words he manipulated in the courtroom. Genesis who didn't have anything in his life that he didn't have a use for.

The first shot split the air; bullets zipped by my face, and they were so close I felt the heat in passing.

"Stop!"

The sound of Genesis's voice brought relief . . . along with a whole new source of terror.

I couldn't stop shivering. Every part of my body was shaking.

He walked toward us. It only took him a few quick long strides to get to where we were standing. When he stood in front of me, I was too disgusted, too ashamed of his sin to even look him in the eyes.

Foreign jotted over to Genesis's side. "You came to watch this one happen live and direct? You wanna do the honor? Pull the trigger?"

Genesis's shadow stopped at my feet. I watched the dark shadowy version of him on the ground. He shook his head, holding his hand up, silencing Foreign. In his other hand he held something else.

"You're pregnant." Genesis didn't ask, he spat the words like poison.

"What difference does it make to you?"

He threw the pregnancy test down at my feet. I'd forgotten all about those damn things. When I looked up, he was running his hands over his head.

"I don't know what the fuck it means. I told you I didn't want kids."

"Why not? You scared you won't be able to keep your nasty hands off of them?"

No sooner had the words left my mouth than I found myself on the ground with Genesis standing over me, blocking out the sun.

"Nah, I want kids. Just not with you."

Even though I thought he was disgusting and foul, his words stole my breath. Chief and Foreign looked at each other and shared a smirk at the harsh way I was being handled.

Genesis snapped his fingers. "Put her somewhere. Somewhere nice and cozy so she can have the kid. And when it's here, you let me know."

He stood in front of me and leaned down until his face was a hair's space away from mine. "You trying to take my baby girl from me? You gonna watch me take that motherfucka from you because I do not give a fuck about you or it."

I watched Chief shake his head out of the corner of my eye as Genesis stormed away.

"Man, shiiiit," Chief said over the wind with what sounded like regret in his voice. "We ain't never did no pregnant bitch before. Seem like some bad juju-type shit, like killin' a spider in the house or steppin' on a grasshopper. Typa shit you don't think about that'll come back and fuck you up later."

Gravel scraped against the black pavement under the heel of Foreign's scuffed Jodhpur boot. "Yeah, well, if it's in my house or if it fits under my boot, I'm squashing it," he spat in Chief's direction. "I don't believe in juju, karma, luck—none of that. I control what *I* control. And it can't be all that bad if we're making bank. You heard what Kane said. Let's just find somewhere to put her until it's time. Gotta be somewhere good too. She knows too much." Foreign directed his frost-blue gaze down at me before glaring back at Chief. "She knows too much about *all of us now*, you included," he said with a sneer.

Yeah, I'd learned a lot about their fake asses, and I hated every single thing about them. From the way they'd all played me to the left, right, down to the way they'd all betrayed me.

Either way it went, Genesis Kane was going to kill me.

Justus

That's it? That's all there is? My fingers held the brown leather journal in a death grip. The dingy reddish-brown splatters on the page blurred and came back into focus. Maybe it was blood. I ain't need nobody to tell me that it was my mom's. My fingers avoided those spots like they were acid. They were scattered across the page running over flowery handwriting. I tried to convince myself that they were old juice stains or hot cocoa. I read my mother's words again. *Genesis Kane is going to kill me.* Tears burned my eyes, and my heart pounded away in my throat. When I got to the last word I slammed the leather book shut with both hands.

"Justus?" Aris yelled through the house. "Boy, what are you doing? Bryan is about to blow out the candles on his cake."

She cracked my door, peeking into my bedroom without knocking. Something I'd told her a thousand times not to do, but she never listened. It felt like Aris was always watching me for some reason.

"Damn, I'll be there in a minute," I barked back, throwing one of my J's toward the door. My brother's birthday wasn't as important to me as what I'd been reading. Not right this second anyway.

"My bad. Didn't know you were in there having you-time. Wash your nasty hands and hurry up," she snapped before closing the door.

I looked at Aris in a whole new light now. There was a reason why her voice was deep for a girl, and she was always pissed off and strong as fuck too. Aunt Shan tried to say it was because she hadn't gone through *the change* yet. I think part of it was because Aris was mad. She didn't have any of the boobs or the booty that the chicks in school had. That was fuckin' with her worse than the change itself. The other part was Aris was as much of a dude as I was. We all took the same sex-ed classes. She probably didn't understand why she had a dick but had been treated like a girl his whole life.

Aunt Shan had always told me that my mom had abandoned me and Bryan, but she hadn't. Her name blared at me in letters etched deep into the cover. *Novie Deleon.*

I shook my head, swinging tears across her journal. My vision blurred. *That couldn't be it. Nah, there was no way the story ended like that.* But deep down, I knew that was the end of her story. I could almost sense it. My insides felt like they were vibrating from the years of grief and sadness. I'd shoved all those bullshit emotions that came from not having my mom deep down into my gut. The feeling swelled up inside me, made me rock back and forth on the edge of my bed like the addicts I'd seen in the park. I couldn't tell if it would swallow me whole or make me implode from the inside out. I'd never felt anything like it.

"Justus, your BP level is abnormally high," the mechanical bitch's voice sounded off from my wrist.

I clawed at my life tracker bracelet trying to rip it off.

The bracelet made its usual annoying warning blips before announcing, "Your Aunt Shan has been alerted."

Getting it off was pointless. I don't even know why I tried.

Rain tapped against the window outside. I sat with my legs hanging over the side of my bed, bracing myself because I wasn't ready to face the fact that my pops the murderer and my Aunt Shan were just as foul.

The life tracker wirelessly signaled for him sending a message to the life tracker he wore to monitor mine. She'd be busting up in here in about zero-point-three seconds like this bitch was on fire. These fucking bracelets were un-fucking-removable, and they tracked every-fucking-thing . . . my mood, where I went, what I ate, and what the fuck I did. Mine was mostly for a heart condition I'd had ever since I was a baby. Everyone thought I'd grow out of it by now, which sucked because I hadn't. Dying didn't scare me, and neither did having a janky heart. Why the fuck do they make us pick our career path and start training fresh out of preschool anyway? Nobody takes the kid with the fucked-up heart, especially not when it comes to playing sports.

Even though I was only sixteen and already six-three, Aunt Shan was just happy she had an excuse to keep me out of the "legal slave trade," as she called it. She wanted me to be a lawyer like my father so fucking bad, and he wasn't even a real lawyer his damn self. That isn't even what hit me the hardest. Now, I knew the real truth. I knew if it wasn't for him, I probably wouldn't even have this heart condition. And I probably wouldn't have gotten passed over to play basketball.

Now my heart was pounding so hard I could feel it booming in my forehead.

"*Justus?*"

Aunt Shan yelled for me, shouting through the house. "Son, are you all right?"

Nah, I wasn't all right. I'd been wronged from day one. Shit, from *before* day one, when my mom was standing there for both of us. I felt full but hollow as fuck, pissed off and sad at the same. I couldn't believe it when I'd found it. A real book, written by hand, and not only that, it was written by my mom to me. It'd taken me almost a month to read it, especially since we streamed books now. I wasn't about to get caught dead walking around with an antique book tucked under my arm.

I'd found it in a crumpled cardboard box in the back of the garage behind some old tires. Aunt Shan had either forgot it was in there, or she wasn't trying to touch it. It was covered with spiderwebs, dust, and rat shit, with the words *Novie's Stuff* scratched out and *Trash* written underneath.

The tightness in my throat made it hard to swallow . . . hard to breathe. The walls were closing in on me, and I wasn't even allowed to leave them. It cut me to my core to know my pops had done so much wrong in his life when I wasn't allowed to do anything. No socializing, hanging out—no dating. That's exactly why nobody knew anything about the one person I needed right now. I sent Asa a message to come scoop me up ASAP. If I didn't get out of this house, I'd lose my mind or snap.

"Justus, are you good? What's going on?" Aunt Shan bust up into my room looking panicked and freaked out. Sweat was pouring off her forehead.

I hated that they could do that, just come in and out whenever they wanted, but she'd taken the lock code off my door back when I was six. I had a seizure, and no one could get in.

I flopped back on the bed and stared up at the ceiling. "I'm straight. You know this bracelet trips sometimes."

"Better to be safe than sorry. Let's at least go take your vitals, Justus."

She started to come toward me, and I couldn't stand it; I couldn't stand her. The thought of being around her, having her near me, made my chest tight. My name didn't even mean anything anymore. What did that nigga know about Justus? Nah, I wouldn't be able to fake this, not when I knew what I knew.

I jumped up, knocking her hand away before she could touch me. "I said I'm good. I'm goin' out," I gritted the words through my clenched teeth.

"Where the hell are you going? And who the fuck you raisin' up at?" she roared.

I sneered. This bitch didn't deserve my respect, and after what she did, she didn't deserve an answer for my disrespect either. My hands felt like they didn't belong to me as I grabbed things and started throwing them into my backpack.

Aunt Shan stepped everywhere I stepped, stalking me, watching me.

"So now you think you too grown to answer me, boy? You ain't too sick to catch one."

Still no answer. I gripped the closet door handles, imagining her neck, my pop's neck in between my fingers as I flung it open. The door derailed from its track, slamming into the wall and falling to the floor.

Aunt Shan grabbed my shoulder, spinning me to face her. Her fist was raised. She'd never beat me the way I'd seen her beat Aris. She'd never even hit Bryan, and he was always doing crazy shit back in the day. Aris caught the worst of it, and now I directed every ounce of hatred, hurt, and anger that I had in me toward her. It was like the wind left her sails; her fist came down, and she took her hand off my shoulder. She deflated right in front of me.

"Just tell me what's wrong, baby. If you're in trouble, I can fix it. Whatever it is, I won't be mad."

"You helped killed my mom?"

There . . . I'd said it.

Her eyes dropped to the floor. It looked as if I'd punched her hard in her doughy gut.

"Why did he give me to *you?*"

She didn't even have to answer my question. The way she'd reacted was answer enough. I went back to grabbing some of my things.

"Baby, there's a lot you don't understand and don't know. Your mom . . . I gave up everything for her. She took so much from me."

"So you took everything from me!"

When I threw the hood to my hoodie over my head I didn't look back, and she didn't stop me.

Fat cold raindrops smacked me in the face as I marched across the street toward the silver truck sitting at the corner. I tried to let my feelings roll off my back with the rain and tears rolling off my cheeks.

"Hey, you," Asa called out as I climbed into the truck cabin.

I wanted to answer, but I couldn't say the words that had been filling my stomach ever since I read them. Asa could sense that something wasn't right with me.

"What's the matter, Jus?"

Asa was trying to look through me, but I didn't need that shit right now. I grabbed the back of his neck, pulled him toward me, and I kissed my man like the world was on fire. His lips tasted like Dr. Pepper and spearmint gum. He moaned before pulling away from me.

"Aww, shit . . ." Asa whispered.

His eyes were staring past me, over my shoulder. I didn't have to turn around to know what the fuck was back there. Wind rushed against my back, rain pelted against the back of my neck. The door to the truck was yanked open. I was snatched out by the hood on my sweatshirt. The wet pavement skinned my palms as I fell backward.

I caught a glimpse of Aunt Shan's face as she rushed past me with her teeth bared and hands clenched. She barreled past me into the cabin of the truck. She looked possessed.

"Keep your fucking hands off my fucking baby! Don't bring that nigga around here. You promised! You fucking promised!" Aunt Shan howled at Asa.

Her elbow was flying back; she landed blow after blow. Asa wasn't even defending himself. He was probably in shock. My life-tracker bracelet started beeping and kicking off warnings. All of my levels were off the chart. It made Aunt Shan's go off too, and she turned to look back out at me, still holding a fistful of Asa's collar. And I launched, using that moment to yank her backward out of the cabin of the truck.

I hopped in and slammed the door almost catching her fingers.

"Go . . . go . . . go! Drive, nigga!" I smacked the dashboard trying to get Asa to move his ass and get us the fuck out of there.

Aunt Shan stood on the sidewalk staring after us. I watched her in the side mirror until she disappeared. I'd always been afraid of coming out, afraid of telling the world that I didn't feel anything for women. That I actually liked men. Now she saw the truth for herself.

It was quiet as fuck as we splashed through the streets heading toward the highway. Silence sat between me and Asa like a thick curtain. The quiet was good. I wasn't in much of a talking mood. Asa always knew when to talk and when to stay quiet. Must be something that comes with getting old. Not that my boo was old, but he wasn't in high school. I don't even know if he graduated high school, but he was old enough to be my dad, and I didn't give a fuck. We needed to figure out how to get my life tracker off or someone would always be able to find me.

After a few minutes I broke the silence. "Asa . . . I found this, and I read it." I held up the journal I'd been hiding for so many months. No one carried books anymore, not real ones anyway. Everyone streamed anything that was written or typed. Any books that still existed were worth a grip, and they were either in museums or art galleries. Bryan and Aris would've joked me for the rest of my life if they'd seen me with it.

Asa's eyes went wide as saucers. The truck swerved.

"Where did you get that shit?" he asked in a strange whisper.

"Found it. Tucked in a box full of Mom's shit." I sucked in air like I was drowning. "My dad killed her. She wrote it, and she said he'd kill her. I think Aunt Shan helped. She's been lying to me for all these years."

Asa took a shaky breath. "I never told you this, but me, your dad, and your Aunt Shan go way back. I love you, and I loved your dad. More than life itself. But he has always had a way of looking at something and only seeing what he wants to see in it. Your Aunt Shan's the same exact way."

"Like how she only sees me as a lawyer?" I asked in a dry voice.

"Yeah. Something like that. Let's take a drive and I'll explain."

I pulled my soaked hoodie over my head and sat back.

"It all started with Tima. Your dad's first wife." He cleared his throat. "Your dad's name was Jarryd back then, and he worked with me on the FBI bomb squad. I found out Tima was cheating on him with some wack-ass lawyer from an office in Downtown Norfolk. I did what any homeboy would do. I looked out for my boy's best interest. Yo, I told that lawyer leave well enough alone, but he didn't want to listen. So I set that nigga up good. Called in a bunch of scares all over the place to keep the bomb boys busy. The only real one was in that garage. But somebody must've seen me comin' or going. Because your dad somehow got sent out there seconds before it went off. He wasn't supposed to be anywhere near that explosion. But I made that bomb, and I was one of the best bomb technicians, so it was perfect. Nobody would've been able to stop it except me. My heart was in the right place. I wanted to tell him for years, but he'd never seen it like that. So I never told him. And then he took that nigga's identity. He became this Genesis Kane, and every time he loved someone it made my heart bleed. Your mom was smart. She figured him out. And she probably figured out the bloody hearts I was sending him too. But he never saw me. The nigga just looked right over me."

The wheels were spinning, but there were certain things that they kept kicking back at me, making my brain slam on the brakes.

"If you knew my mom, why didn't I see your name in her journals?" I asked, curious about the way Asa seemed to be hanging onto these stories about my dad.

The truck sped up. Rain tapped against the roof and the windows. Traffic went by in a blur.

"Li'l nigga, I care about you the same way I cared about his rusty ass back then. The only difference is that I actually love you. Fell in love with you. I followed around behind that nigga like a fuckin' puppy, and I would've done anything he asked me to if it gave me a chance to get closer to him. He wanted to get rid of you; he said it over and over. When he saw you, he started acting weird. That nigga wouldn't have given me the time of day, no matter what I did. My boy Chief suggested that we give you to Shandy, but it didn't even make a difference."

My pulse thumped hard in my neck. I didn't even see this nigga for who he was, and he'd been sitting right in my face the whole time.

"*You're* Foreign." I didn't ask. I accused him of that shit.

My man, my boo, the dude my aunt Shandy called my uncle Asa, was Foreign with the electric-blue eyes, permanent dark stubble, and rough demeanor. He wasn't even a real uncle. I'd felt so sick to my stomach with guilty and disgust, I couldn't eat for a week after the first time we hooked up. Every time someone said something to me, I was paranoid that they could see my dirty secret, that I was gay, and that I snuck out three and sometimes four times a night to fuck my uncle Asa in his truck around the corner from my house. This secret perversion I was carrying around with me.

"Yo, just take me back," I commanded.

Foreign or Asa or whoever he was ignored me. He sped up until the odometer was over a hundred miles an hour. His eyes were glued on the road.

"Nah. We not goin' back. You know how many years I waited? I dealt with his wife, his girlfriends, side bitches, and baby mommas. I waited and waited for that nigga, but he was too homophobic to just let shit happen. And now I have you. Justus is mine. I have his heart."

He finally looked at me. There was so much crazy in his eyes that I couldn't figure out how the fuck I hadn't seen any of it before. His hand was warm as he reached over to squeeze my knee.

"You love me, so you'll forgive me, and you'll accept this. You're mine."